The Staff and the Sandals

Advantage™
FICTION

N. YVONNE BUNN

The Staff and The Sandals by N. Yvonne Bunn

ISBN: 1-59755-057-4

Published by: Advantage Books™
www.advantagebooks.com

Library of Congress Control Number: 2006929836

First Printing: April 2007

07 08 09 10 11 12 01 9 8 7 6

Printed in the United States of America

Acknowledgements

Thanks to my husband who listened to my stories.

To my two nieces who helped me format this book.

To my friends who helped type the manuscripts.

Chapter One

Beriah awoke as dawn was breaking in the eastern sky. Bleary-eyed, he crawled up through the opening of the dark underground tunnel, which traveled beneath the Holy City of Jerusalem. The subterranean passageway had many spurs. Some led to areas with vaulted ceilings. Others led to underground water pools. While another passageway was created to move troops of soldiers under the city to surprise the enemy.

Beriah, as a small child, had been shown these underground passages by an elderly man whose name was Jobah. Finally, old Jobah had taken the crippled, orphan child under his wing until Beriah was age fifteen. At which time the old man died. Beriah, with the help of a friend, placed the body of Jobah in an open niche hewed out in Jobah's family tomb. It was now ten years later and Beriah lived in the dark cavern. It was here Beriah took refuge from the cruelties from the world above.

Beriah was clothed in a clean, brown robe and sandals so thin he could feel the cobblestones of the street above the cavern. Beriah stopped and breathed in the fresh morning air. He listened to the birdcalls in the bushes and took in the beauty of the rosy sky which hung over Jerusalem. Looking towards the Temple Mount, he thanked Yahweh for this glorious day and asked for guidance and blessing.

This was the time of day that Beriah loved most. The air was cool and fresh; like the water that trickled down the ancient rock formation in the cavern home.

Birds and small animals were already in quest for food. The Holy City of Jerusalem was beginning to come alive. Bees droned as they set out for the day. Donkeys brayed and camel's bells jangled with the rhythm of prodding. A steady hum of humanity was already moving to a crescendo. The rosy sky was beginning to change as orange sunrays shot across the heavens, and the moon was fading like a gliding ghost. Fires from the early morning meals were sending smoke spumes spiraling heavenward. The aroma for food mixed with the odors of animals, and the dew drenched flowers, with the sweat of humanity.

Picking up his belongings, Beriah moved in a crab-like gait toward the bazaar. He still had some coins left from the alms of the day before. The bazaar was already set up and opened for business. The open-air stalls, with their multi-colored canopies, were piled high to catch the eyes of strolling man and to assail his nostrils. Fowls and mutton rotating on spits were tantalizing to the eyes and nose. The sweet odor of ripe fruit and melons vied with the pungent odor of herbs, fresh bread, and sweetmeats. The senses of the customers were bombarded as these smells wafted in the air.

There was a steady hum of activity as Beriah moved from stall to stall. First, he bought a handful of figs, and then four apples. He purchased a fresh loaf of bread and a chunk of goat cheese. Lastly, he chose a round bun covered with dates called sweetmeat. He tied his food in clean cloths and placed them in his shoulder bag. Beriah then worked his way through the thronging masses that were astir in the narrow, twisting streets.

Reaching the well, where the shopkeepers drew water, Beriah spread out a small rug. Here he spent his days seeking alms from those entering Jerusalem. He began to think about the day as he played his harp. He wanted to get candles before going home; and he needed to pick up the crushed crates Tola, the Coppersmith, left behind his shop. A small fire in the evening was a comfort to Beriah as he ate his evening meal. The fire also drove away shadows in the high-vaulted room in the cavern. Hopefully, he would have enough alms at the end of the day to buy tomorrow's food and a chunk of old Shua's lye soap. If people were generous, he would fill his flagon with goat's milk. These were happy thoughts.

The shopkeepers were kind to Beriah. Amos, the tinsmith, had given him a cooking pot and an assortment of pans that were flawed yet usable. Beriah was pleased with the gifts. He often came early and swept the entrance with a willow-with broom. This was his way of saying thank you.

Though Beriah was crippled in the body, he was not crippled in the mind and spirit. He was an exceptionally bright young man. His friend and mentor, old Jobah, had been a scholar who was down on his luck when he became old. Jobah had spent many evenings telling Beriah stories from the Torah. At an early age, Beriah felt a kinship to Abraham, Isaac, and Jacob. Also, to Joseph, who was sold into slavery as a boy. Yet, Joseph had risen to the position of Governor of Egypt. Beriah never tired of the story of Moses as a baby, floating down the Nile River, in a basket. He escaped the wrath of Pharaoh only to grow up and lead his people out of the land of Egypt. Nor did he tire from hearing about the Israelites looking for their Messiah.

The remembrance of the flight of the Jews out of Egypt was the reason for the influx of people in Jerusalem this week. Again, it was Passover. A time to remember that God had spared His people from Pharaoh and the Death Angel. During their flight from Egypt, God had caused the Red Sea to roll back and make a way where none existed.

During Passover week the people in Jerusalem would swell between forty and fifty thousand persons. Jews would come from the far reaches of the known world. Every Jew wanted to be in Jerusalem at least once in his or her lifetime. All other Jews when praying would face in the direction of Jerusalem and their hearts would cry out for Zion. Even the God-fearers would travel to the Holy City when possible to pray to the eternal God.

The Jews would eat the unleavened bread, bitter herbs, and roasted Passover lamb. They would retell the ancient story of breaking the yoke of bondage. As their forefathers had said, "Lest we forget." Each would make the long, hard pilgrimage to the temple to pray and seek the holiness of His Presence.

Old Jobah had also taught Beriah to read and do numbers. Beriah's mind was like a sponge and Jobah filled it with Greek, Latin, music, arts, and the land beyond Jerusalem.

Today Beriah was happy as he settled down by the well. From under his arm he brought out his treasured harp. The harp had been a gift from Jobah. After the evening stories and lessons, Jobah would teach young Beriah to pluck the lyre-like musical instrument. Its sounds could be joyful, soothing, or sad. The sounds Beriah liked best were the soft, soothing melodies he himself had composed. Sometimes he made words to go with the tune but mostly he just played.

Often weary travelers stopped at the well for a cup of water, or paused to watch Beriah's long nimble fingers pluck the strings of the harp. At times, Beriah sang in his soft, clear voice. Many travelers smiled and dropped coins into his cup before moving on. Beriah enjoyed making others happy. This, he felt, was earning his daily alms.

The travelers came by litters, donkeys, oxen, and carts. Others came astride horses, rocking on long-legged camels, by boats to the seaports or walked. The clothing of the travelers was as different as the modes of travel.

There were the country folks from Galilee and Judea in their brown and black and striped robes. The outpost of Transalpine Gaul wore blue and white linen. Antioch and Tyre were adorned in rich purple and gold and embroidered togas, which were flung over one shoulder. Macedonia and Mesopotamia favored white linens; with brightly colored silken threads. Their clothing was both short and long. Asia Minor had people resplendent in rich brocades of ivory, blacks, and deep reds; Africa had sarongs and flowing robes and Achaia wore bright silk tunics.

Whether rich or poor, young or old, from near or far, everyone wanted through the arched gate leading into the Temple courtyard. It was here they had come to pray and give sacrifice to El Shaddai, the Almighty.

The merchants did not complain about the crab-like cripple. They often told Beriah his music helped them relax over their work.

Occasionally, Roman soldiers would stop for water. For the soldiers, Beriah would play more lively tunes. This caused the soldiers to momentarily laugh and relax. Tola and the other merchants knew by the rhythms of the harp that the Roman soldiers were near. To them, this was better than a town crier.

The neighboring merchants watched over the gentle cripple. They gave him many small, useful gifts. Tola made sure Beriah had wood from the packing boxes. Hur, the Potter, gave him various pieces of pottery, which had slight flaws but were still usable. Carmie, the merchant of fine cloth, gave him scraps of material and shipping straw to line his pallet. Rosh, the weaver, made sure Beriah had a change of robes and a warm cloak. He even wove him a small rug to sit on while playing the harp. Elon, who bought and sold leather and skins, gave Beriah four warm off-colored sheepskins for his pallet.

In return for the gifts, Beriah would often go early and stay late to dust and sweep for the merchants. Beriah even took Rosh's tangled yarn home and returned it the next day wound in neat colored balls. Hiram, the candle maker, saved his imperfect candles for his young friend. Hiram always refused pay. He would chuckle and say the music was worth a dozen candles. Abe, the tent-maker, made Beriah a small blue and white canopy for shade.

All in all it was a contented neighborhood. Seasons came and seasons passed for Beriah and the merchants. Each day was a day the Lord God Jehovah made and a day to rejoice.

Each one was contented as long as; the Roman soldiers, the priest, and the tax collectors did not place undue pressure on their way of life. However, unbeknown to them, this was the day that all this would change. Word soon reached the merchants of the overnight arrest of the much talked about Messiah.

Word quickly filtered from shop to shop. Customers told tidbits of the arrest ordered by the greedy Priests Annas and Caiaphas. Also about the shuffling of Jesus before King Herod who angrily declared he would not do Pontius Pilate's job. "After all," Herod told the Roman Centurion, "I'm still being criticized for beheading the prophet John the

Baptist." The Roman Centurion tried to hide his revulsion of Herod. He too, had heard the rumors of a drunken King Herod lusting for his stepdaughter Salome; and granting her wish. Unfortunately, the wish was for the head of John the Baptist on a platter.

Other people brought news of the coming trial of Jesus by Pontius Pilate. All these things were discussed in subdued tones. It was said that the high priests were so sure of getting a conviction, that they had sent the hard-nosed young priest Assir to have a cross made the night before the trial. Temple rumor had it that Assir was a taskmaster on the laws of Moses. If you so much as deviated from the law, Assir would seek the death penalty. When it came to this new fanatical group that followed the Galilean, Assir all but snorted fire. He vowed to put a stop to such religious rebellion. Assir was heard to say, "Kristo, the Anointed One indeed! When He's hanging on a tree they'll see that He was just a blow-hard rabble rouser."

A weary old man sitting nearby shook his saged head and responded, "Hasn't that young whippersnapper read from the prophet Isaiah who said, 'When you have lifted up the Son of Man, then you will know who I am and that I do nothing on my own.... But I, when I am lifted up, will draw all men unto myself.' Beware Assir that in your zeal to do well; in the eyes of Hasham, the Almighty, you do not murder His only begotten Son. Who knows, Rabbi Yeshua may be that Son. Although the law says, 'Anyone who is hung on a tree is under God's curse.' Perhaps God views our sins as such repulsive deeds that it's sin He wants to nail to the tree. And the blood of the spotless Lamb is the only thing that will wash away the stain of sin. Therefore, the only spotless lamb worthy is His only beloved Son – Yeshua. Even the angels in heaven sing 'Worthy is the Lamb, Worthy is the Lamb of God.' And this praise will last throughout all eternity. Long after you Assir, myself, and other sinners have returned to dust; the angels will still be singing 'Worthy is the Lamb of God.'"

There was an atmosphere of anxiety and fear among the merchants. Those along the outer wall pieced together Jesus' triumphant entry into the city. Also, how the crowd waved palm branches and lined the street with branches for Jesus' donkey to walk on; while they sang, 'Hosanna to the Son of David! Blessed is He who comes in the name of the Lord! Hosanna in the highest!'

Others told of the High Priests Annas and Caiaphas and their cohorts trying to incite a mob to demand the innocent Jesus to be crucified. While others discussed Jesus' betrayal by His disciple Judas Iscariot and the night arrest in the Garden of Gethsemane where Jesus had gone to pray.

The merchants and customers shook their heads in shocked disbelief that the priests and Suducees would be so daring. The news was so horrifying it was hard to conceive that such a thing could happen at this joyous season of the year.

While these events were being discussed, Nadab, the cobbler stumbled down the narrow, twisting passageway. He was out of breath from hurrying. Sweat streamed down his face and he shook like palsy. The merchants gathered around their own. Catching his breath, Nadab told how he was an eyewitness to the terrible beating of Jesus and how the soldiers had mocked and spat on Him. "They even put a scarlet robe on Jesus, then jeered at Him saying, 'Hail, King of the Jews!'" By now Nadab was weeping openly.

"Then what happened?" asked Hur, the Potter.

"Pontius Pilate tried to pacify the mob." Continued Nadab. "He would release one of the prisoners for Passover."

"Which shall I release?" Pilate asked. "Jesus or Bar-Abbas?"

Aghast, Amos the Tin-smith asked, "Who did they say Nadab?"

Trembling Nadab said, "The mob shouted Bar-Abbas! Bar-Abbas!"

Pilate held up his hand for the mob to be quiet. He then threw out his arm and pointed to the beaten Nazarene. Then sneering at the priest he said. "And what shall I do with this Jesus?"

"What was the answer?" probed Rosh, the weaver.

Shaking his head in disbelief, Nadab spoke words that struck terror in the hearts of the listeners. "They yelled, 'Let Him be crucified!

Crucify Him! Crucify Him!' I tell you they were like a bunch of wild dogs."

"And what did Jesus say?" asked a weeping Beriah.

"Jesus just stood; looking broken-hearted. And He said nothing in his own defense. Two big rough looking soldiers grabbed him by each arm. Jesus' legs were about to collapse. He looked back over His shoulder as they dragged Him over to one of the praetorian. He reminded me of a sheep being led to slaughter," Nadab told them.

By now Nadab was on the verge of collapse. Tola, the Coppersmith, seated Nadab on a folding stool. Beriah hobbled across the street and brought Nadab a cup of water. The group of merchants waited while Nadab gulped down the water. The news of the trial had been inconceivable.

Fearfully Tola quizzed, "What did Pontius Pilate say to the demands of the mob?"

Nadab slowly shook his head in sorrow. "That's what's so mystifying," stammered the now weeping man. "Pilate looked at Jesus and then ordered a pan of water, and washed his hands. Holding up his wet, dripping hands to the priests and the mob he said, 'I am innocent of the blood of this just Person.' And the people shouted, 'His blood be on us and our children!'"

A loud gasp rent the morning air as the group of Jewish merchants heard this terrible curse that was placed on the Jewish people. They were appalled. Nadab sagged into Tola's arms and continued weeping. Beriah scurried to get Nadab another cup of water. The little group of merchants seemed to be frozen in time and place. No one spoke and no one moved.

The merchants were still in a huddle when they heard the rhythmic feet of the Roman soldiers moving in formation on the cobblestones. The procession was not moving fast but the soldiers were shoulder to shoulder. Their red togas were thrown over their left shoulder. Shiny, plumed helmets were on their heads and shields were on their breasts. Swords were in their sheaths and lances were in their hands. The soldiers were well trained and on guard for trouble. The might of Rome was depicted on their battle-hardened faces. Only one appeared to the unhappy about his assignment to crucify Jesus. He was the tall, young Centurion who was in charge of carrying out Pilate's orders.

Behind the front guard of soldiers was the staggering Jesus dragging a heavy wooden cross. His hands were bound with rawhide cords to the cross beam of the cross. The day before, two other heavy simplex beams had been delivered to the hill of Golgotha by the strength of two strong donkeys. They were for the two thieves sentenced to die in yesterday's tribunal.

Yet, here was Jesus, being used as a donkey. Not only was He carrying the heavy cross beam, but also, the long simplex pole. Jesus' face was battered, bruised, and swollen in an array of angry purplish and blue colors. One eye was partially closed and the other was bloodshot. The skin and flesh on His back and sides hung in long, bloody shreds. The white of His bones could be seen where the flesh was missing. In Jesus' left side could be seen parts of His internal organs and upper bowel. A rent in His chest showed a small section of lungs inflating and deflating in laborious flutters. Fresh blood ran in rivulets over the already dried blood, which covered His body. The stripes and flesh punctures caused by the whip of nine tails tied with metal and bones were criss-crossed around and over His body in a pattern of no rhyme or reason. Blood ran down Jesus' forehead and face from a cruel crown of two-inch long thorns from the Acacia tree.

The blood mingled with His sweat and dropped onto the cobblestones in slick, sticky blotches. Ninety percent of Jesus' beard had been ripped off leaving His chin exposed like removing the skin off a grape. Sand and grit was clinging to the raw flesh. Green flies smelling blood, were swarming about His face. However, the flies were no match for the Jerusalem red fire ants; upon smelling the fresh blood of a crucified victim, the ants would crawl up the cross and further torment the victim, providing they were still alive, with biting that was unbearable to the crucified one.

Jesus, weakened from His inhumane beating, stumbled and fell to His knees, further bruising His hands and ruffling the skin off His kneecaps and leg bones. Jesus tried to lean His face into His shoulder to wipe the blood out of His eyes. Gasping for breath, Jesus looked up at a soldier who had just prodded his lance in an open wound and ordered Him up. The sneering soldier looked into Jesus' eyes but quickly stepped back. He could not hold eye-to-eye contact with the man on His knees. Though Jesus' body did not look human, the soldier reacted as though he had looked into the eyes of a King.

Jesus' slowly staggered to His feet. Lifting the cross, He stumbled as far as the well where Beriah stood with a cup of water for Nadab. Jesus again fell on His knees. Quickly the crab-like cripple lifted Jesus' head and put the cup to His swollen lips. A moment later, a soldier of the rear guard kicked Beriah backward and the cup went flying. Lying on the cobblestones, Beriah looked Jesus in the eyes. Never had Beriah seen such love and felt such compassion as was in the eyes of the battered Nazarene.

Jesus, weakened by lack of food and sleep and the cruel beating, was unable to rise. During all this drama a crowd of followers and sightseers, along with His accusers, had been keeping pace with the procession. A soldier of the rear guard jabbed a tall, muscular man with his lance, "You!" he demanded, "What's your name?"

With dignity the large man stepped forward. "Simon sir…Simon of Cyrene."

"Well, Simon of Cyrene," sneered the soldier, "Carry that cross for the weakling Nazarene or we'll never get this day's dirty work completed!"

Without a word or a change of expression, Simon untied the rawhide cords and released Jesus' arms. He then lifted the heavy cross from the bloody shoulders of Jesus. With the cross on his own back, Simon leaned down and gently helped Jesus to His feet. In a low compassionate voice Simon said, "Come Master, let me help you." Slowly, the procession began to move toward the dreaded hill called Golgotha.

Quickly, the merchants locked their shops and followed the crowd. Beriah went across to the distraught Nadab and helped him to his living quarters. Then he gathered his belongings and in his slow crab-like gait proceeded along the Via Dolorosa to the Hill of the Skull. Climbing was difficult for Beriah. He held on to protruding rocks and scrub bushes to help him up the rough terrain. As he climbed he could hear the hammer driving the metal spikes into Jesus' hands and feet. Each ring of the hammer was like a blow to Beriah's compassionate heart.

Out of breath, Beriah arrived at the top of the stony hill. Already three undressed men were hanging on crosses. The time was at the third hour. The battered and bleeding Jesus, with beard torn off, was sagging from the center cross. He was being crucified between two thieves. The scene was one that caused Beriah's blood to run cold. The face of the first man was contorted in pain, fear, and helplessness. The face of Jesus was one of anguish and deep sorrow. The face of the third man was one of rage, bitterness, and hatred.

Beriah moved off to one side and seated himself in the shade of a scrub cedar tree. Twisted by the elements of time, the cedar had dug its roots into the cliff rock like a falcon holding onto a wire. The tree leaned at a precarious angle thus casting shade upon the unholy ground. Here, Beriah prayed fervently for God to deliver Jesus from His suffering.

The crowd that was gathered on the hill was a diverse group. The Roman Soldiers soon split up. Of the thirty soldiers, one group stayed on guard while the other group passed the time casting lots. The soldiers were disgruntled. The sweat was running down the sides of their faces. Their metal helmets were a conduit for the hot sunrays. If this fracas lasted too long, their brains would be fried. The heat of the breastplates, shields, and lances felt like they had come out of a furnace.

And to make matters worse, they were wearing red cloaks, which added more heat. This was the end of the week and they should be able to relax in the baths and have a few tankards of wine. Instead, they were given extra duty because a mob of dirty Jews were filling the streets of Jerusalem this week-end to worship a God they couldn't even see. Bah!

The Priests, Saducees, and the Pharisees stood to one side gloating. Near the cross was a small group of women dressed in dark robes and headdresses. The one in the center was making a high, keening sound. A young man was trying to console the weeping women. It was whispered that this was Mary, the mother of Jesus. Other onlookers were milling around or talking quietly in little groups. A Hawker was selling sweetmeats to the soldiers. The merchants from near the Via Dolarosa huddled together in silence. Their faces registered horror, concern, and compassion. A few of Jesus' followers stayed on the fringe of the crowd.

Rat, the young pickpocket relieved the Priest and three Pharisees of some gold coins. He bought a sweetmeat from the vendor and sidled over to sit in the shade beside Beriah. In a mocking voice he asked, "Why are you here crab man? You come to watch the Tragedy Play?" Beriah did not answer. After a large bite of the sticky roll, Rat continued, "I've got to give the foxy old priests credit. This tragedy is as good as the Tragedy Plays Sophocles wrote about the ancient Greece." Beriah still said nothing. "So why did you come Crab man? It must have been hard, considering you're a cripple," said Rat.

Beriah looked at the dirty brash young man. He hesitated then answered. "I felt compelled to come. I wanted to show Jesus that some of us care about His abuse and the mockery of justice. After all, what if He is the Son of God? If Jesus is the Messiah, will God hold us accountable because we didn't come to His defense?" With tears in his eyes Beriah lowered his head. His cripple shoulders shook.

"Whoa man, be careful what you say! Don't let the soldiers hear such seditious talk against Rome, or you'll be the next one hanging on a tree. Maybe even today if you incite a riot," warned Rat. Both young men were silent for a while as they watched Jesus and the thieves struggle to lift themselves in order to get a breath. Moans escaped the parched lips of the men on the crosses. Flies swarmed and vied with the fire ants to suck the fresh blood. The flesh of their hands and feet was beginning to tear from the pressure put on the wounds when the body was lifted up and down for breathing. The sound of breathing made an eerie sound like feet being pulled out of slimy mire. It was a deep throated, sucking, pulling, labored sound which came from deep in the chest cavity and from lungs that wheezed like dry, decaying bellows.

The sky above the crosses was a clear blue without a cloud anywhere to be seen. The sun was beaming down hot on the bowed head. And high overhead the vultures sailed in broad circles. The naked heads, slightly crooked beaks, dark feathers, and blue claws cast ugly moving shadows across the hot, dusty earth. Occasionally, the birds of death flew lower and looked at the horrendous scene. Then being upset, they vomited, as their nature was, and returned to their wide circle pattern. Their wings moved effortlessly, gliding while they watched and waited. Off and on their eight foot wide wing shadows cast evil looking dark shadows across the watching, uplifted faces of the waiting crowd. The shadows appeared to be searching for the secret sins hidden in the souls of each man and woman who watched the Lamb of God being slain.

Finally, Beriah asked the cynical young man with the matted, black hair, "Why'd you come?"

Rat's reply was not the one Beriah expected. Nodding his head in the direction of the High Priest, Rat replied, "See that gloating old Priest with the twelve big jewels on his ephod?" Beriah acknowledged that he did. "He's wearing a King's fortune on his chest and I intend to own it someday. In fact, not only the stones but also the golden bells around the hem of his garment and the gold on his miter. Let the old fool wear a plain headdress like Phineas, who works in the Cheesemaker's Valley." Grinning Rat continued, "I'll be magnanimous and let him keep the multi-colored pomegranates between the gold bells. They're only made of string. Yes sir, I've taken quite a fancy to that outfit."

"You're crazy!" gasped Beriah. "You can't get away with something like that! God designed the clothing for the priest. You talk about sedition. Why you couldn't find a place to hide in all Jerusalem. Every Jew would stop working and look for you if you robbed the High Priest!"

Sighing Rat continued, "You're probably right, but it was fun to dream of skinning that old fox like he does the poor people each day at the Temple."

Talk became less and less as the morning moved slowly on. The thrill seekers who had followed the soldiers and the beaten and battered Nazarene were beginning to be uncomfortable. Strangely, as they looked at a man who did not look human, they only saw love peering out of His good eye. There was an aura of holiness about this man who had done no wrong. What was even stranger, it was as though they themselves were on trial. It was an uncomfortable feeling, as though each was being weighed and was found wanting.

Laughing and boisterous talk slowly subsided and a sense of shame and remorse for being a part of this unholy scene seeped in. A few brave men bowed their heads in shame and left the hill. They walked bent and stooped. They had aged in hours. Their shame was like lead upon their shoulders and sorrow in their hearts. Oh to be able to turn back time. But alas, time is lived but once and can never be returned.

The day heated up and the air was close and stifling. A putrid odor of sweat and blood permeated the atmosphere. The soldiers, getting tired of their game, cast lots for Jesus' clothes. The winner was the young Centurion who was in charge of the execution. He picked up the robe made without seams and left the rest of Jesus' meager belongings on the ground. Looking none too happy about his winnings, he carefully folded the robe, almost reverently.

Beriah shook his head in bewilderment. "Now what will Jesus be buried in?" he whispered.

At last Rat reacted, "I say friend, that was a selfish thing to do to a dying man." Shaking his dirty mane of matted hair, Rat continued. "It doesn't seem fair. In fact, nothing about this diabolical farce of justice seems fair." After Rat's outburst of injustice, Beriah felt a growing affinity toward the brash young man.

Along about the fifth hour, a foreboding sense of doom descended upon the crowd. The wind began to pick up as the sky turned a strange ominous gray. Then the gathering clouds began to swirl and change each minute. Sometimes the color was pewter, then a dirty yellow-green mixed with indigo and black. The vultures stopped circling in the air and went to roost on the limbs of a tall, dead tree. Their black-feathered wings were gathered close to their turkey size bodies. The jaundiced, yellow eyes stared in fear as the wind lifted their neck feathers around their baldheads. The white bleached tree was now decorated with somber puffballs. Thus creating a giant, grotesque funeral arrangement for the reaper of death. The whole macabre scene was surreal. Though the clouds rolled and tumbled, they continued to get darker and lower. The dark turbulent clouds soon engulfed the very tops of the crosses. Meanwhile, a mysterious fog began to creep up from the ground. No one spoke. Fear caused people to move closer together. The weeping women fell to their knees, still praying to the Great Jehovah.

Apprehension became tangible in the restless moving of the soldiers. Shields and lances were held in ready positions and swords were checked in their sheaths. To Beriah, it seemed that the God of Israel was angry about the barbaric scene. The Priests and the Pharisees cast uneasy glances at the dying Jesus. Then along with many fainthearted followers began to scramble down the rugged path and headed for the gates of Jerusalem.

Suddenly, as though an invisible hand had thrown a switch the wind ceased. An eerie silence descended on the hill of Golgotha. The birds and insects made no sound. Not a leaf rustled nor a blade of grass stirred. Not a breath of fresh air lifted the clouds. All eyes were on the central cross. In agony, Jesus moaned and asked for water. A soldier dipped a sponge in vinegar and gall. Then on a long reed he lifted the sponge to Jesus' lips. After tasting the pain-killing gall, Jesus refused to drink. Nearing the sixth hour, the land of Israel was as dark as a night without moon or stars. Never had such a strange phenomenon happened since the death angel killed every first-born male child of the Egyptians.

The soldiers lit torches from scrub bushes and built a small fire to see by. The dancing flames of the fire magnified the grotesque, mutilated body of the man beneath the sign that read 'King of the Jews' which had been ordered by the Roman Procurator, Pontius Pilate. The Priests and Pharisees had declared the sign blasphemy but Pilate commanded it to be hung.

Watching the eyes of Jesus, Rat whispered, "I'm almost persuaded the Nazarene is who He claims to be."

Beriah agreed. "We could be witnessing the monstrous murder of the Son of God."

By the flickering flames Jesus looked down on the remaining crowd. With eyes filled with sorrow and His voice choked with compassion; He prayed aloud. "Father, forgive them; for they know not what they do."

The thief to Jesus' right cried, "Master, remember me when You come into your kingdom."

Jesus answered with love, "This day, thou shalt be with Me in Paradise."

A Pharisee made a feeble protest saying, "The poor diluted fool thinks He's God. We all know it's blasphemy and the demented wretch is already paying the ultimate price!"

Nearing the ninth hour, Jesus again asked for water. In false bravo someone jeered, "Leave Him alone! Let's see if Elijah will come to save Him!"

Jesus' body was getting weaker and His breathing much labored. In a heart rendering loud voice He cried out, "My God, My God, why hast Thou forsaken me?" The anguish in Jesus' voice sent chills up Beriah's spine and onto his scalp. Rat too was reacting to the heart-wrenching cry. At the moment Rat had crossed his arms and was rocking back and forth, tears were streaming down his face as though he too felt Jesus' torment. All signs of brazen bluster had disappeared from the young man. Beriah, without speaking, put his arm around Rat's shaking shoulders and thus they remained. After Jesus cried, "My God, My God, why hast Thou forsaken Me?" the wind picked up and began to swirl the dirt and leaves. It bent the trees and bushes in a bowed position.

Beriah whispered in a choked voice, "Old Jobah said when the Messiah comes, every knee shall bow."

"From the strength of the wind those soldiers may do more than bow, they may be face down before Jesus," replied Rat.

At that moment part of the soldiers were stamping out small dry grass fires started by blowing embers. A flock of crows were caught in the swirl-winds with tail feathers blown up like open fans. Their frantic cries of "caw, caw, caw" could be heard as they went over.

At the ninth hour, a putrid odor of sulfur mingled with the ground fog. It burned the eyes and noses of the onlookers. Between outbreaks of the crowd coughing, Jesus looked up toward the heaven and again cried out, "Father, It is finished!" and yielded up His spirit. His lips closed on His last agonizing breath. His head slumped forward with such force that the crown of thorns fell to the ground. Jesus' eyes were closed in death. His brown hair fell forward and His body sagged on the metal spikes. Quickly, a frightened, young soldier thrust his lance through Jesus' side. As the lance was pulled out water and blood gushed out and ran down Jesus' long bare legs. When the last breath left Jesus the wind died down to a soft gentle breeze. The blood and water continued to flow from the dead Nazarene. It poured off His feet, down the cross, and onto the stony ground. Mary, Jesus' mother, screamed a heartbroken cry and flung her arms around the bloody feet of her beloved son. A soldier stepped forward to remove her but was stopped by the Commanding Centurion. "Leave her in peace to mourn her son." He commanded with compassion.

As Rat & Beriah watched, a rumbling sound could be heard and the earth began to tremble. Then it began to shake violently. The earth spewed up dirt and boulders and a scrub tree was uprooted. Strong men fell down, others prayed aloud. The crosses of the two thieves tilted at a precarious angle. Only the center cross remained erect and untouched. A bright shaft of light broke through the clouds and illuminated the bowed head of the crucified Jesus. The earth continued to shake. Mary, the mother of Jesus, clung tighter to the bloody feet as though trying one last time to protect her dear son.

The Centurion looked up at the radiant head of the slain Jesus and said, "Surely, this must be the Son of God." Gradually, the earth stopped shaking. Quickly the thrill seekers got to their feet and fled down the side of the hill. The soldiers just as quickly began taking down the bodies of the two thieves. However, they did not touch the center figure. The young disciple whom Jesus had entrusted with His mother began to loosen Mary's hold on the cross. With the help of the other women they led the weeping mother off the hill of Calvary.

The soldiers worked quickly and soon with the two thieves, they too descended the hill. Up the hill, the dead, bleached tree leaned to the east. The ground around the base of the tree was littered with black feathers. The backs of the vultures were naked. Their baldheads were tucked under their massive wings as though hiding from the wrath of God. Tenaciously, the claws of the birds clung to the dead white limbs.

Beriah and Rat remained crouched behind a huge boulder, which had been spewed up by the earthquake. Except for the crucified man called Christ no one else was left on the hill. There was a deathly hush. A cool breeze began to blow. It blew Jesus' brown hair partially over His face as though hiding it from the cruelty of mankind. After what seemed an eternity of hiding, Beriah and Rat heard a sound. Shaking, they curiously peered around the boulder. Before them were two men which Beriah recognized. One was the wealthy merchant, Joseph of Arimethea, and the other was Nicodemus, a member of the Sanhedrin. Unbeknown to priest and Pharisee, both of these men were followers of Jesus. Joseph had obtained permission to remove Jesus before sundown according to the Jewish law. This act also prevented Jesus' body from being left on the cross for days to be devoured by vultures.

In preparation for burial, Joseph and Nicodemus anointed Jesus' body with myrrh and aloes. Nicodemus had brought spices and Joseph brought fine linen cloth. Carefully, they wrapped the body of Jesus. By performing this pious act both men were considered unclean by Jewish law. Therefore, they would not be able to participate in the Passover ceremonies. However, theirs' was a labor of love and this did not deter them. The men did not linger on the hill. With the aid of Joseph's servants, the linen wrapped body was carried away. Beriah and Rat overheard Joseph tell Nicodemus they would lay Jesus in a new tomb he had recently purchased for his own use.

After the burial party left, Beriah and Rat crept out from their hiding place. Nearby lay the small pile of clothing belonging to Jesus. Rat reached down and picked up a pair of sandals. Holding them out to Beriah he said, “I guess no one wanted these. You take them Crab man. Yours are worn out.”

Beriah hesitated, “Maybe the soldiers will want them.”

“Naw,” answered Rat. “Roman sandals are designed differently. Go on, take them.” Reluctantly Beriah took the sandals and clutched them to his chest. “Come on Crab man, let’s get back to the city. Here let me carry your things and you lean on me for support,” said Rat. “I’ll help you back to your dwelling.” The darkness had lifted a little. Beriah took a last look at the three empty bloodstained crosses silhouetted against the lonely sky. The tragic drama had now been played out – or had it?

Chapter Two

Rat picked up Beriah's rug and bag and slung them over his shoulder. Then put his arm around the crippled man. Beriah, clutching the sandals and harp to his aching heart, was glad for Rat's support. Together they moved slowly down the rock-strewn path. Neither man looked back again.

The beauty of the sun-drenched morning was gone from the land of Judea. The burning odor of dust particles mingled with the pungency of green broken cedar. Scrub oaks lay broken along the cliffs and the surly-gray face of the limestone skull was weeping grit and sand tears from the shifting earth tremors.

Beriah had a deep sense of despair that was squeezing his heart. The death of the Galilean seemed to amass agonies in his soul. The sharp, serrated edges of the rocks, which had been spewed out of the bowels of the earth, scratched and tore at their hands and legs as they cautiously worked their way down the slippery path.

Night was on them by the time they reached the walls of the Holy City. Surprisingly, the gate was not locked. The city was in darkness except for the weak light of the pale greenish moon whose face appeared to show revulsion for the evil bloody scene on Golgotha's hill. The normal sounds of the evening were muted. There were no human voices, no dogs barking, no camels complaining, no birds twittering, and no donkeys braying at the end of the day. The only sound was the incessant scrapping of cricket legs which seem to say, 'Will you have me crucify your King, your King, crucify your King, crucify your King, your King?' And across the Kidron Valley came a reply, 'Whoo, whoo,' and a bird replied, 'Not I, not I, not I.' Other than these sounds, it was as though the world was dead. The silence was more terrifying than the darkness. Every shadow was frightening. The two young men only spoke in whispers. Rat's arm was still around Beriah. Perhaps he too needed the comfort of another person.

At last Beriah asked in a low voice, "Where do you live friend?"

"No place in particular. I just curl up on trash piles in the alleys," said Rat.

"Doesn't it get cold at night?" inquired Beriah in concern.

"Sure, some nights. Especially if the wives throw their dishwater on me. You wouldn't believe it, but some do it on purpose and tell me to move on."

Beriah was quiet while he mulled over in his mind how to help his new friend. Finally he said, "You best come home with me." In truth, Beriah needed company tonight as badly as Rat needed a safe place to sleep.

Slowly, Beriah led the way along silent, winding streets. The shades of the storefronts were closed. The doors locked – and upstairs living quarters were in total darkness. Beriah continued along the narrow corridors until they neared the outer wall. Here among bushes and large boulders Beriah stopped. Rat was puzzled at the location. Suddenly, Beriah said, "Wait here and I'll light a candle." With that remark Beriah dropped into a crevice in the earth. A short time later, he bobbed up again holding a lighted candle.

Rat was mystified. "Now," directed Beriah, "hand my bag in first, and then carefully lower yourself through the opening. I'm standing on solid rock. There are hand-hewn steps leading to my living quarters. Come don't be afraid. It's quite safe." Cautiously Rat lowered his tall, lanky frame through the opening. There was the fleeting feeling of fear about the unknown that bothered Rat. This fear was as old as time itself. A fear, which was implanted in man when Adam and Eve ate the forbidden fruit of the tree of knowledge. Fear had dogged man's footsteps throughout the centuries after having learned good and evil.

Rat was surprised that he was in an underground passageway. Beriah asked Rat to carry his belongings while he carried the candle, harp, and the sandals of the Nazarene Jesus. Holding the candle high, Beriah led the way down the worn steps. After several twists and turns of a narrow passageway, they came to a room with a high vaulted ceiling. The room had been hewed out of stone. Beriah then torched some wood for a much needed fire. The room quickly filled with light. Rat stood in stunned silence. Beriah lit a pine knot jutting out from the wall. He placed the candle on a packing box table. Then gesturing with his hand he said, "We have a spring for water." Rat followed the movement of Beriah's hand to where the limestone rocks encircled a small pool of water. Nearby sat a clay water jug with two handles. A gourd dipper was hanging from a branch, which had been wedged into a crack in the stonewall. Over the spring, little patches of pale green moss and white lichens had over the years penetrated the porous stone. The water looked cool and inviting after the long, hot day.

"On a lower level we have a pool for bathing. Again Beriah motioned in the direction of the pool. Rat stepped forward to the pool. He was surprised to see that it was formed by water emerging from an underground source. It cascaded over a small precipice forming a miniature waterfall before falling into a bowl-like rock formation. Over the pool was a small fissure, which in day, let in a narrow shaft of light, which fed the ferns in cracks and crevices." At last Rat spoke in awe. "This is a pool any Greek would love to have in his garden!"

Beriah replied, "The smoke from our fires go down other passageways which travel under the entire city. This way, I can heat water and food. We have mats near the fire for sitting, and mats near the walls for sleeping. I keep my own cooking pots and pans to the back. Over to the left, we have a place to wash up and do laundry."

Nodding to a mat on the right side of the fire, Beriah said, "Sit down and rest." As Beriah was talking, Rat's eyes had been trying to take in the comforts of the large vaulted room. His excited curiosity was about to get the better of him.

Rat could not hold his excitement any longer. "It's marvelous! How did you discover this place? How long have you lived here? Why man; you have everything you need. Who else knows about this place?"

Beriah sat quietly until the young man ran down. "Let's eat first and then I'll answer your questions." Beriah arose and washed his hands and dried them on a scrap of cloth, which Carmie had donated for his comfort. Beriah emptied the water in a crevice near the wall and refilled the pan with spring water. Next, he placed a kettle of water near the fire.

Rat was told to wash up while Beriah went about the evening meal. Although the day's events were foremost in both of their minds, they refrained from talking about it at the moment.

Beriah set two pottery cups and bowls on the box. Then Beriah took a clay jug and filled it with cold spring water and set it near the box. Rat returned to his mat as Beriah was untying the cloths holding figs, bread, cheese, sweetmeat, and apples. He removed a knife from his pouch and divided the food, placing the figs in a small bowl.

While all of this was taking place, no word had been spoken between the two men. When the water was poured into cups, Beriah bowed his head, and said, "Now let us give thanks to the Great Jehovah for this food." Rat watched Beriah's face as he prayed and was touched by the sincerity in Beriah's voice as he said, "Father, we thank thee for these and thy mercies. Bless this food to our use, and our lives, to thy service. Amen." With this Beriah looked at Rat and said, "Friend you are welcome to my table and humble home."

Rat gave a half smile at Beriah. "It's strange," he mused, "I really believe you mean it." With tears in his eyes the young man continued, "This is the first kindness and the first home I've been invited into since I reached this city a year ago. In the future, you're my friend Beriah, and I will cease calling you Crab man. My name is Adonis and I'd be honored if you would call me Adonis instead of Rat."

"Adonis is a nice Greek name. How'd a Jewish man come by that name?" asked Beriah.

"I'm not Jewish," answered Adonis. "My home is in Athens."

"Then how did you end up in Jerusalem?" quizzed Beriah.

Adonis gave a sad smile, “Easy friend Beriah, I jumped off my father’s ship at the Port of Sycaminum. I traded a rich man’s clothing for a dirty woolen cloak and joined up with a camel caravan. Many days and many miles had passed along with much hard work. And for the first time in my life, I arrived in Jerusalem. I wanted to be free and see the world.” Putting a fig in his mouth, Adonis leaned back on one arm in the Greek style of eating, then sheepishly said, “It was easy—no?”

Beriah looked at the daring but foolish young man. “No Adonis, not easy. You left out the sore feet, the blistered hands and aching back that wasn’t use to hard work, and feeling rather foolish for leaving a good life behind.”

Adonis nodded, “Friend Beriah, you have the wisdom of a Socrates.”

To Adonis’ surprise, Beriah said, “I too have studied your Socrates, Plato, and Aristotle. Flattery was not one of their teachings. However, cleanliness and clean living was important, as well as, the searching for the inward man. Have you been searching Adonis?” Pointing to the other side of the room, Beriah continued, “Over there is my old friend and teacher’s pallet. You’re welcome to use it and wear his clean robes if you stop stealing and show yourself worthy. There’s plenty of water here for bathing. A razor and soap are near the wash pan. Adonis, you can stay here for a while providing you can be trusted. I’m willing to give you a try. There’s an extra sheepskin near your pallet. We’ll talk more tomorrow about you finding some honest work.”

Adonis insisted on washing the cups and bowls. After the table was cleared, Beriah and Adonis sat around the fire drinking juice. At last, Adonis broached the subject of the crucifixion. “Beriah, one day I overheard an elderly man in the temple courtyard telling a weird story. It was about the Hebrew children while following Moses in the wilderness. It seemed they were being bitten by poisonous snakes and were sick and dying. The old man said that God told Moses, their leader, to make a serpent of bronze and put it on a long stick and whoever looked upon the bronze serpent lived." Adonis went on, "He also said that a prophet named Isaiah said that the 'messiah would be lifted up and draw all men to Him'. Beriah, do you know anything about these legends and do they have anything to do with today's grisly business?"

Beriah's eyes filled with tears. "The old man was referring to the scroll of the prophet Isaiah. That was one of the lessons that my mentor and friend Old Jobah insisted I memorize," answered Beriah.

"Could you say it for me?" asked Adonis.

Beriah, through tears, looked into the flame of the fire. Then in a soft tone, he quoted in a voice that wavered. "Who had believed our message and to who is the arm of the Lord been revealed? He grew up before Him like a tender shoot and like a root out of dry ground. He had no beauty or majesty to attract us to Him, nothing in His appearance that we should desire Him. He was despised and rejected by men, a man of sorrows and familiar with suffering. Like one from whom men hide their faces, He was despised, and we esteemed Him not. Surely, He took up our infirmities and carried our sorrows. Yet, we considered Him stricken by God, smitten by Him and afflicted. But He was pierced for our transgressions, He was crushed for our iniquities; the punishment that brought us peace was upon Him. And by His wounds we are healed. We all, like sheep, have gone astray; each of us have turned to his own way, and the Lord has laid on Him the iniquities of us all…"

As Beriah finished quoting Isaiah's Suffering Servant, his face was wet with tears. Across the fire, Adonis also had a wet face. "It's getting late Adonis, tomorrow evening we'll talk about this again."

Adonis said, "Goodnight," covered himself with the sheepskin, and was soon fast asleep. Yet, Beriah's mind was tormented by the images of the day, as he went over and over the horrifying scenes until the wee hours of the morning. Even then, he relived them in his dreams.

Surprisingly, Beriah did not wake until mid-morning. Lighting a candle, he looked around the room. Adonis' pallet was smooth and his sheepskin cover folded, but there was no sign of the young Greek.

Slowly, Beriah straightened his own pallet. He washed the sleep out of his eyes, put on a clean robe, picked up his bag and belongings, and was ready to find something to eat. Today, being the Sabbath, most shops and bazaar stalls were closed. Jews were forbidden to buy or sell on the Sabbath. Only the Gentiles broke the Sabbath law. As usual, Beriah spent the Sabbath playing his music for the camel caravans, entertaining the travelers. It was here that Beriah first heard the news about the temple. A trader told how the veil of the Holy of Holies was rent from top to bottom as though an angry God was showing displeasure at the cruel crucifixion of a saintly Rabbi. Some didn't believe the story saying it was too far fetched. A young man spoke up, "My uncle is a Priest and he said it was torn."

"What was the veil like?" asked an Arab merchant.

"According to my uncle, it was blue, scarlet, and purple with Cherubim's. The rent marred its beauty," said the young man, who was from the tribe of Levi.

Beriah played his music softly so he could overhear the conversation as men came and went throughout the day. One such story said that Herod had fled to his retreat in Caesarea. Another story had King Herod drunk and screaming "John the Baptist is in the palace hunting for his head!" Supposedly, the King's physicians had to subdue him with medication.

A group of men arrived shortly after the noon meal and told about graves being split asunder, and buildings being shifted off their foundations. As the day progressed, the stories became more alarming. Questions passed back and forth about the tombs and cemeteries. There was speculation that the earthquake too damaged them. If so, who would be brave enough to go into the dark recesses of the earth to see if the angry God had spewed out the dead. Stories of unrest in the city continued to pour in. Each new person returning to the caravansary was interrogated. One person told about a man at the Temple, who said that Pontius Pilate walked his balcony all night, only stopping periodically to wash his hands.

By evening, Beriah's spirit was as low as a camel's belly lying in the sand. Though his cup was overflowing, his heart felt like lead. At the end of the day he had bought enough herbed rice and mutton for two meals. This was placed in a small leather drawstring pouch. Next, he bought dates and a loaf of barley bread. On his way back to his underground home, he remembered the traders' talk about the cemeteries and tombs being damaged. Perhaps tomorrow he should check in on Old Jobah's family tomb and see if any of the ancient Jewish crypts had been disturbed. This was a disquieting thought. In his heart, he hoped that Adonis would return again tonight. Beriah knew he would welcome the young Greek's company. Near the edge of the city, Beriah bought a small flagon of fruit juice and some pomegranates.

The day had remained semi-dark. It was as though the light of the world had been removed. Beriah's footsteps grew more weary as he thought about spending the evening alone. Carefully he dropped into the crevice and descended the stone stairs. The cool air of the underground tunnel felt good against Beriah's flushed face. Tonight his twisted back ached. This was caused by the tension of the strange rumors. Beriah's clothes and hair had a thin layer of dust that still floated in the air from the earthquake. His eyelashes and nostrils also had dust and grit from the fallout. The dust had a putrid odor. Throughout the day, Beriah had wet a cloth in the watering trough trying to keep the sickening odor out of his nose and off his face. But the air over Jerusalem had a smell and a gloom of death.

As Beriah rounded the corner leading to his living quarters, his heart leaped. There before him was the smiling Adonis. He had on a clean robe and his hair had been washed and combed. It was now a shining mass of black waves. "Greetings friend Beriah!" Beriah was so over-come with relief he hugged the amused Adonis. The young Greek had been busy. A fire was burning and the table was enlarged by adding a box. A scrap of pretty material covered it. In the center of the table burned a candle and a bouquet of wildflowers were in a pottery jug. The table was set for two. A fresh melon and sweet rolls lay beside Beriah's plate. Even more surprising the wash area was clean and tidy.

More packing crates had been brought in and a makeshift cabinet had also been created. The cabinet now displayed Beriah's pots and pottery. Robes had been washed and draped over the protruding rock formation that surrounded the small pool. A metal tripod had been erected for Beriah's kettles. The area in their living quarters had been swept with a willow broom. The mats by the table had fresh straw under them to make sitting more comfortable.

Adonis watched Beriah's face as he surveyed the day's labor. Adonis was more than rewarded by the expression of gladness on Beriah's face. Tears of joy overflowed Beriah's eyes. Adonis quickly said in a way of explanation, "I took your advice Beriah. I have been doing what Socrates taught and searched my inward man."

"And what did you find Adonis?" asked Beriah.

The smile left Adonis' face, "I didn't like what I found. So I have set about to rectify my life. I want to get back on a straight course. Tomorrow I'll seek honest work even if I have to muck out the stalls at the Camel Caravansary."

Beriah smiled, "You've made a wise choice Adonis. Now let's eat the nourishing food we brought home." With this Beriah located two bowls and wooden spoons. He ladled out the herbed rice and mutton. The rich aroma tantalized their nostrils, as Beriah placed a wooden spoon by each bowl and filled a small pot with dates. He then laid the bread on a board and cut off two large slices. Next, he poured the juice. Sitting down on the mat, Beriah smiled, "Now let us pray." Both men bowed their heads. Beriah's soft voice began, "Father God, I thank you for sending Adonis to be my friend. Father you know I've been lonely since Jobah died. Now you have replaced him with someone who plans to set his life on a course of clean living. Father, whether he stays with me a long time or a short while, I will always treasure his friendship. Also, for the compassion and care Adonis showed to me yesterday when the man of God was crucified and the earth shook with your wrath. Wherever his footsteps lead, please keep him from all harm. Now Father I thank you for our food and humble abode. Amen."

During the meal, Beriah related the many stories and rumors he had overheard at the Caravansary. Adonis listened with great interest. When Beriah had finished Adonis said, "I too have overheard many strange tales. In the Temple one group believes this crucified Jesus will come out of His tomb after three days. In the Temple courtyard the soldiers were placing bets on this wild story. Other soldiers scoffed and laughed and declared that if Jesus comes out of His tomb, Herod would lose his mind. It was whispered the disciples and followers of Jesus were in hiding.

I overheard a man saying the secret sign of the believers, in the teaching of Jesus, was a picture of a fish. Due to Jesus saying to His followers 'I will make you fishers of men.' The High Priest had not been seen since the earthquake and Pontius Pilate is still walking his balcony and periodically, washing his hands." Adonis continued, "An old man who was in the outer court of the Temple at the time of the earthquake said when the veil was rent in the Holy of Holies, it sounded like a sail being ripped in a hurricane. It was also whispered, the Golden Candelabra in the Holy of Holies had been turned over during the quake and the priests were having a hard time getting the altar fires to burn. I tell you Beriah, these are troubled times.

This semi-darkness that has hung all day gives me the creeps. There's an aura of doom hanging over this city. The pilgrims who traveled so far to be in Jerusalem during Passover have been shuffling along in long lines waiting to give sacrifices to the Great Jehovah." Beriah noticed that Adonis was shivering at times when he spoke. Adonis continued speaking and shivering, "The pilgrims' voices and footsteps are muted. Even the moneychangers and merchants plying the sales of the sacrificial lambs and doves are doing business in voices just about a whisper.

It seems the cruel crucifixion of the Holy Rabbi from Nazareth has staunched the laughter and joy of the Passover Festival. Thousands of the visitors fled Jerusalem yesterday after the quake. And others are leaving as soon as they make their sacrifices. It looks like the greedy Priests have cut off their noses to spite their faces this time. The

Temple Coffers won't be ringing with the usual abundance of silver and gold. Already the merchants and Inn Keepers are complaining about the loss of revenue. The only thing normal about the Temple Courtyard are the old men sitting in their usual places. Even their daily debates, gossip, and story swapping is transpiring in low tones."

Beriah nodded his head, "This cloud of doom bothers me too. In fact, I heard similar stories about the dead rising. I need to check on Jobah's family tomb. Maybe the earthquake damaged it. There are twelve people buried there."

After a lull in conversation, Adonis spoke, "Beriah, I don't know much about this God of the Jews, however, if He raises the Nazarene from the dead, I intend to find out more about Him." The two men talked far into the night. The fire died down to a heap of glowing embers. Long grotesque shadows moved on the wall as Beriah and Adonis moved or shifted their bodies. The talk finally came to a halt; yet, the men were reluctant to go to bed. It was well past midnight before they lay down. Even then, sleep did not come easy.

Morning came in; much like the day before. When Beriah awoke, Adonis had already made up his pallet and left. Momentarily, Beriah felt a sense of loss. Then he prepared for the first day of the week. The shops were already opened as Beriah settled down by the well. The sun had come up bright. It helped to lift the feeling of gloom, which had held the city captive since the crucifixion. Merchants and customers could be heard haggling with each other over prices and workmanship. With the sun, an atmosphere of normalcy began to return.

That is everything on the surface appeared normal. Yet, underneath, hidden from the eyes of man, lay a multitude of emotions and questions. The biggest question being, 'was this – the crucifixion of Jesus of Nazareth – the greatest crime ever spawned by madmen?"

Beriah soon settled down by the well and began playing his harp. Except today there was no joyful lilt to his music. Rather, the strings took on a sad, wistful sound that seemed to be searching the recesses of the soul. Rosh's humming sounded much like a funeral dirge as he slowly worked his loom. Hirah was hanging an assortment of colored candles on a line, while singing: "Shema Israel, Adonai Elohener, Adonai echad.

Hear, O Israel: The Lord our God is one.

Hur, the Potter sang out, "God is our refuge and strength,
An ever-present help in trouble.
Therefore, we will not fear, though
The earth gives way and the mountains fall
Into the heart of the sea."

Across the way, Tola, the coppersmith, sang back,
"Yes – be bold and strong,
Banish all fear and doubt,
For remember, the Lord your God
Is with you wherever you go."

He then resumed striking metal with a wooden hammer – making a melancholy sound. Next to Tola, Old Shua sang in a mediocre voice,

"If I rise on the wings of dawn,
If I settle by the sea,
Even there your hand will guide me,
Your right hand will hold me fast."

Beriah listened to the uplifting words and plucked the strings of his harp to the rhythm of the surrounding noises. But his mind was a confused mixture of thoughts and emotions. The brutality of the crucifixion kept running through Beriah's mind. Was Jesus the Jewish Machiach and the Samaritans' Taheh? The Restorer? The Awaited One? The Coming One? The Anointed One? And if Jesus was the Anointed One, what calamity had man brought upon mankind for all eternity by murdering Him?

Passersby were generous with their coins as they stopped at the well. A feeling of 'all is not well' lingered in the air. The merchants went through the act of running business as usual until an excited voice shouted, "The Nazarene has disappeared! The tomb is empty!"

"What do you mean – empty? "What happened to the body?" "Was it stolen?" "Did He arise from the dead?" These questions came flying from all directions. The man who had brought the news was bombarded with more inquiries. "That's all I know," answered the carrier of the story. Then he hurried on to spread the news.

Immediately, the business transactions stopped. The customers fled in the direction of the Temple to glean more news about Jesus. Throughout the day the rumors flew. There were those who said the Priests were livid. Supposedly, Pilate had the soldiers who were guarding the tomb up for insubordination. Whoever heard of Roman soldiers sleeping on the job, much less, seeing mysterious, heavenly beings? There was a full-scale investigation of who broke the seal and rolled away the stone. Furthermore, how did a body evaporate through grave clothes and not disturb them? One woman was so bold as to even say she had seen the risen Jesus!

Thus the stories continued to fly. One of the Palace servants said Herod's wife, Herodias, fearing Jesus, demanded her daughter to get rid of the head of John the Baptist. Salome, still having the head of the Baptizer on the platter, rebelled at first, but relented and had the monstrosity placed in her own sepulcher! Herod, after hearing about the empty tomb, had to be put in bed again. He declared to his physician, there were worms crawling under his skin. Just before closing time, three men came by who told about graves opened all around the city. Some of the people, who had been dead for years, were seen walking around. One rumor has it that the deceased talked to neighbors and family members!

With this news, Beriah decided to call it a day and return to his cavern home. On the way, he stopped at the bazaar and bought rice and beef stew, bananas, bread, cheese, and a flagon of goats' milk. Then he hurried home. Adonis still hadn't arrived. Placing the milk in cold spring water, Beriah lit a torch. With a feeling of dread and fear he traveled down the long passageway that exited near the tomb where Jobah was buried.

When Beriah entered the family tomb from a broken door, dank, putrid air assailed his nostrils. Lighting a candle, he could immediately see something was amiss. The covers of some of the vaults were lying on the ground. Some were broken and others lay at odd angles as though a powerful hand had pushed from the inside of the crypt. Four yellowed linen bodies remained untouched while others had vanished. With trembling hands and a heart that was pounding, Beriah approached Jobah's niche. To Beriah's horror, old Jobah wasn't there! Jobah too had disappeared. Staggering, Beriah retraced his steps back to his living quarters.

Adonis had arrived and had a fire going. Upon seeing the ashen face of Beriah he hurried to his side, "Beriah, you look as though you've seen a ghost! Are you ill? Here, sit down on this mat." When Beriah was seated, Adonis quickly brought him a drink of water. At last Beriah gained self-control and told Adonis about his harrowing experience in Jobah's tomb. To Beriah's surprise Adonis was ecstatic. He whirled and danced around the room. Beriah thought the young Greek had lost his mind. Suddenly, Adonis came to a halt and declared, "It's wonderful! Don't you see what this means Beriah?" Numbly, Beriah shook his head. "It means that since time began, it has finally been proven; there is life after death! Rejoice Beriah, this is a time to celebrate!"

Slowly Adonis' words seem to sink in. 'Life after death' thought Beriah. "Then Adonis, this must mean that Jesus is alive!" By now Adonis' happiness was contagious.

"This calls for a celebration," declared Adonis.

Jovially, the two young men spread out their evening meal. Both tried to talk at once. They tossed out questions in rapid succession. As the night progressed, they delved deeper into the spirituality of the soul. At death where does man go? What were the teachings of the Nazarene? What did you have to do to live forever? Did bad men go to the same place as good men? Or was there more than one place? "I'll tell you what Beriah," said Adonis. "I'll find out where the followers of Jesus meet and we'll attend their meetings. In fact, I helped a camel merchant unload his caravan at Joseph of Arimethea's warehouse. In the corner of the storeroom I saw the drawing of a small fish. Tomorrow I'll go back and let it be known that I want to know more about Jesus' teachings." Finally towards dawn, two excited, young men lay down – only to arise early.

Again the day was filled with distraught. The influx of people who had come to Jerusalem for Passover had gotten wind of the trouble and were making a hasty exit out of every gate of the city. They were leading laden donkeys carrying packs on their backs, riding horses, camels, wooden carts and wagons, along with the rich; who were riding in silk-curtained wains pulled by oxen.

As far as the eye could see were streams of frightened, disillusioned humanity. They weren't taking time to talk. A quick goodbye and 'God go with you,' was about the extent of the conversation. Once again, the Jews were making a hasty exodus, like they had done when they left Egypt. The Roman soldiers seemed to be everywhere. They interrogated the young and old alike. Pilate was determined to find the perpetrator who hypnotized the guards and stole the body of the Nazarene. All the known followers of Jesus were rounded up for questioning. The men and women were warned not to get involved with this fanatical plot to make Rome look bad. A report that Roman soldiers could not guard one dead Jew would not sit well with Caesar.

Beriah was not questioned but Rosh, Hur, Amos, and old Shua were interrogated for over an hour. When the soldiers left, the weeping, old woman closed her soap stall and went home. The others gathered in Tola's shop to discuss the new danger. Beriah was not invited to the meetings. Yet he kept a close eye out as the merchants continued to migrate toward Tola's shop. Along about the ninth hour, a young man stopped at the well. He was wearing a robe with a cowl. He was clean-shaven. As he drank, he kept his head bowed and turned to one side.

Beriah recognized the young man as one of the followers of Jesus who stood on the fringe of the crowd at the crucifixion. However, today, he was missing his black curly beard. The young man's face looked tired and his eyes weary. After drinking he sat down to rest. In the distance came the sound of Roman soldiers. The startled young man looked terrified. Beriah leaned down and scooped up dirt by the well and dumped it over the young man's head and clothing. Then shoving his alms cup into the stranger's hand, Beriah sketched a fish in the dust. Just as quickly, he erased the fish with the heel of his sandal. At the same time, he began playing a lively tune on the harp. "Thank you," whispered the now dirty man. The Roman soldiers came down the street. They glared at Beriah and the young man, but did not slow down.

Marching in formation, they continued on around the twisting cobblestone passageway. Beriah stopped playing. He laid his harp down and began dusting off the stranger. Humbly, the stranger said, " I owe you a debt of gratitude."

Beriah smiled, "I'm sorry about the dirt, but you needed a quick disguise."

"What I really need is a safe place to hide." Stated the man.

"I have a safe place," said Beriah. Without another word Beriah handed the man his leather bag and rug. Then, in a laborious walk, Beriah led the way. Covered in dirt, the stranger looked like hundreds of other workingmen in Jerusalem.

Beriah left his bag and harp with the stranger in the shade of the fig tree while he bought food. After procuring the day's provision he led the way to his cavern home. Adonis still hadn't returned. Lighting the fire Beriah motioned his visitor to sit down. Smiling Beriah said, "My name is Beriah. I saw you at the crucifixion."

Nodding, the stranger said, "I'm a follower of Jesus." Reaching out his hand, he said, " My name is Joshua."

Beriah shook the extended hand. "Why did you take a chance of being seen after stealing the Nazarene's body?"

Joshua sadly smiled. "I came out to warn our friends to go into hiding. We won't be able to meet openly again. Also, we didn't steal the body of Jesus. Rather, He arose from the dead."

Beriah gasped, "Are you sure?"

Nodding his head Joshua said, "Jesus appeared to two of my friends on the road to Emmaus and later to the disciples. It's true Beriah, Jesus is alive."

"I want to believe you but it seems impossible. I have heard of Jesus' miracles but I've never heard Him talk. My first time in His presence was at the crucifixion. I was there with my friend Adonis. My friend and I want to attend some meetings that tells about Jesus' teachings."

A short time later Adonis came, carrying a staff and filled with news. Introductions were made and the evening meal was set. Beriah gave his mat to Joshua and sat on his own rug. Adonis told of various interrogations and several arrests. Beriah invited Joshua to stay in the cavern until it was safe. During the evening, Beriah asked Joshua if some of his friends would like to hold meetings in the passageway. Joshua pondered the invitation. "Many need to go in hiding. Of course, for a while, all meetings will have to be in secret. Otherwise, the streets would be filled with crosses. This would be an ideal place, except for one thing."

"What's that?" Beriah asked.

"A lot of people coming and going into the shrub bushes would invite suspicion, " said Joshua.

"I wasn't thinking of my opening or my quarters. These underground passages travel beneath the entire city. About a mile from here down another passageway is a hidden opening. In fact, it opens behind brambles, boulders, and trees on the side of the Cheesemaker's Valley. Since that's always a busy area they might go unnoticed. Tomorrow I'll show you the opening from the outside. It's not too far from the bridge that crosses the valley to the Temple." There was a lull in the conversation.

Finally, Adonis brought forth the staff he had carried home. Approaching Beriah, he said, "I brought you a staff to help you walk. It might need to be shortened."

Beriah was touched by Adonis' thoughtfulness. Accepting the staff, Beriah felt the smoothness of the wood. It felt warm to his hand. Surprisingly, it was not heavy. Balancing it on his outstretched hand Beriah said, " It's a wonderful staff. Did you make it Adonis?"

Adonis looked at Joshua – then back at Beriah. He remembered his promise about clean living. Adonis hesitated then softly said, "I found it in the Garden of Gethsemane. I was there the night of the arrest."

"What were you doing in the Garden of Gethsemane?" asked Beriah.

Adonis replied, "You see, I was in the Garden taking a nap when voices awoke me. It was already after the supper hour. I saw this man called Jesus kneeling and praying aloud. It was a heart-wrenching prayer. Beriah, you won't believe this, but Jesus' sweat looked like drops of blood. It coursed down His face and hung in His beard. It was the color of the juice of wild berries. I don't know what God He was talking to but it gave me the shivers. I tell you, Jesus' soul seemed to be in agony. Truly as bad, if not more so, than when He hung on the cross. Jesus seemed to be trying to come to some sort of decision and it was tearing Him apart."

Joshua, who had been listening intently, leaned forward, "Do you remember anything Jesus said while He was praying?" Adonis shook his head no. "Take your time Adonis – try to recall the whole scene. It's very important. You see, you were hearing the inward thoughts of the Son of God to Yahweh, His Heavenly Father." Beriah's eyes were opened wide in astonished wonder as the two men talked back and forth to each other. Unconsciously, he clutched the staff. Adonis stood, then began to pace. "Think Adonis! Let your mind go back to that evening in the Garden," coaxed Joshua. Slowly, in a soothing voice, Joshua continued, "Was it pitch dark?

Adonis shook his head again. "No the moon was just rising."

Joshua's smooth voice continued, "But there were no other sounds?"

Adonis stopped his pacing. With brow furrowed and eyes turned toward the darkened passageway, he softly said, "A donkey brayed." The firelight lit up the young Greek's face as Joshua and Beriah watched. Adonis seemed to be in a trance. He didn't seem to be aware of his surroundings. Rather, he was re-living the evening in the Garden of Gethsemane. Finally Adonis said, "The katydids were keeping up a steady hum. A few birds in the scrub bushes were chatting. An owl hooted in a hollow tree and an answer came from the direction of the Mount of Moriah." There was a long pause.

"Go on Adonis, what else do you remember?" asked Joshua.

Adonis continued, "There was a shepherd crossing the Kidron Valley. I thought that was late to be moving his flock."

"Was there anyone else in the Garden, Adonis?" asked Beriah for the first time.

Adonis turned toward Beriah. His black eyes still did not focus on the immediate surroundings. "There were several men, but they were asleep. I don't know how long they had been there before I woke up. Of course, they didn't see me. I was behind a bunch of scrub bushes." Again, Adonis stopped talking and began to chuckle. Joshua and Beriah exchanged puzzled looks. Without urging, Adonis picked up his story. "The biggest man was asleep. He was slumped against an olive tree. His mouth was open and he was snoring. The fireflies were still low on the ground and I wondered if he would suck one in his mouth. If so, would the bug continue to light? – Just a silly thought. At one point, Jesus stopped praying and asked the men if they could not wait and watch with Him for just one hour. He seemed hurt that they did not share His grief and agony."

"Then what happened?" asked Joshua.

Adonis' mind moved to something else. "I held out my hand and a little lightening bug lit on it. As it flickered on and off, I remembered something an old man said at the Temple."

"What was that?" asked Beriah.

Adonis replied, "The old man said 'Jesus was the light of the world.' Gently I blew on the lightening bug and sent it airborne. Jesus returned to the boulder, knelt, and continued to look heavenward and prayed. The men went back to sleep."

"Did you sleep Adonis?" asked Beriah.

"No, I was too uncomfortable lying on sand and pebbles. Besides, a foolish grasshopper jumped from a tall, swaying weed to a limb, over my head. It happened to be the one where a small, brown lizard was waiting for his supper. Just as I flipped the foolish insect off, I heard Jesus speak," said Adonis.

"What did he say?" urged Joshua.

With a puzzled expression Adonis answered. "Something about letting a cup pass from Him, if it was His Father's will. Shortly after that, a group of soldiers came. I'm afraid I've not been much help for I stayed hidden."

"You're doing fine Adonis. Anything else?" asked Joshua.

Adonis hesitated, "Yes. A man stepped forward and kissed Jesus. In a voice filled with sadness Jesus asked, 'would you betray your master with a kiss?' I believe He called this man Judas. Shortly thereafter, I was alone in the Garden. That's when I noticed the staff leaning against the tree. I don't know whom it belonged to. I went back today and it was still there, so I brought it for Beriah."

Chapter Three

The following evening found Beriah and Joshua crossing the Cheesemaker's Valley. They continued in the direction of Mount Moriah. It was here, behind brambles, bushes and boulders that Beriah found the hidden opening into the underground tunnels.

Lighting candles, the two men explored the passageway. Finally, they came to a high vaulted area, much like the one Beriah occupied. Joshua explored the area and found a source for water. Nodding his head, he turned to Beriah, "You're right. This could serve as a meeting place for my friends. In fact, in case of danger, we may need to hide out here. Thank you Beriah for showing me this haven of refuge."

It was nearing dark by the time Beriah and Joshua had bought food for the evening. Beriah's legs and back were aching and his walk was slow and laborious. Joshua had been carrying everything except the harp. Nearing the cavern, Joshua said, "You're tired Beriah, I'm afraid I overexerted you." Beriah smiled at Joshua's concern. "In fact, I've been wondering why you didn't use the staff that Adonis gave you."

For several moments Beriah said nothing. Then softly, he answered, "The staff belonged to a man of God and I'm not worthy using it. Neither have I worn the sandals." Joshua wasn't sure what sandals Beriah was referring to.

Later, after Adonis had returned home and the evening meal was over, the men began to talk. Adonis told about helping a camel trader unload his string of camels. "I tell you," Adonis stated, "Camels are the most contrary beasts on four legs. One of Abdul's camels bit me on the seat of my pants while I was bent over. As if that wasn't enough, the brute sat down on my foot. It took the threats of Abdullah to get it off.

Then the dumb animal had the nerve to spit on me and then grin!" By now Beriah and Joshua could not hold their laughter. Adonis said with wounded pride. "Go ahead and laugh, but how would you like to work with a ten foot long, stubborn camel?"

Suddenly – Beriah stopped laughing, "I would give all I own to be able to do such work," said Beriah.

Adonis leaned over and patted Beriah's crippled back. "I too would give all I own to see you well Beriah."

There was a short lull in the conversation then Joshua said, "I need a job Adonis. Do you think you could get me one helping you?" After the discussion of getting Joshua a job, the stilted atmosphere was broken and talk moved again to other things.

After discussing the many opening of graves, Adonis told some exciting news. "The priests are about to pull their hair out. There have been rumors and reports of sightings of Jesus all over the countryside. People are now calling Him the Christ, or the Messiah." Adonis continued, "Jesus seems to be getting more attention since His crucifixion than before. I think the priests are afraid that Jesus will pay them a visit."

"The old hypocrites should be scared," declared Beriah.

"Anyway," continued Adonis, "rumors have it that Herod has tripled his guards. Also, there seems to be Roman soldiers everywhere. So I suspect Pilate is also uneasy since he gave in to pressure and let Jesus be crucified."

Joshua finally entered into the conversation. "According to Peter, one of Jesus' disciples, Jesus said 'He came into the world to die as an atonement for sin. Also, to lay down His life and that no man taketh it."

"These are deep, profound statements," said Adonis.

"Why would He want to die for our sins?" asked Beriah shaking his head in bewilderment.

"It's simple," stated Joshua. "God loves us so much, He sent His only Son, who was without sin, to be a sacrifice for our sins."

"But why a sacrifice?" asked Adonis.

Joshua continued, "God commanded Moses to sacrifice a lamb for our sins. Only a spotless lamb can he sacrifice at the Temple for our sins. So by the Father sending His Son as an unblemished lamb in our place, we can be forgiven and have eternal life."

"Is it that simple?" asked Beriah with eyes filled with wonder.

Joshua nodded, "If you just believe in Jesus and accept Him as your Lord and Savior."

"Is this why so many people are placing their lives in danger by believing in Jesus?" quizzed Adonis.

Joshua nodded his head yes in answer to both questions. "For tonight, just think about the reason Jesus left His Heavenly home and came into this world. When we have our next meeting I'll take you with me. Then you can hear some of the followers tell about Jesus' teachings." Far into the night Adonis rolled on his mat and thought about Joshua's words and about the strange happenings of the last ten days.

Two weeks later Joshua let it be known that a secret meeting was to be held the following night. He invited both Adonis and Beriah to join him. Both men were exuberant about attending a meeting where the followers of Jesus would gather. Neither man knew what to expect. They only knew that it was to be held in the passageway. "There's only one thing that I ask," said Joshua. "I want you both to keep an open mind."

The following morning, Joshua went with Adonis to seek work unloading the camels. Beriah was late arising. His back was stiff and painful. It was the first time in ages that he wanted to crawl back under his sheepskin and let the thronging masses of humanity go. However, remembering the coming meeting with Joshua's friend caused him to get up.

Throughout his morning preparations, Beriah was aware of excruciating pain in his twisted spine. He was more bent over than usual. Each step he took added more pain. At last, taking a quick breath and wiping tears from his luminous brown eyes, he staggered and fell to his knees. In agony, he cried aloud, "Father God, please help me."

While on his knees, his right hand brushed against the staff that Adonis had brought home. Wrapping his fingers around the smooth wood, he slowly staggered to his feet. For a few seconds he swayed. Then gaining his equilibrium, he felt a tingling sensation in his fingers. The tingling began to travel. It moved up his right arm, across his shoulder, and down his spine. Immediately, a feeling of warmth flooded his entire body. As the warmth receded, so did the pain. In stunned astonishment Beriah looked at the staff. There was nothing unusual about it. It was just an ordinary looking walking stick. One like hundreds of others that could be seen carried by the people entering in Jerusalem. A feeling of joy filled Beriah's being. Holding tightly to the wonderful staff, he made his way to the well. For him, the morning took on a new dimension. Under his breath he thanked God for taking away the pain and for Adonis' gift. Along about mid-morning, Hiram, the Candlemaker, came to the well. After drawing water, he stood talking to Beriah. "You must be feeling well today Beriah," he commented.

"Oh I do!" replied Beriah. "But how did you know?"

Hiram smiled, "By the joyful lilt and rhythm of your music." Hiram lingered for a moment. During this time he kept squeezing, first one hand, then the other.

"Are your hands hurting again?" asked Beriah with sympathy.

Hiram nodded, "In the worst way. I'm letting them rest for a few minutes. By the way, I'm glad that you have a staff to help you walk," said Hiram as he picked up the staff, which was lying on the ground. Slowly he ran it between his hands. Then with a puzzled expression on his face, he laid the staff down. Without a word, Hiram crossed the passageway to his stall. Beriah played automatically but kept his eyes on the Candlemaker. Hiram still stood with a perplexed countenance. Slowly, he flexed his hands, and then did it again and again. Next, he wiggled his fingers. A smile broke out on his face. Shaking his head, as though mystified, he returned to work.

Later in the afternoon, a young couple stopped for water. They were very distraught. The mother was trying to pacify a small baby who was red and wet with perspiration. "She's burning up with fever," the young woman said to her husband. The weak, young cries touched Beriah.

Laying aside his harp, he asked the young mother, "Could I hold her under my canopy while you draw water?"

The husband nodded and the young mother passed her baby down to Beriah. "Her name is Rebecca," she whispered.

Beriah looked at the fretful little face. It was almost too weak to pucker up to cry. While the parents drew water and wet a cloth, Beriah ran his hand over the staff and then laid his hand on baby Rebecca's forehead. Immediately, the skin began to cool. Her eyes opened and the crying ceased. Rebecca's little rosebud mouth gave a small smile; she fell into a natural sleep. Beriah felt love rushing warm and filling his whole being. Crooning softly, he rocked the sleeping baby. In wonder, the young couple watched Beriah with Rebecca. Looking up, Beriah smiled, "The fever broke," he said in way of explanation. All these wonders Beriah kept hidden in his heart.

By the time the three friends had crossed the Cheesemaker's Valley, darkness had fallen and the stars were out. The city was once again a low hum of noise. Women could be heard calling children. Men's voices were raised in debate. There was laughter and quarreling and an occasional song. Dogs barked, goats bleated, and insects hummed. Life went on as though the events of Passover week had never happened. Leaving behind the odors of cooking food, cheese aging, the sweat of animals and humanity, the air became cooler, cleaner and more pure. Cautiously, the men approached the boulders and trees on the side of the hill. Lingering behind the rocks, they waited to see if they had been followed. A short time later they saw two, dark cloaked figures bent low among small scrub bushes working their way in their direction. Joshua reacted immediately. "Lie down and fringe sleep," he whispered. "If asked, we're shepherds looking for lost sheep – which is true."

Dropping to the sandy earth, the men curled up as though asleep. Beriah's mind was confused. Was Joshua a shepherd when not on the run? Waiting for the approaching dark cloaked figures was nerve racking. Beriah noticed Adonis slumped up against a rock but his knees and hands were in a springing position. Joshua was lying on his stomach with right hand outstretched where it could grab a weary ankle. Beriah, with left arm over his forehead, peered through the gloom toward the edge of the boulder. His heart had accelerated and his breathing was shallow. Somewhere nearby, the grass swished and a twig snapped. Then all was still. Overhead, an owl hooted and two dark figures rounded the rocks. Then everything seemed to happen at once. Joshua's hand snaked out and caught an ankle. Adonis sprang and the next person was down. There was a flurry of arms and legs flailing, long hair tumbling, and frightened whimpers of muffled cries. Joshua reacted first. "Father in Heaven, its women!" he cried.

A frightened voice stammered, "Joshua, is it really you?"

Joshua was by now on his feet and pulling up his captive. "I'm sorry Joanna. We were just trying to create enough commotion to divert the attention away from the passageway." Adonis too had pulled a young woman to her feet. He began to brush the sand from her cloak while Beriah retrieved her headdress.

A stammering Adonis said, "Sorry madam."

A soft sweet voice answered, "That's all right. I'm still a little frightened but not hurt. My name is Kasiah and it's Miss."

"I'm Adonis and this is my friend Beriah," handing over the headdress Beriah acknowledged the introduction. Finding his voice Adonis said, "It seems a shame to cover such a cloud of hair." Introductions were made and a little talk took place.

Holding on to each other, the little party entered the passageway. Cautiously, they traveled several feet in darkness before lighting a torch. Joshua, thinking ahead, had brought the torch in the folds of his robe. By torchlight they continued until they came to the followers of Jesus. The little group was sitting in a semi-circle. The leader was in the process of expounding on the teaching of Jesus. Quickly the newcomers sat down behind the seated men and women. After a smile and a nod of greeting, the leader continued, "Remember friends: Jesus is the Christ, the Son of God, and believing, you may have life. Jesus said, 'I am the way, the truth, and the life; I am the light of the world. I am the Good Shepherd. I am the Door of the sheep. I am the Bread of life. I am the Vine and you are the branches.' So you see," the man, continued, "when we think of these precious words, we begin to see a picture of Jesus doing as He said and conquered death, hell and the grave. This means if He lives-we too will be resurrected to live forever in the 'Land of fadeless days.' As the Good Shepherd He will lead and direct us to green pastures. As the Door of the sheep, He will keep us safe and we can find peace. Jesus is the true vine and His Father is the Husbandman of the vine. If we believe that He is the Son of God, we become the branches and will bear fruit." The speaker had tears in his eyes as he spoke lovingly of his Savior. "Jesus' resurrection gives us a living hope that we will live throughout eternity. Friends – never forget what Christ said, 'I am the Way, the Truth, and the Life; no man cometh unto the Father, but by Me.' Do not be deceived; there is no other way. Jesus, the Christ, is the only way to Heaven. If we reach those Heavenly shores, it will be through Him. Jesus just paid our sin debt on the cross. Don't turn down His free gift. Now let us pray." The meeting continued for another hour. The members took turns sharing their recent experiences, hopes, and fears.

It was nearing the midnight hour when the little trio arrived at their underground home. After sharing some fruit, each man settled on his own pallet, each to think over the words of the Nazarene Rabbi.

Early on the fourth Sabbath, following the crucifixion, Beriah was again at the camel caravansary. There was much hustle and bustle. A caravan had arrived from Port Sycaminum. It was a long train consisting of thirty-six camels and their drivers. Jacob, who owned the inn, was beside himself trying to find room to unload the camels, and to find food and water for the animals, and for the hot, tired, and irritable men. In order to accommodate the new arrivals, everyone who had spent the night, had to give up some space. A large dog, from the newly arrived caravan broke his rope. Realizing that he was free, the dog ran pell-mell among the resting camels. Pandemonium also broke loose within the caravansary walls. The camels ran around the compound in disorderly haste. In their headlong race, they knocked down tents and overturned supplies. In their confusion, the camel drivers bumped into each other. A string of Arabic curses filled the hot, humid air while they tried to gain control. With fangs exposed, the dog snapped at first one camel then another. The men gave chase to the camels and then the dog. Each time the men would corner the rogue dog he would somehow elude them. At last, the gray wolf-like dog bounded at Beriah. Sitting very still, with what seemed to be his heart in his mouth, Beriah waited for the dog to snap. Instead the dog came to an abrupt stop and sniffed at Beriah's feet. Hardly daring to breath, Beriah waited while the dog smelled the staff. Then with tail wagging, he licked Beriah's feet and in contentment he laid down his head on Beriah's lap. With trembling hand, Beriah reached down and stroked the large dog's head. Anger slowly dissipated from the faces of the men. Knives were replaced in sheaths and sticks thrown away. Then laughter broke loose among the rough men.

The leader of the caravan stepped forward. "Young man, for miles this rogue has tormented and bluffed my men. Yet, he sniffs at your feet and lies down like a tame housecat. Do your sandals have magic in them?"

Beriah looked down at his feet. He had forgotten about breaking the strap to his old sandals; or how he had changed into the sandals left on the hill of the skull. "No sir, they aren't magic. But they once belonged to a holy Man." Changing the subject away from the sandals, Beriah asked, "What's your dog's name?"

The big burly man shrugged and shook his head. "I don't know. He's not my dog. He jumped the ship that was unloading at the Port of Sycaminum. The sailors couldn't get him back. He trailed us for miles. We finally caught him just outside Jerusalem. He's a fine dog but he plays havoc among the camels. Scratching his beard and squinting his eyes, the caravan owner asked, "How would you like to have a fine dog?"

"Me?" asked Beriah.

"Why not?" the Arab continued. "You're the only one he's taken to. It's better than the men killing him."

Beriah looked at the dog and with doe-like eyes the dog looked at Beriah. Nodding, Beriah said, "I'll keep him."

Rubbing his hands in satisfaction, the Arab asked, "What will you name him?"

Beriah answered quickly, "Samson – after a strong warrior."

"Good, good," laughed the man. Opening his purse, he put a handful of coins into Beriah's cup and turned to the frightened camels. A round of cheers went up and laughter broke out among the tired men. Beriah strummed his harp. The dog, worn out from the chase was now fast asleep.

As the day progressed, one by one the men approached the crippled young man and put coins into his cup. The dog slept most of the day. At last, Beriah bought bread, rice, mutton and fruit for four. Since this was a good day indeed, Beriah was able to purchase sweetmeat for a dessert. Then gathering his belongings, he prepared to call it a day. The caravan owner brought Beriah the dog's rope. Beriah smiled, took the rope and tied his rug on Samson's back. Then picking up his leather bag, he secured it, as well, to the dog's back. Among laughter and well wishes, Beriah and Samson started for home. Going by the bazaar, Beriah filled his flagon with juice. Samson walked close to Beriah often rubbing up against his leg. Away from the camels the dog was well behaved but ever watchful.

Inside the cave Beriah lit a fire. After taking his belongings off Samson's back, he gave the dog a pan of water. Leaving Samson to explore his surroundings, Beriah set the table. Then sitting down, he waited for his friends and to think over the day's events. He could hardly believe that only a month ago he had been so lonely. Now he had two friends and a dog to share his home. Beriah felt truly blessed.

An hour later, Adonis and Joshua arrived home. Rounding the corner, a strange sight met their eyes. Lying on the mat was a large gray wolf and Beriah was asleep – curled up beside it. In fear Adonis cried out, "Beriah!" The startled Beriah sat up just as Samson lunged.

In the blinking of an eye, Adonis was on his back with the dog on top. Beriah grabbed the staff and Joshua a stone. Then to their amazement, Adonis began to laugh and Samson gave joyous barks! There were hugs and slobbery kisses. Between laughter and hugs Adonis pulled the dog off. Then laying his head on the thick fur he said, "Thor, old boy, is it really you?" Slowly Beriah laid down the staff and Joshua, his stone. There was no doubt in either of their minds; the dog had found his master.

Around the evening fire, Beriah told how Samson had wreck havoc with the camels and that the Arab camel master had given the dog to him. Adonis told how Thor liked to travel with him on his father's ship. "By chance, did the Arab tell you the name of the ship?" asked Adonis.

Beriah nodded, "He called it the Athena."

Adonis hugged the dog. "I knew I was right. This is my dog and the Athena is my father's ship."

Joshua smiled at the happy reunion of the man and dog. "Thor is a Norse name. Why did you choose that instead of a Greek name?"

Adonis smiled, "Thor means 'god of thunder.' When Thor growls in his throat it sounds like low thunder."

Beriah finally said, "I've called him Samson all day, for the great Jewish warrior who slayed a thousand Philistines with the jawbone of an ass."

Adonis was intrigued by Beriah's new name. So for the next hour Joshua told stories about Samson. At last Adonis said, "I like Beriah's choice of name better. So I'll call him Sam until he adjusts to the longer name."

Beriah then related how Samson had carried his things home and guarded him at the bazaar.

"That's great Beriah. It'll do your back good to be relieved of a load. In fact I'll rig up a better way for securing them to Sam," said Adonis.

At last, Joshua got around to the all-important question. "If Sam snapped at all the men and the camels, why didn't he attack Beriah?"

Stillness came over the little group. "You're right," said Adonis. "Sam snapped at everyone but Beriah." Turning to Beriah, Adonis continued, "Tell us how Sam reacted to you Beriah." Joshua and Adonis watched as Beriah looked down at his feet. There was a short pause before Adonis excitedly said, "That's it! He sniffed at your feet?"

Beriah nodded and reached for the staff. Joshua looking perplexed said, "Isn't that the normal way a dog checks out a person?"

"True," answered Adonis, "but Beriah had on special sandals and was holding a special staff. You see, Joshua, Beriah was wearing the shoes of the crucified Nazarene. Plus, holding the staff that was left behind by the Nazarene in the Garden of Gethsemane." Slowly the significance of Adonis's words sank in.

Joshua carefully reached over and touched the soles of the sandals. "Is there power in the staff and sandals?" he asked.

Adonis shook his head, "No they're just common leather and wood. What Samson smelled was the essence of the previous owner. His spiritual scent of goodness still lingers. We as humans cannot smell the odor, yet it's there. Therefore, Sam felt love and safety. At least that's my belief."

After this, Beriah told how the baby at the well was healed. He then recalled how Hiram's hands were hurting. However, after he held the staff, he returned to work. Last of all, Beriah told about picking up the staff and feeling a hot, tingling sensation flowing through his arms and back. Softly, Beriah whispered, "Then all of a sudden, that excruciating pain in my body disappeared." Tears filled Beriah's eyes and he humbly bowed his head. Sam slowly left Adonis's arms and ambled around the fire. He lowered himself down on the mat beside Beriah and laid his head on Beriah's lap. Beriah placed his face against the gray fur and his shoulders shook with convulsing sobs. There wasn't a dry eye as Adonis and Joshua witnessed Beriah's humbleness. The little trio lay down and began to meditate on the wonderful staff and sandals.

The next morning Samson accompanied Beriah to the well. The merchants admired Beriah's dog and chuckled about him carrying

Beriah's belongings. Elon quietly studied the height and breadth of Samson and without a word, returned to his leather shop. Mid-morning Elon returned, carrying a strip of sheepskin and a set of saddlebags. "Beriah, I've shortened these bags to fit your dog. Also, here's a saddle blanket."

Beriah was astonished. "How'd you do this in such a short time?" he asked.

"Oh that was easy. I just shortened the center section of a set of saddlebags I had made for a small donkey," explained Elon. Beriah was delighted.

Throughout the morning the merchants dropped by the well to pet the dog and admire Elon's gift. Samson settled down beside Beriah and enjoyed the attention he was getting. All went well until mid-afternoon, when six burley Roman soldiers, with hardened faces, arrested Tola and Hur. With arms bound behind their backs, they were led away. Samson immediately stood, hackles raised, fangs showing, legs prepared to lunge, when Beriah touched Samson's back with the staff. Looking confused, the dog returned to the rug and lay down. Slowly his fur went back in place.

Fear ran rampant up and down the narrow street. At last, Beriah loaded his saddlebags and crossed the street to Rosh's shop. The shuttle was still as Rosh untangled skeins of yarn. Tears flowed freely down the tired worried face. Without speaking, Beriah sat down on the floor and began to untangle the colored yarn. Rosh took out a large handkerchief and mopped his face and blew his nose. Samson laid across the door but stayed alert for trouble. "Beriah, you'd better not be seen with the merchants on this street," stated Rosh. Beriah did not look up nor answer. Instead he drew a picture of a fish in the dust. Swiftly, Rosh reached a trembling, wrinkled hand down and erased the fish. With compassion, Beriah raised his head and looked into Rosh's eyes. The old man gave a nod and a faint smile. "God bless you my brother."

It was close to dark when Beriah left Rosh's shop and made his way to the Bazaar. By the time he bought food, the stars had begun to appear in the sky and the noise of the city was down to a low drone. Removing the saddlebag, Beriah coaxed Sam down into the crevice. As he and the dog started down the steps, they met a worried Adonis and Joshua on the way up. “We were just coming to look for you,” a relieved Adonis said.

Chapter Four

The following day was a busy one. There was a new influx of people entering Jerusalem. Many had heard about the empty tomb and wanted to see where Jesus had lain. Others wanted to witness the frustration of the hated Romans and the despised King Herod. A few wanted to hunt for the 'stolen body' of Jesus, hoping for a reward from the frantic High Priest; while others wanted to satisfy their grotesque curiosity to see the ruptured and open graves. Yet another faction wanted to loot the tombs of the ancient dead.

Beriah watched and listened to the people who lingered by his well. Little by little, he pieced together the attitude of the people. It was an inharmonious atmosphere; as well as, the fact that the general populace was in fear and suspicion. The merchants were just as scared and worried as anyone. They still had no news of Tola and Hur. About the sixth hour, Beriah and Samson paid a visit to the elderly weaver. Rosh, looking befuddled, was sitting in the midst of his tangled yarn. His white hair was standing on ends and his black cap was askew. Old Rosh welcomed Beriah's help and company. "These are troubled times, my brother. I don't think the soldiers will hold our friends. They don't have any proof that we are followers of the Nazarene Rabbi. However, it will be hard for us to meet in order to discuss our new found faith." Beriah helped the old man and listened to him talk for over an hour before returning to the well.

Nearing the ninth hour, two unsavory looking characters and a young, nervous looking man lingered near the well. Listening carefully, Beriah heard the tallest man speak first, in an undertone he said, "I say that we should open the tomb of Absolom instead of King David. After all, King David felt guilty over his officer killing his own son."

"Absolom deserved to die," said the second man. "He was trying to take over his father's throne."

"True," said the tall man. "But like any father, King David filled the mausoleum full of treasure."

The young man was more hesitant. "Barak, I'm not sure that robbing a tomb is such a good idea."

"Why not?" demanded the tall man. "Naaman has no complaints. Have you turned yellow Heber?

The youngest of the trio began to squirm. "Not exactly, but I didn't think we would break into such well known tombs."

"That's what makes it so ideal," said Barak. "Who would think thieves would dare to rob King David's tomb – or his family's. No one!" Barak turned to Naaman, "Come, we'll need to purchase some strong bags. Heber, you sit down and decide if you're for us or against us." With this, the two men moved in the direction of Elon's leather shop while the young man, Heber, waited by the stone well box.

Beriah smiled at the young man. "Have you come far?" Beriah asked, feigning ignorance.

The young man nervously answered, "North of Jericho."

How did you get mixed up with those two? Are they relatives?" Beriah probed.

Heber shook his head. "I was without a home or food. They shared their food and water and invited me to come to Jerusalem. I had never seen either of them until two weeks ago."

"Do your folks live near Jericho?" asked Beriah.

Heber kept an eye on the leather shop. "I'm an orphan. I stay where I can, sleep where I can, but I do work for food."

"Do you really want to get involved with those two?" Beriah inquired, nodding his head toward the two thieves.

"No, but I don't know how to get away from them," said Heber in a scared tone.

Beriah spoke softly, "If you really want to get away from them – I'll help you."

"Please tell me how," begged the frightened, young Heber.

Beriah motioned toward his cloak. "Quickly, slip on my cloak and pull the cowl over your head. Cross the street, then two shops down is a path to the alley. The alley runs behind the shops all the way to the area of the bazaar. Stop at the end of the alley and wait for me. I'll help you find a place to sleep and get work. If you stay with these men, the soldiers will kill you."

Young Heber said, "I've never stolen anything in my life. I've always worked and been honest. But Barak is ruthless and I'm afraid of him."

"Then hurry!" urged Beriah, shoving his robe into Heber's hands.

"I'll wait for you," whispered Heber, as he hurriedly put on the robe. Beriah watched until Heber rounded the corner in the direction of the alley. Then slowly tied his belongings on Samson's back.

Just as Beriah picked up his staff and harp, the two would be thieves returned. "What happened to our friend?" demanded Barak.

"What friend?" asked Beriah.

"Don't act dumb with me; or is your brain as warped as your back?" snarled Barak as he grabbed Beriah by the arm. Immediately, Samson had Barak's arm in his mouth and just as quickly, Barak pulled the staff out of Beriah's hand. He raised it to strike the dog. Instead of his arm coming down, it quivered violently but would not lower.

The man Naaman yelled, "Don't just stand there Barak – hit the brute before he goes for your throat."

A terrified Barak yelled, "Help me fool!" Naaman reached for the staff and he too became stuck to the walking stick. Beriah watched Barak's frightened face as his eyes rolled like a stallion that had panicked, while Naaman's eyes bulged in their sockets.

Then Beriah reached over and relieved both men of his staff. Beriah touched Samson and he released Barak's arm. In a quiet voice, Beriah addressed the two men. "If you're looking for a place to stay, there's the Camel Caravansary just outside the city walls. They rent places to sleep and serve good food. Or if you're looking for a place to worship, the temple is on the Temple Mount. Perhaps your friend has gone to worship. It never hurts to give thanks to God for our blessings or to ask for forgiveness for our sins." Beriah watched as the two men stumbled in the direction of the Temple. Then he and Samson followed the path leading to the alley behind the business section.

The alley was, as usual, a maze of discarded boxes and trash from the various shops. And here and there were containers of garbage from their connected homes. From the lines overhead, hung freshly washed clothes, drying and flapping in the breeze. The garbage cans gave off a putrid odor. The back of the shops was in a deteriorated condition. All in all, it was an unpleasant sight. Beriah would often use the alley as a short cut to the bazaar.

At last Beriah overtook Heber. Beriah asked no questions. He just said, "Follow me." With the trust of a child, Heber followed the crippled man and his dog. Coming to the fig tree near the bazaar, Beriah instructed Heber to wait in the shade with the dog and Beriah's harp. Then Beriah hurried to the stall that sold ducks. He bought a roast duck and herbed rice. Next, he bought a nice melon. Placing these in his shoulder bag, he then bought a whole loaf of baked bread, a chunk of cheese, and some raisins. Returning to the tree, Beriah handed the shoulder bag to Heber. Then smiling, he said, "Now, let's go home." If Adonis and Joshua were surprised to see a new face, they did not show it. Beriah made the introductions. Another packing box was added to the table. Adonis gave up his pallet and sat on the sheepskin cover. Joshua and Adonis had also bought food and juice. Before eating, Beriah asked Joshua to say the blessing. He then delegated Adonis to carve the duck, Joshua to pour the juice, and Heber to slice the bread. Beriah served the herbed rice. Samson was given a portion and waited impatiently for the bones. Finally, Beriah told the story of Heber's escape from the thieves who planned on robbing the tombs.

Joshua was quite upset about Barak and Naaman's clandestine plan. "Do you know when this is to take place?" he asked Heber.

"Tomorrow night. They're going to look the situation over tomorrow. Then after dark they're going back with tools," said Heber.

"Aren't they afraid of getting caught? After all, it will take several days to chisel an opening big enough for a man to crawl through," said Adonis.

"Barak says with so much damage to the graves and tombs, even if it is discovered, people will think it happened in the earthquake. Besides, the earthquake may have already damaged the tombs. Of course, Naaman may back out. He is so superstitious," said Heber. Shortly before midnight, a pallet was made for Heber. Joshua and Adonis would get him a job unloading camels tomorrow. As the fire died down, Beriah thanked God for the rescue of a young man from a life of crime.

The following day had some good news. The Roman Procurator for lack of evidence had released Tola and Hur. Both had been warned about getting involved with the Nazarene radicals. Tola and Hur were still shaken from the interrogation. One by one, the merchants visited each friend and welcomed him back. Beriah waited until late afternoon before making his call. Both men welcomed Beriah as a believer in Jesus. Yet warned him about openly discussing his new found faith. After leaving Tola's shop, Beriah stopped by Carmie's shop and purchased enough white remnants to meet the needs of Joshua and Adonis. Later Beriah hurried home.

Joshua and Adonis were providing the evening meal. However, Beriah took time out to buy some cheese and fruit. Joshua, Adonis, and Heber had arrived before Beriah and were busy going over their plans for the night.

During the evening meal, Joshua said, "I think our 'would be tomb robbers' are probably strangers to Jerusalem, because Absolom's tomb is across the Kidron Valley on the lower slope of Mount Olive. Close by is the tomb known as Zechariah's tomb, and the family entombment of Bnei Hezir, which is a priestly family. The Bnei Hezir family tomb stands out with it's Greek – Oriental design. It has a small porch and Doric Columns. It could easily be assumed for the tomb of King David.

However, King David is buried on the western hill called Mount Zion. Since one tomb lies in the east and the other to the west, they won't be at both the same night."

"I think you're right," said Adonis. "So I say we stake out the one across the Kidron Valley. Beriah heard the leader say Absolom's tomb would be filled with treasures."

Shortly after dark, the trio crossed the Kidron Valley toward the lower part of the Mount of Olives. Once there, they quickly made white cloaks with loose cowls to cover their bodies and heads. Each man powdered his face with flour. Standing on the porch of the tomb of the House of Hezir, they waited for the 'would be tomb robbers.' Joshua stood in the middle and Heber to his right and Adonis to his left. Heber was wearing a long, black wig. Adonis had blackened his eyes and lined them with a circle of charcoal. His face gave a grotesque illusion of a skull. Adonis held a mowing scythe in his hand. Joshua carried a lantern with a greenish globe. The lamp was left unlit while they waited for Barak and Naaman to arrive at the mausoleum called Absolom's tomb. "Does that tomb, with the Doric columns and the upside down cone, really hold the body of King David's son?" whispered Adonis, as they watched the sepulchral.

"No one knows for sure," answered Joshua. "Some say yes and others believe Absolom was buried in one of the chambers of King David's tomb over in Mount Zion. They've been buried for generations. The locations have been handed down by word of mouth. So no one is sure."

A few moments later, voices were heard. Crossing the Kidron Valley were two men and a reluctant donkey. "What a comical sight they are." Adonis said to Joshua and Heber. The trio sat down on the porch of the Bnei Hezir tomb and leaned back against the columns and waited.

The two men were arguing. Naaman could be heard saying, "Why not King David's tomb? It should be full of riches."

"Because we can't LOCATE KING DAVID'S TOMB YOU TWIT!" snarled Barak. Joshua stifled a laugh. "But we have found Absolom's, so I say we open this one."

"Well Barak, while you drank wine all day, I found a man who told me where to find King David's tomb," gloated Naaman.

Barak's face showed by the moonlight. He scratched his beard and spat, "And where might that be, 'Mr. Josephus' himself?" he growled.

With a sneering voice, Naaman said, "Right there before your nose!" and pointed to the tomb where the trio sat.

Instantly, Joshua lit the lantern and the three men slowly arose and stood in the glow of the greenish light. "Are you looking for my tomb Barak?" asked Joshua in a loud, commanding voice. "Or were you looking for my son Absolom?" With this, he pulled the cowl off Heber's head – exposing the long, black wig. The wig resembled the long, black hair of Absolom. Both, Barak and Naaman, were frozen in their tracks and unable to utter a sound. Then swinging the greenish light over Adonis and his scythe, Joshua continued, "Or were you looking for the Angel of Death? After all, only the dead belong here." Having said this, Adonis stepped forward and raised the mowing scythe.

"Great God Jehovah help us!" screamed Naaman, as he and Barak fled and stumbled down the mount. Barak could be heard yelling at Naaman for running too slow and being in his way.

The made-up trio waited until the 'tomb robbers' were out of site; then they laughed so hard their stomachs ached. Joshua slowly let out a sigh, "Let's take the donkey and the scythe to my uncle. We'll clean up there before going home," he said.

"Joshua do you mind if we sit down until my legs stop trembling?" asked Heber in a shaking voice. Joshua put his arm around Heber's shoulders and with this, the trio sat down and leaned back against the columns of the sepulchral. The night was still except for a few insects and nocturnal birdcalls. A cool breeze moved the grass and the stars peeped out from an indigo sky. The pale moon rose higher, while inside the tombs, the dead slept on.

At last, Adonis asked, "Who lies in the tomb with the pyramidal roof?"

Joshua answered in a soft voice, "That's the tomb of Zechariah, and over there is the tomb of Jehosaphat. Below are the fields of the dead. It's for the common people. However, part of it is referred to as the burial field of the kings. Supposedly, King Uzziah was buried here. It's a good thing his grave wasn't opened."

"Why?" asked Heber.

"Because he died from Leprosy," answered Joshua.

Adonis whistled a startled sound. "You're right. That sarcophagus would have been working alive with leprosy germs, even after all these years. It seems Barak and Naaman got off easy with just a little scare. Any tomb could be filled with all types of germs and diseases." Said Joshua thoughtfully.

Shortly after midnight the trio arrived back at the cavern. A worried Beriah had waited up. He had a large bowl of fruit and cheese on the table and fruit juice being cooled in spring water. By the time the nightly escapade was told and the laughing died down, two hours had passed. "Do you think Barak and Naaman will try again to rob a tomb?" asked Beriah.

"No way," laughed Adonis. "When Joshua held that lantern above my head and they saw my scythe, they almost fainted! I haven't seen men run so fast since an Olympic game."

"I agree with Adonis," smiled Joshua. "I don't think they'll try again."

"Beriah, I'm so glad you rescued me," said Heber on a more serious note. "I knew it was Adonis, but my heart felt like it would jump out of my body. Man, you talk about scary; why that greenish light, on his pale face, and his eyes blacked out was like looking at death itself."

"When was this charade hatched up?" asked Beriah.

"Today, while we unloaded a camel train," smiled Adonis. "In Greece, I belonged to a small theatrical group who put on plays periodically. Anyway, it worked out and that's what counts."

The following day, Beriah kept a lookout for Barak and Naaman but didn't see them. Beriah visited Tola, Hur, and Rosh and quietly told them about his newly found friends. He also told Tola that there were passageways and rooms beneath the city if someone needed refuge from the Roman persecution. Beriah said he would show Tola a more secluded entrance, in the event Tola and his friends wanted to lay in supplies for future emergencies or secret meetings.

Tola's eyes filled with tears of gratitude. Hugging Beriah, Tola said, "This is the answer to my prayers. Thank you Beriah from the bottom of my heart. At the moment, we're new followers of Jesus. So our faith is weak. We need to continue to fellowship and worship together. That way, we will gain strength through togetherness. Jesus said, 'Where two or more gather together in my name, there I will be also.' Thank you again Beriah." With this said, Tola kissed Beriah on each cheek.

Beriah smiled. A warm glow filled his being. "I'll show you the way when you're ready." Beriah then returned to the well.

Picking up his harp, Beriah began to pluck the strings and soft melodious sounds floated through the warm air. Shortly after the ninth hour, Beriah loaded Samson's saddlebags. Then he picked up a sack-full of tangled wool from Rosh, the weaver, and started home. Stopping by the bazaar, he purchased fish, rice, and fresh vegetables. Stepping into the shrubbery, which surrounded the opening into the cavern, Beriah stopped. Samson could smell the food, but being well trained, waited patiently. The bond and understanding of man and dog was astounding. Beriah searched on the ground for sturdy sticks to be used as spits. He was careful not to break limbs from trees and bushes. He wanted nothing to look out of order. At last Beriah located four nice, long sticks, which would serve his purpose. Beriah was thankful that Adonis and Joshua had taken on the duty of collecting boxes and firewood. The two men had chosen to do this after dark so they wouldn't attract attention with their coming and going. By going up and down alleys, Joshua and Adonis had collected quite a surprising amount of wood: which they placed in a special storage area.

The cool subterranean living quarters felt good to Beriah. He placed the fresh fish and vegetables in cold water, lit a small fire, and laid down to rest before his friends arrived.

That evening, around the fire, the little group roasted the fish and related their day. Beriah told about Tola's and Hur's release from jail. He also told his friends he was going to show Tola a different passageway so he and his group could meet and worship in secret. Joshua and Adonis nodded in agreement with Beriah's plan. "It won't always be like this," said Joshua. "Someday the followers of Jesus will be able to worship in the open. In the meantime, we'll meet in homes or caves. But we won't be stopped."

The next morning when Beriah awoke, he found his three friends had already left for the upper city to unload the camel caravans. Beriah was tired and sluggish from lack of sleep the night before. However, he dressed with care. He strapped the bag of yarn and his belongings on Samson. Beriah carried the harp. It was too precious for the dog to carry. Arriving at the well, Beriah began to play soft music. Today was forty days since Passover. The farmers were busy harvesting their wheat; as well as, gathering the early grapes and figs. Pentecost or Feast of Weeks should complete the harvesting. Pentecost – meaning fifty days after Passover, which comes in the month of Sivan. The Jews look forward to the celebration of Shavat – as they call it. The celebration marks the end of the grain harvest and the beginning of the fruit harvest. It was a time to rejoice and give thanks to God for His bounty. Each farmer would give the priest two loaves of bread, baked from their finest flour, to offer to God and make an animal sacrifice. When Pentecost arrived, the Holy City would once again be teeming with people who come to worship. It was a joyous season. Beriah looked forward to days that would be filled with happiness instead of gloom and suspicion.

In the afternoon, Beriah returned Rosh's yarn. He visited a short time and decided to leave early. After acquiring food for the evening meal, Beriah returned to the cavern, lit a small fire, and laid down to rest. In minutes, he was fast asleep. It was almost dark when the trio arrived home. Beriah was still asleep. Too excited to keep their news, Adonis shook the sleeping cripple. "Wake up Beriah. Joshua has the most exciting news."

Beriah sat up with a start. Wiping the sleep from his eyes, he looked into three faces filled with wonder. Looking at Joshua, he asked, "Have they caught Barak and Naaman?"

"No, no, nothing like that," interjected the excited Adonis.

"Then what's happened?" asked Beriah.

"Let's sit down and I'll tell you what I learned from my uncle, who heard it from one of Jesus' disciples." By now Beriah was all ears. Joshua waited until everyone was seated. "My good news is that Jesus went back to Heaven," said Joshua.

"How? Why? Will He come back?" Beriah's questions rolled off his tongue as he became concerned. "Are you sure this is good news Joshua?"

"I'll tell you what. Let's go over this while we have our evening meal," said Joshua. "Heber will you fetch more wood? Beriah can set the table and Adonis can cut the bread. I'll say the blessing then while we eat, I'll answer your questions." Each man set about his assigned duty and soon everyone was seated.

After the blessing and the serving of food, all eyes were turned toward Joshua, who said, "I'll start at the beginning. Adonis, Heber, and I stopped by my uncle Jethro's, house to check on the little donkey. Uncle Jethro had just gotten back from taking the donkey to his son Ezra, who lives in the Essene quarters of the city. This being harvest time for wheat, he felt sure Ezra could use the little donkey to haul the sheaves. While there, Uncle Jethro heard that Jesus' disciples had arrived back to the place where they had shared the Last Supper with Jesus before His crucifixion. For lack of a better name for the borrowed place, I'll call it the Upper Room. Anyway, Uncle Jethro decided to visit the disciples Peter and Andrew, whom he knew from Galilee. When he arrived at the Upper Room, they were singing and rejoicing. After fond greetings, Peter told an exciting story." As Joshua talked, the men ate automatically and kept their eyes glued to the storyteller.

The fire crackled and gave off warmth and light in the cool cavern. Sitting expectantly, Beriah's tiredness began to ebb away. Heber was no longer frightened and Adonis, who had heard the story before, was even more intrigued by the re-telling. Joshua let his eyes roam from the dog, which was waiting patiently for tidbits of food, to the eager faces filled with anticipation. Smiling, he resumed his story; "According to Peter, the disciples had been with Jesus off and on for the last forty days. This particular day they went with Jesus to Bethany; the town where Lazarus, Mary, and Martha lived. You see Adonis these were three of Jesus' friends. In fact, just a couple of months ago, Jesus raised Lazarus from the dead. After visiting around, Jesus then went up to the Mount of Olivet." Pausing from the story, he said to Adonis, "Bethany is just a day's journey from Jerusalem in the direction of Jericho. Heber may have passed through it on the way here with Barak and Naaman." Heber affirmed they had passed through the village.

Joshua continued, "Here, Jesus began to speak, He said He was going away. 'I'm going to my Father's house; where there are many mansions.' He said 'Then I will return, so that where I am, there you may be also.' Some questioned Him on the way and the time. He again reminded them, 'I am the Way, the Truth and the Life, no man cometh to the Father but by Me. As to when I will return, no one knows, except My Father; not even the angels in Heaven know.' Jesus instructed His disciples to feed His sheep and to go into all the world and preach the gospel to the ends of the earth." At this point, Joshua stopped. "Adonis, Jesus referred to Himself as the Shepherd and His followers, His sheep. To feed His sheep – was to tell them His word and His teachings."

"Go on," urged Adonis.

Joshua took a sip of water and continued, "Then before their eyes Jesus was lifted up and a cloud, from God, like the one that filled the Holy of Holies, covered Jesus from sight. As they stood looking up, two angels appeared. The angels were dressed in shining, white raiment. The angels called them 'men of Galilee.' So they knew the angels were from God.

"What else did they say?" asked Beriah.

"They said 'Jesus, who had ascended into Heaven would come again in like manner.' So Beriah, Jesus will come back some day. He also told the disciples that He would never leave them nor forsake them, even until the end of the age. Jesus said that He would also send a helper, His Holy Spirit! Peter said they were instructed to return to Jerusalem until the Pentecost; that's when the Holy Spirit is supposed to arrive and endue them with power from on high. Then they are to take His word or gospel to the ends of the earth. Beginning first in Jerusalem and then in Samaria and Judea, even to the ends of the earth.

Jesus was with His disciples and other followers for forty days after His resurrection from the dead. He taught and instructed them on teaching about His crucifixion, death, and resurrection. They are to preach about the atoning grace through His shed blood, the forgiveness of sin, the baptism of the Holy Spirit, the resurrection of the dead, and life everlasting." Joshua got another drink of water and continued, "Jesus' living, eating, and teaching His disciples before He ascended into Heaven, is infallible proof that He is alive and the Son of God. The disciples obeyed Jesus and hurried to Jerusalem. There are about one hundred twenty souls waiting for the Helper or the Holy Spirit, which Jesus will send."

"Who are these people?" asked Beriah. "Jesus had twelve disciples and Judas hung himself for betraying Jesus. That leaves only eleven."

"True," said Joshua. "However, the others are followers of Jesus; as well as, His mother, brothers and sisters. Uncle Jethro said they were in one place and one accord in prayer and supplication. Uncle Jethro said their happiness was something to behold!" Talk around the fire continued until the fire died down to glowing embers. The men took to their pallets only to think their own thoughts and mull the events of the day. These were strange times indeed.

Chapter Five

On the morning of Pentecost the streets were filled with people who had come to Jerusalem to celebrate the Feast of Harvest. Already, a throng of people had filled the Temple Courtyard and others were going in that direction.

Beriah and Samson went to the camel caravansary. Beriah sat down by the gate to play his harp. The caravansary was an interesting place. A camel train had arrived from Egypt and one from Asia Minor. Beriah wished he could see the wealth of things that were strapped under the leather-covered parcels. These new exotic supplies would be sold to the Arab and Gentile merchants who made up the many businesses throughout the city and at the bazaar. There were other travelers who had spent the night. A man and his servant from Parthian had shared a room with three men from Mesopotamia. While out in the courtyard, travelers from Mede, Cappodocia, Phrygia, and Libya were trying to communicate by sign language to merchants from Pontius, Judea, and Pamphylia. Three Romans sat by themselves and ignored two Elamites. Each traveler spoke in his own language. Some knew Greek or Aramaic to make their wishes known.

All the different sounds and dialects reminded Beriah of the story of the Tower of Babel. When Beriah was young he had asked Old Jobah why all the people couldn't speak alike. Jobah told young Beriah, that in the beginning, all men did speak the same language. Beriah asked what happened. Jobah said, "Because men became so wise they thought they could build a tower to God. Of course, God let them labor and sweat and argue among themselves. Then God showed the people how foolish their human wisdom was beside His. God gave them different languages. Therefore, they could no longer understand each other. The construction stopped and the foolish people dispersed. Each with the ones who spoke their new tongue."

Beriah smiled as he remembered the twinkle in old Jobah's eyes as he said, "Don't ever try to get bigger than your breeches Beriah. If you do, God will take you down a notch or two." Clearing his head of reminiscing, Beriah picked up the rhythm of his music. Nearby, a camel began shaking his head, which rang his camel bells. The camel then looked down his nose as if to say, 'I like the sound of bells better.' The antics of the camel brought a round of laughter from the men of different countries. The sight and sound of harp and bells was universally understood and appreciated. A round of applause arose. Beriah gave an embarrassed bow. The camel blinked his long eyelashes and raised his head higher, which caused more laughter. And so the day passed swiftly; and it was time to go home, when suddenly a new phenomenon began to occur. There was a sudden sound from Heaven. It came as of a mighty, rushing wind. It reminded Beriah of Old Jobah's story about Elijah, the prophet, who had hidden from the wicked Queen Jezebel. Jobah said that God has passed by and tore into the mountain of Horeb. So great was it's force that it broke rocks into pieces. Perhaps such a wind as this sounded as the Spirit of God hovered above the waters as God created the heavens and the earth. The roar of the wind filled the air. It seemed to be moving in the direction of the Essene quarters of the city. This was the area where the disciples and Jesus' followers were praying and rejoicing. The travelers from different countries began to gesture, 'What is this? What does this mean?' Then, in one accord, they began to hurry toward the Essene quarters as if trying to catch the wind.

Beriah bought the supper meal from Jacob, the Innkeeper, and hurried toward his cavern. When he arrived, no one was there. Lighting the fire, he sat down to think about the sound of the mighty winds.

It was well after dark when Joshua, Adonis, and Heber arrived. They were in an elated mood. Beriah was suspicious. Cautiously, he asked them, "Have you been tasting new wine?"

Laughing, Adonis answered, "Oh yes Beriah, we have been filled with the new wine of the Holy Spirit." With this, he collapsed on his mat and continued to laugh joyously.

Joshua quickly picked up the conversation. "Beriah, my uncle took us to meet the disciple Peter – the one called the 'Big Fisherman.' He was telling us that before Jesus ascended into Heaven, He breathed on His disciples and said, 'Receive you the Holy Ghost.' Then directed them to wait in Jerusalem until Pentecost for the Holy Spirit. While Peter was telling us the wonderful things that Jesus had taught, after His resurrection, a mighty, rushing wind filled the house where they were staying. It had the sound of a tempest at sea. The wind seemed to enter their beings. Peter began to shout, 'Don't be afraid! It's the Holy Ghost sent by God to be our helper! This Holy Spirit will energize us with His power!'" After this, Joshua stopped speaking. He sat with a radiant expression on his face.

At last Heber spoke, "Go on Joshua. Tell Beriah about the fire that was wiggling all over the floor."

Joshua waited so long to answer, that Adonis also began to prompt him to go on. Looking into the fire, Joshua said, "The next manifestation of the Holy Spirit's presence and power was the cloven tongues of fire."

As Heber said, "It sat on each of the disciples and one hundred and twenty followers of Jesus."

Beriah gasped, "Why fire Joshua? And why cloven?"

"Wind and fire are outward signs of a great spiritual miracle," answered Joshua. "Fire is symbolic of divine power. Remember God appeared to Moses in a burning bush – a bush that was not consumed! His glory was so great that Moses could not look upon Him. Fire gives warmth and light and it purifies. The outpouring of the Holy Spirit filled the room with the love of God and caused the disciples and followers to be on fire for God. You asked why the fire was cloven? It could possibly be that one side was for the word of Jesus to the Jewish people; while the other side, could be for the word of our Lord to the Gentile nations. It also made the followers want to tell the world about

Jesus, who is the Light of the world. Beriah, the whole groups of people were baptized in the Holy Ghost and began to speak in tongues. What was it Peter said? Oh yes. They spoke tongues, 'as the Spirit gave the utterance.'" Beriah looked questionably at Joshua.

"It's true Beriah. What they spoke was not gibberish," said Adonis. "I, being a Greek, heard some Greek speaking travelers say that they were told about Jesus Christ! Many other nationalities that come to Passover, heard about Jesus as well. One Arabian was overheard saying; that he could hear them speak, in his tongue, the wonderful works of God! Peter was so energized by the Holy Ghost that he preached with boldness; telling the crowd to: repent, believe that Jesus is the Son of God, and be baptized. What I am going to tell you next will be hard to believe. But over three thousand people believed, were baptized, and filled with the Holy Spirit! It was truly great! Isn't it marvelous Beriah? Just think, the Holy Spirit of God will live in all believers. He will be our constant Helper and Guide. The Giver of gifts. This is the fulfillment of Jesus' promise when He said, 'I will never leave you nor forsake you.'"

The men were rather quiet while they ate. They seemed to be reflecting on the events of the day. At last Beriah told how they had heard the sound of the mighty, rushing wind at the camel caravansary. He relayed the different places and languages that were represented by the travelers: Egypt, Asia, Parthian, Mesopotamia, Mede, Libya, Greece, Elamite, Hebrew, and Aramaic. Beriah smiled, "I could understand the camels better than all the different dialects. However, all the men had one thing in common."

"What was that?" asked Adonis. "When they heard the sound of that wind from heaven, they forgot their camels and chased after the wind."

"Chased the wind," said Joshua. "That's wonderful Beriah. This means they believed and were baptized and are now brothers in Christ."

With tears in his eyes, Beriah looked at Joshua and asked, "Do you think Peter would baptize me? For I truly believe Jesus is the Messiah."

Joshua, Adonis, and Heber looked with love at the humble cripple who had so touched each of their lives. "I'll make the arrangement with Peter to come here. He can baptize you in your pool," said Joshua.

The following day, the men again returned to work. Beriah held his new found faith close to his heart. He cherished the words and stories he had heard about Jesus. Throughout the day, stories circulated from shop to shop about the mighty wind that blew from Heaven and the strange manifestation of the day before. The Priests had gotten news of speaking in strange languages and three thousand people being baptized. They immediately tried to disclaim that this visitation was from God. Rather, they declared demons and evil spirits possessed the fanatic followers of Jesus. The masses in the temple courtyard were confused as to whom to believe.

Beriah had packed his things on Samson and was ready to go home when Hiram, the Candlemaker, rushed out of Old Rosh, the Weaver's shop. He hurried across the passageway to Beriah. "Come quick, bring your staff. Rosh needs help!" Beriah and Samson hurried after Hiram. Beriah assumed Rosh would once again be sitting in a pile of tangled yarn. To Beriah's horror, the old man was lying on the floor. His face was blue and he was gasping for breath. He seemed to be dying. Beriah leaned over his friend; whose bulging eyes were filled with terror. Feebly, Rosh reached a trembling, blue-veined hand to his throat.

Without hesitation, Beriah touched the staff to Rosh's throat and said, "Be healed, in the name of Jesus." Immediately, there was an eruption from Rosh's mouth and a large wooden button flew across the shop. Color returned to Rosh's face and his breathing became normal.

Hiram helped the weeping, old man to a chair. In amazement, the two men looked at Beriah in awe. Rosh reached out a trembling hand and Beriah took it. Looking into Beriah's face, Rosh said, "Thank you my brother. Indeed your faith is greater than mine."

Beriah wrapped his arms around his friend and humbly said, "And Hiram's faith is greater than mine." In a crab-like gait, Beriah, with his harp and staff, stepped out into the fresh air. Petting the dog's head he said, "Come Samson old boy, let's go home."

That night around the evening meal, Beriah related the story of Rosh getting choked on a wooden button. "Why would he have an object like that in his mouth?" asked Adonis.

Beriah smiled, "Rosh's shop is filled with piles of yarn that seems to be forever getting tangled. Anyway, the button came off his robe and Rosh put it in his mouth for safekeeping until he had time to tie it back on. Unfortunately he sneezed and the button became lodged in his air passage. He couldn't breath. Hiram, the Candlemaker, found Rosh on the floor and ran for me."

"Ran for you Beriah?" asked Joshua. "Why you? What did he want you to do?"

Beriah lowered his voice and said, "He wanted me to bring my staff. You see: Hiram had picked up my staff the day his hands were hurting him and the pain went away."

"What happened when you got to the weaver's shop Beriah? Think carefully and don't leave anything out. Take your time and try to recall the scene," Joshua encouraged.

"I had already packed my things on Samson and was ready to return home. A flustered Hiram ran across the street and began to pull me after him. 'Come quick, and bring your staff' Hiram said. I could hardly keep up. I didn't understand the necessity of hurrying until I stepped into the shop," said Beriah. "It took a few seconds for my eyes to adjust to the dimness of the interior of the weaver's shop. It was then I saw my old friend and follower of Jesus on the floor. His face was blue and his eyes bulged. He was in a panic and so was I. At first, I thought his heart had given out until he clutched his throat. Then I knew Rosh was choking." At this point Beriah stopped talking and sat looking into the fire.

Joshua pressed his finger to his lips, indicating that Adonis and Heber not speak. The trio waited for Beriah to gain control of his emotions and to continue. Heber added another piece of wood to the fire and Adonis refilled the mugs with juice. Joshua sliced the cheese and leaned back.

At last Beriah picked up his story. "I knew if something wasn't done quickly, Rosh would die. I remembered last night when you were 'drunk' on the Holy Spirit and you talked about your new found faith." Looking at Joshua, Beriah said, "And like a burning image branded on my mind, I recalled our conversation. Joshua, you told us Jesus said we could perform mighty miracles in His name; so I reached out the staff and touched Rosh's throat and said, 'In the name of Jesus, be healed." Beriah stopped talking and looked around the fire at his friends. Their faces were lit with wonder.

"There came a deep rumbling in Rosh's stomach; and it erupted with such force that the wooden button flew across the shop. Rosh gasped and began to breathe. Slowly his face became rosy. He was breathing normally and Hiram helped him to a chair," finished Beriah. With this, Adonis began to whoop and Heber started laughing, and clapping his hands. Beriah was embarrassed.

Joshua smiled and waited until Beriah had eaten a pear before he again returned to Rosh's recovery. "But that's not the end of the story. Do you want to share the rest with us?" asked Joshua. A special understanding seemed to flow between Joshua and Beriah. Adonis and Heber were perplexed. What more did Joshua want to know?

Shaking his head, Beriah said in a humble voice, "Old Rosh hugged me and said, 'Thank you my brother. Indeed your faith is greater than mine."

"Was it the staff that healed the weaver? Is it a magic staff?" asked Heber.

"No Heber. The staff has no magic," said Joshua shaking his head. "The miracle was due to Beriah's faith in our Lord and Savior, Jesus Christ. He simply pointed the staff in the area to be healed. He commanded a healing in the name of Jesus and Jesus did the healing. In other words, Beriah became the intercessor between Rosh and Jesus."

"I still don't understand how Beriah healed Rosh if the staff has no power," continued Heber.

"I too, am confused," said Adonis. "Earlier, Beriah handled the staff and the pain in his back went away. Hiram, the Candlemaker, handled the staff and his hands stopped hurting. In fact, that was probably why he ran for Beriah to bring his staff and help Rosh. Remember how Beriah ran his hand over the staff and touched the baby at the well? The baby's fever broke."

"Yes," spoke Heber. "Beriah said that Barak and Naaman were going to hit Samson with the staff and couldn't."

"That's right," butted in Adonis. "And Samson had been snapping at the camels and drivers, but when he smelled Jesus' sandals and the staff, he laid his head on Beriah's lap. How do you explain all of this Joshua?" asked Adonis.

"I believe the essence and odor of Jesus is embedded in the wood and leather. However, I feel whatever part of the staff and sandals play, is the fact that Beriah believes they belong to the Holy Man. In fact, Beriah believes that Jesus is the Son of God. Beriah's faith is interceding between the healing, or turns of events and Jesus. No my friends, the staff doesn't work magic. Beriah's wonderful faith is the catalyst of the healing. The love he has for his friends, neighbors, and his fellow man, unconscientiously even, he has been the intercessor beseeching healing and peace," said Joshua.

"Are you saying, that because of Beriah's faith, he is what set all these miracles into motion?" asked Adonis.

Joshua nodded his head yes.

"Then could I do the same?" asked Adonis.

"Jesus said you could do miracles but your faith must be great Adonis. Because what you're really doing is asking Jesus to do the miracle you beseech. But you must have faith that He will answer. Do you have that kind of faith Adonis?" asked Joshua.

Adonis sadly shook his head, "My faith is weak. However, I have high hopes that as I learn more about Jesus, my faith will grow by leaps and bounds. I want to study about Jesus under his disciple Peter. When I have learned more of Jesus' teachings, I plan to go home to Greece. I want my mother and father, along with all our neighbors, to share this wonderful word of God and His salvation."

"Could I go with you Adonis?" pleaded Heber.

Adonis looked at Heber; then threw his arm around his young friend. "You most certainly may. Why once we learn more about Jesus, we can sail to Greece on one of my father's ships. Like Peter told us on the Day of Pentecost, 'Jesus said we were to go two by two and spread the word to all nations." Joshua and Beriah looked at the excited young men. Suddenly, Adonis looked at Beriah and Joshua, "Say, why don't you two come along also? It would be great and you could see some of the world beyond Jerusalem."

"Thanks, but no thanks," smiled Joshua.

"What about you Beriah? Will you come with us?" asked Adonis. Beriah's eyes filled with tears but he slowly shook his head. Suddenly it dawned on the foursome that their lives were getting ready to travel different roads. The men had forged a strong bond of friendship, and parting would be hard. "What will you do Joshua?" asked Adonis.

"I've been thinking of tracing Jesus' footsteps along the Sea of Galilee. I'd first like to visit Bethlehem where Jesus was born, then to Bethany to talk to Lazarus. That's the man Jesus raised from the dead. In fact, I'd like to visit all the villages and places Jesus went. I'd like to hear the people tell about what Jesus did and taught," said Joshua.

"That's marvelous Joshua. I'd like to do that also, but first I want to know my family has a chance to be saved," said Adonis.

"I understand, Adonis. And I admire you for your decision," said Joshua. "However, I was hoping to talk Beriah into coming with me."

Beriah's head snapped up. "Me, Joshua?" he asked as tears flowed freely down his face. The thought of losing his friends was breaking Beriah's heart; he wasn't sure he could continue to live alone year after year in the dark cavern.

"Yes Beriah, you," laughed Joshua.

Sadly Beriah said, "I've never been away from Jerusalem except through Jobah's stories and the stories of the caravan drivers. I'm sure I couldn't walk so far; but thanks for asking me."

"Who said anything about walking?" asked Joshua. "What I had in mind was riding."

"Do you have a camel Joshua?" asked Beriah.

"No," laughed Joshua, "but my uncle Jethro is keeping that gentle, little donkey for me. Remember when the thieves, Barak and Naaman, abandoned him?"

"Beriah, this is a wonderful plan," laughed Adonis. "The little donkey is really a pet. You'll love him." Beriah was bewildered. His life was changing too fast: his head, a cloud of emotional thoughts. Adonis pushed on, "Beriah, if you go with Joshua, I won't spend the rest of my life worrying about you."

Excitement leaped into Beriah's heart. "Joshua, are you sure I wouldn't be a burden to you?"

Joshua chuckled, "If you were, it would be a delightful burden."

"The dog," said Beriah. "What is to become of Samson?"

Adonis looked at his dog, which at the moment had his head in Beriah's lap.

"Samson belongs to you Beriah. When I'm in Greece, I'll know you're protected," said Adonis.

For the next two months, what time the trio wasn't working, they were at the Temple. The disciple Peter, filled with courage and power of the Holy Spirit, preached on Solomon's porch and in the temple courtyard. The followers of Jesus continued to grow. Before long, their number had swelled to five thousand. Peter's message was simple. God loved the world so much, that He sent His Son, Jesus, to pay our sin debt. On the cross, Jesus paid a debt He did not owe; a debt, we could not pay. Peter continued to preach on believing in Jesus, repentance, and to be baptized. From there he sent the believers out to spread the word of God to the ends of the world.

The Romans were unhappy about the rapid growth of the new movement of Jesus. The priests were beside themselves. If the movement continued to grow, their revenue would diminish. These Jesus freaks had to be stopped at all costs. Or the Temple coffers would be empty of silver and gold. Not to mention all the lambs, bullocks, and other offerings brought to the temple. Why their very way of life was in jeopardy. Perhaps even their position and power would cease to exist.

Each evening around the fires and the talk at the well, the whispers of the travelers on the winding, narrow streets, tales from customers and the happenings at the Temple, were discussed and analyzed. It was a frightening, yet exciting, time to be alive. The disciple Peter had healed a man who had been a cripple for forty years: in the name of Jesus. Adonis laughed, "You should have seen the scowls on the faces of the Priests. They knew if they arrested Peter, the crowd would rise up against them."

"You're right Adonis," said Joshua sadly. "However, I'm afraid the time is coming when the anger of the Priests will overcome their fear. When this happens, Peter will be put in prison."

"What about the young disciple John? He may not be as loud and forceful as Peter, but he draws a following. In fact, in his soft voice he explains the love and compassion Jesus had for us. I'm truly sorry I didn't meet Jesus in person," said Heber.

"I too wish I had known Jesus in person," said Beriah. "However, all of us now know Him in our hearts."

Chapter Six

Three weeks later the trio came home with the news that Peter and John had been arrested and put in prison by the Priest, the Captain of the temple, and the Saducees. Because it was evening, Peter and John would have to wait until the next day for their hearing. "What will be their charges?" asked a disturbed Beriah.

"There will be charges against them for teaching Jesus' resurrection and about Him being the Son of God. They don't like Peter saying we are commissioned to preach the gospel first to the seeds of Abraham and then to the ends of the earth. Which means we are to preach to the despised Gentiles," stated Joshua. The arrest of Peter and John, and what this would mean to the believers, was discussed far into the night.

The following day, after the sixth hour, news came to Hur, the Potter, that the High Priest had reprimanded Peter and John. They were warned not to speak of Jesus; but Peter, being full of the Holy Ghost, let it be known, that Jesus Christ of Nazareth, whom they crucified and God raised Him from the dead, was indeed 'the stone whom you have rejected and has now become the Chief Corner Stone.' Hur had told Beriah that Peter refused to stop preaching Jesus. "I'm afraid it's just a matter of time before Peter and John are arrested again or killed," said Hur in concern. Shortly before Beriah's return home, he had another visitor. This time it was old Shua, the Soap Maker. Without asking she sat down beside Beriah. Then removing two apples from her pocket, she handed one to Beriah. He thanked her and waited for her to say what was on her mind. Beriah hoped she wasn't going to ask for a healing of some kind. He was quite surprised when she asked him,

"Beriah, do you remember anything about your life before you met Old Jobah?" Beriah nodded no and his face clouded up in a puzzled frown. "Didn't Jobah tell you how you came to live with him?" asked Old Shua.

"Not that I recall," answered Beriah, wondering where this was leading. "Jobah was good to me and was always there for me. He said that I was an orphan and he didn't know who my parents were."

"And that's all you were told?" asked a now agitated Shua.

"Jobah said it was hard to find a home for a child; much less a crippled child. I've always loved Jobah and I am thankful he gave me a home," said Beriah in a humble voice.

"Then it's about time that I tell you a few things." After a long pause Shua said, "You were found lying alone on the seashore near Joppa. It was miles from the nearest house. The only thing you had on was a wet night shirt and a chain around your neck with a coin on it."

'Why is she telling me this' Beriah was asking himself. Beriah asked Shua, "What kind of a coin?"

"I don't really know, except it had two heads on it, one on the front and one on the back. You were about four years old. According to the owner of a camel caravan, you were covered with sand, cuts, bruises, and insect bites. Your back was broken and you were running a fever. In fact, you were delirious. Fortunately, the caravan owner had a big heart. He laid you on boards and strapped you down. Though the man was kind; he was not a physician. However, he took you first to Joppa. No one knew you. Then the man brought you to Jerusalem; where kindly Old Jobah took you in and loved you like a son," Shua told him.

"I wonder why he never told me such things. Surely he would have known if I was lost I would want to find my parents," said Beriah in a bewildered tone.

"I don't want to speak ill of the dead, Beriah," said Shua, "but at the time you came into Jobah's life, he had reached rock bottom. He let wine get the best of him. The old man went from being a respected scholar, who taught different languages, art and music to the children of the wealthy, to being a beggar at the gates in order to have food. After you came into Old Jobah's life, he stopped drinking and took odd jobs around the shops and inns. We were so happy for him; that we decided to stay quiet."

"Who do you mean by we Shua?" asked Beriah.

Old Shua nodded up and down the street. "All the merchants who knew about you, when Jobah died, we decided that we would look after you and be your friends."

Beriah, a little agitated responded, "If you've stayed quiet all these years, why are you telling me now?"

"Times are now filled with trouble and uncertainties. We felt you should know your background." Reaching into her pocket, Shua withdrew a chain and a silver coin. Holding the chain and coin out she said, "Here; this belongs to you." She pressed the necklace into Beriah's hand.

For a few seconds Beriah sat staring at the silver chain and coin. Closing his fingers tightly around it, Beriah said, "Shua, how did you come by the necklace?"

Looking off in the direction of the upper city, Shua said in a voice just above a whisper, "Years ago I lived in the upper city with the well to do. I was young and life was filled with wonder; and I was in love with a good-looking scholar named Jobah. We were married; yet no children came to bless our household. After a few years, Jobah began to take more wine with his meal than the usual glass or two. Soon, his reputation as a worthy teacher was tarnished. He lost his job. Soon we lost our home and moved to the lower city. Then Jobah moved out.

I began to make soap from my grandmother's directions. Next, I set up shop and supported myself. In order to eat, Jobah became a beggar. Oh Beriah! Jobah had such a brilliant mind!" At this, Shua began to weep. "He changed after he adopted you. He brought me the chain so he wouldn't sell it when tempted to drink. He knew he could trust me to save it for you, Beriah." Shua wiped her eyes on the tail of her garment…Shua stood and took a few steps then stopped. Turning back, she said, "Beriah, the few words you could speak were Greek.

You knew no other language. You kept saying 'Me, Nico, Me, Nico." Once these words were spoken, Old Shua crossed the street.

Beriah's heart was racing as he studied the coin. Perhaps his own dear mother or father had placed it around his neck. But what was the meaning of the two heads? For the next hour Beriah studied the coin. Oh if only these heads could talk. At last he slipped the chain over his head and concealed it with his robe.

Around the ninth hour, Beriah and Samson left the well. They traveled down the alley to the bazaar. Here Beriah purchased the evening meal. His mind was still churning with the information that Shua had told him. He was debating whether or not to share his news with the trio.

To Beriah's surprise, Adonis, Joshua, and Heber had returned earlier. There were also two strange men around the fire. The younger and smaller of the men was sitting. He smiled as Joshua introduced him as John, one of Jesus' disciples. The taller, rough-looking man, in a brown homespun robe, was introduced as the disciple Peter. Introductions were acknowledged. To Beriah's surprise, Peter reached out and took the staff out of Beriah's hand. Carefully, Peter looked the staff over. Then his penetrating eyes bored into Beriah's. "Where did you find this staff?" he asked in a gruff voice that shook with passion.

Before Beriah could answer, Adonis spoke up, "I'm the one who found the staff and gave it to Beriah." Peter looked first at the young man and then the others. It was hard for Adonis to keep eye contact with the overpowering Peter, but he did. Running his tongue over his lips, Adonis swallowed and said, "I found the staff in the Garden of Gethsemane the day after the crucifixion. It was leaning against a gnarled, old olive tree. In fact, you were leaning against the same tree the night before."

"What was I doing?" asked Peter cautiously.

Adonis hesitated, and then said, "You were asleep sir, but so were the others." Adonis said hastily. A look of sadness crossed the Big Fisherman's face.

Shaking his head sideways he said, "But that was no excuse for me. When Jesus needed us most, we let Him down; and I more than others. I told Jesus I would never forsake Him. Yet I slept while He prayed. When He was arrested we fled in fear. I followed at a safe distance; but denied knowing Jesus three times before the cock crowed just as Christ predicted." There was a profound silence in the room. Slowly, Peter ran his hands up and down the smooth wood. His eyes misted over. He then appeared to look beyond the other men. In a low voice he said, "I made this staff for Jesus. He often referred to Himself as our Shepherd. In jest I gave Him a staff to guide His sheep. Jesus enjoyed my humor. After that, he used the staff when walking."

Around the evening meal, Adonis related how he had acquired the staff. After many questions Joshua said, "Why not let Beriah tell you about the miracles surrounding the touching of the staff."

Reluctantly Beriah related how the pain in his legs and back had gone away, then about the hands of Hiram the Candlemaker. Next, Beriah told about the sick baby and how he had acquired the dog, Samson. "Any other strange occurrences?" asked Peter. Beriah nodded yes, but didn't continue. Joshua spoke up and told about Barak and Naaman, the would be tomb robbers. Then Adonis told about Rosh the Weaver choking.

Peter quietly listened as the stories were related. Next Peter said something that had been on everyone's mind. "If others are healed by coming in contact with the staff, then why not Beriah?" All eyes turned on Beriah. Peter continued, "Do you have an answer Beriah? Is your faith in Jesus weak?" There was a gasp around the fire as Peter handed Beriah the staff.

Still standing, the crippled man leaned on the staff. Then with dignity and courage Beriah looked Peter in the eyes. "I have faith in our Lord Jesus, that when it is His good time, He will heal me, if not in this life, then in the next to come. I don't know why I'm holding His staff and still have a warped back. Though I'm crippled in body, I'm not crippled in faith. And crippled or not, I will forever praise and follow my Lord and Savior." With that, Beriah sat down on his mat.

Peter smiled at the courageous, young man. "I don't know the reason either Beriah. Your faith and love for Jesus is in evidence for all to see. Why you even seem to be gathering all us strays into your home. After we eat, I suggest we get on with the baptizing you so desire."

Beriah's happiness was so great; he had a hard time eating. Toward the end of the meal, Beriah said, "I want to take off my sandals. They're the ones the soldiers gambled for but left them on the Hill of Golgotha." Beriah took off his sandals and set them by his sleeping pallet. After this, he turned to Peter and humbly asked, "Do you think we could break bread and drink the fruit of the vine before I'm baptized?"

Peter smiled, "I think that would be a fitting tribute for the occasion Beriah."

Joshua spoke up, "Sit still Beriah, Adonis and I will get the bread and wine."

A short time later, the little group bowed their heads as Peter said, "Jesus took the bread, blessed it and broke it, and gave it to us and said, 'Take it; for this is my body.'" With this, Peter broke the bread and passed it around. "Then Jesus took the cup, gave thanks and gave it to us saying, 'Drink from it, all of you. For this is my blood of the new covenant, which is shed for the remission of sin.'" Peter took a sip of juice and passed it around. Then Peter said, "The sacrament of the Lord's supper is meant to bring all creations back to God, in Christ and with Christ. This is an experience which seals our faith in Jesus as the Messiah."

Quietly, Beriah left the table and returned with a towel and a pan of water. Adonis watched in amazement as Beriah took off his outer robe. Then pulling his under-garment between his legs: he tied it at his waist. Next, he knelt before Peter and removed his sandals. After washing Peter's feet, he continued around the table until he had washed everyone's feet in the manner set by Jesus at the Last Supper.

A short time after the foot washing, Peter prayed for the group. He then led Beriah into the sunken pool. Lifting up his eyes, he again prayed for Jesus' blessings to fall upon Beriah and to fill him with the Holy Spirit. And thus, before witnesses, Beriah was baptized.

Nearing the day of the Jewish Holy Day of Rosh Hoshanna or Feast of the Trumpets, Adonis broke the news that he would be starting for home the next day. "In fact, Heber has agreed to go with me," smiled Adonis. "Beriah, I hope you understand that I must tell my family about Jesus."

Through tears Beriah nodded and said, "I've known all along that someday we would part Adonis. However, I'm finding parting to be hard."

With this, the two young men embraced. "Are you sure you and Joshua won't come with us?" coaxed Adonis.

Beriah shook his head no. "Maybe someday we'll meet again Adonis. And may you never lose your new-found faith in Christ."

Adonis turned to Joshua who was witnessing the love that had formed between Beriah and Adonis. By the dancing flames of the fire, it had occurred to Joshua an uncanny resemblance between the two young men. "Will you not come along with us Joshua? We're approaching autumn and the grapes will soon be harvested. Autumn is a joyous time of the year in Greece. Abdul's caravan is leaving at daybreak. He had news one of my Father's ships will be in Sycaminum for a week. I hope to be on the high seas and home within eight weeks. That is, if the winds are right."

Joshua smiled, "I'm like Beriah. My pathway is in Judea for a while. But who knows? Perhaps our paths will cross again someday. Don't worry about Beriah; he'll be traveling with me. We plan to trace the footsteps of Jesus." The rest of the evening was filled with hugs, laughter, and tears.

At last Adonis walked over to Beriah. Adonis reached for a chain around his neck and brought out a signet ring. Carefully, he placed the necklace around Beriah's neck. "My father gave me this ring. It has his crest on it. If at anytime you two change your mind, then wait in Sycaminum for one of my father's ships. Just present this ring and you'll have free passage to Greece or to anyplace you care to travel.

Through tears Beriah removed his own necklace and coin and placed it over Adonis' head. Smiling he said, "I'm loaning you this coin. Someday when you get the urge to travel: return it to me. You know where I live and you will always be welcome. That goes for you too Heber."

Adonis hugged Beriah and said, "If it's God's will, we will see each other again someday. If not in this life, then in the new one to come that Jesus promised to the redeemed."

It was almost dawn before Beriah fell into a troubled sleep. When he awoke, Adonis and Heber were gone. Joshua had already been to the bazaar for juice and rolls. When Beriah fully awakened, he looked over at Adonis' and Heber's pallets. The covers on both were neatly folded but his friends were gone. It was then that Beriah gave way to loud, uncontrolled, and anguished sobs. Joshua sat quietly and let Beriah cry like a little boy lost, until there was nothing left but sorrow. Without a word, Joshua got up and wet a cloth in cold water. Still without speaking, he placed it in Beriah's hand and sat back down by the fire.

Normally a fire was not lit in the morning, but today Joshua planned on staying home with Beriah. For Beriah, parting with Adonis had the overtone of parting with a loved one in death. Joshua wanted to make sure that Beriah would be all right. Quietly, Joshua placed the tripod; Adonis had made, over the fire. He hung a kettle of water on the hook. While waiting for the water to boil, he set out cups and bowls. At last Beriah arose and washed his face in cold, spring water. Turning to Joshua, he asked, "You're not working today?" Joshua said, "It will do us both good. Perhaps we can even begin to make plans for our journey." Soon the water began to boil. Joshua made two cups of hot Oriental tea. He laced Beriah's with honey to help calm his nerves.

Over the tea and sweet roll, Joshua began to talk. "I thought we could go first to Bethlehem where Jesus was born. Then we'll come back to Jerusalem and on to Bethany." Throughout the day the men talked and planned. They discussed Nazareth, the Sea of Galilee, the Jordan River, Capernaum, Decapolis, Judea, and land beyond Jordan.

They were also interested in traveling to Gergesenes, the region of Magdala, Bersaida, Cana, and the regions of Tyre and Sidon.

"Beriah, these are but a few of the places Jesus taught or performed miracles. I get so excited just talking about the places," said Joshua.

"I know," repeated Beriah. "It will be an exciting journey!"

Chapter Seven

Joshua and Beriah were two days on the road to Bethlehem. The first night they built a small fire on a little slope of the hill and slept under a tree near the road. Beriah had not complained but he was trying to adjust to riding a donkey with the constant motion of moving back and forth. Beriah was almost in tears from the jolting and jarring sensation of the donkey's hoofs stepping on the hard baked earth. The autumn sun beat down relentlessly on their heads and the hot wind blew gritty sand in their eyes and teeth. Their hair and clothing turned a dirty color from the sand and dust. The grass and weeds were parched. Here and there, a few palm trees were seen. Their shredded fonds hung like beards; fluttering in the wind.

Although the journey was a few miles southward and across a broad plain of Jerusalem, there had been a few snags. Beriah had never been on the back of a donkey. The donkey was also having an adjustment problem. Lately, the donkey had been carrying sheaves of grain, and only once before it had carried a person. The little donkey, which was gentle by nature, wasn't happy about it's new duty. At times the donkey would stall and several times it would sit down. Beriah was sore after the first mile and decided to walk part of the time. Joshua and Beriah rested in the heat of the afternoon. Soon other travelers joined them under a large sprawling olive tree.

After polite inquiries into each other's destinations; the men bound for Jerusalem asked, "Is there any truth to the rumors of the Nazarene Rabbi being crucified and then coming out of the tomb?" For the next two hours Joshua and Beriah told the travelers about Jesus being seen by more that five hundred witnesses before He ascended into Heaven. Joshua told about the mighty rushing wind and the fire at Pentecost; also, how the people were filled with the Holy Spirit and spoke in other tongues.

On the evening of the second day, Joshua and Beriah arrived at the little town of Bethlehem. The town was spread out on a low hill. Its terraced streets ran up the hill and around limestone houses. A few cedar, oak and palm trees dotted the hills. Here and there were rich garden patches and orchards. These gave it the name, 'The House of Bread.' At the foot of the hill was a valley with fields of wheat lying in mounds and an olive orchard. On the hills were flocks of sheep. The shepherds had small fires to ward off wolves and the chill of the approaching night. Their small lights looked like rays of hope for the travelers. To the east, were barren hills of Judea and the desert where John the Baptist lived. In summer the land around Bethlehem was dry and bare. However, in winter, the rains came and the hills flourished with little flowering plants. They seem to spring up everywhere.

Joshua asked directions to the Inn. He had been saving some money from each of his working days. Tonight, he wanted Beriah to rest before they explored the town. A lantern had already been lit in the window of the Khan when Joshua rapped on the door. A short time later, an elderly man opened the door part way. He squinted his eyes as if trying to see through the dusk of twilight. A woman's voice called out from the dining area. "Who's there Abe?"

"We have two travelers Phoebe," the old man called back. "Set them out a bowl of stew, some bread and cheese while I show them a room."

"Before we eat we need to take care of our dog and donkey and wash off some dust and grime," stated Joshua. "Also, I'll pay for our food and lodging now."

"Good, Good," said the elderly man. Pointing a knarled finger he said, "A short way up the hill and behind the inn is a cave stable. That's where we keep our animals. You'll find grain and a watering trough up there. That'll be an extra shekel. Out back are a pan and a pail of water.

You might want to shake the dust off your clothes out there. Phoebe can keep the stew hot until you're ready."

Joshua encouraged Beriah to clean up while he watered and fed Jasper, the donkey. By the time Jasper and Samson were fed and secured for the night and both men were freshened up, an hour had passed. While Joshua and Beriah ate the savory food placed before them; the old woman kept up a constant chatter. Joshua and Beriah listened politely. At last Joshua said, "You have a nice establishment here Miss Phoebe. How many travelers can you accommodate?"

Miss Phoebe – she beamed at the compliment. "We have six rooms that we let out for four people each. Those were the original rooms in Abe's grandfather's days. However, being on the trade route out of Libya, Ethiopia, and Egypt: we didn't have enough room. Years ago Abe built on what we call the Common room, it sleeps twenty-four – another dozen in a pinch. Same with the rooms, when we're crowded, they'll hold six each. We have plenty of sleeping mats. My problem is keeping enough sheets and towels washed. It seems I always have a kettle of towels and sheets soaking."

Beriah smiled and said, "You're blessed to have the hot sun to dry them. I don't suppose the drying period is very long."

Miss Phoebe smiled at Beriah. Her heart seemed to go out for the young cripple. "Here, have some more tomatoes and cucumbers. They've been plentiful this year."

"This is mighty good bread," stated Joshua. "There's nothing that smells better than the aroma of fresh baked bread."

Miss Phoebe's round face was flushed with the pleasure of compliments, as her husband came into the room. Abe addressed Joshua, "I'm surprised you didn't stay at the camel caravansary down at the foot of the hill. It's more up to date than we are."

Joshua laughed, "Our dog Samson plays havoc among the camels. Isn't that so Beriah?"

Nodding, Beriah said, "You wouldn't believe how Samson enjoys teasing camels and their drivers. However, I've been working with

Samson and his manners are improving. I earn my living playing the harp. Some days I play at the camel caravansary in Jerusalem."

"Where's the dog now?" asked the leery innkeeper.

"Tied out back," said Joshua, as he took a bite of bread and washed it down with goat's milk. "Did you make the fig preserves?" Miss Phoebe beamed. "I put up fifty two quarts," she said.

Turning to Abe, Joshua asked, "What's the most people you ever accommodated at one time?"

For a few moments, Abe did not answer. Joshua waited. At last Abe said, "Years ago, we put up 125 people."

Miss Phoebe broke in, "We even had them in the halls. It kept me busy cooking, and cleaning rooms."

"When was this and what caused an influx of people?" asked Beriah.

For a few moments no one spoke. Finally Abe replied, "It all happened before either one of you were born."

"Really? Was it one of our Holy days or just a festival?" quizzed Joshua.

"Neither," replied Old Abe. "Caesar Augustus, mighty emperor of Rome," said Abe with disgust for the fallen leader, "decreed that all the world should be registered for a census. Everyone had to go to his or her own city. Those that were of the House and lineage of David came to Bethlehem. Not only did we have the people, who came to register, but the Roman Soldiers and the usual travelers as well. We were filled up and even overflowing. The caravansary was full and some of the people stayed in private homes. Not to mention: horses, donkeys, and camels everywhere! Some even slept in tents."

"That must have been something," said Joshua. "Did you turn people away?"

"I'm afraid I did," nodded Abe.

At this point, Miss Phoebe interrupted again, "I remember one particular couple that came at the edge of dark. The young wife had already gone into labor and they hadn't been able to find a room. The poor man was desperate. Abe said they could use the stable. At least they would be able to get out of the night air. We had hired a man to muck out the stable that very afternoon and fresh straw was laid down on the floor. I remember taking two blankets and a lantern and guided them up the hill."

"What was the night like?" asked Beriah, his eyes wide in wonder. "Except for the chatter of all those foreign tongues, and the braying of animals, it was a beautiful night. The stars filled the sky and the moon shone its pale, yellowish light. The houses were silhouetted against the hill. Each home had a lighted window. There were bonfires with meat roasting on spits. The air smelled of the aroma of cooking, wood, smoke, and dust. Toward the hill, where the shepherds watched their flocks, small fires blazed. Sometimes when the wind blows in our direction, we can hear the bleating of sheep. Not a frightened bleating but rather a plaintive or mourning sound. Strange, but the cows, back of the inn, were lowing as though in sorrow. The owls hooted as if the coming and going of the people was an annoyance. Even the whippoorwills seemed to ask their age old question in melodic calls."

"Phoebe you're droning on too much. Stick to the story and stop being so fanciful," said Abe.

Phoebe shook her frizzled hair and picked up the narrative. "I took the man and woman to the stable. There was plenty of fresh water in the trough. However, later I took up some clean cloths and a gourd with a jug of fresh drinking water. The young woman was lying down. She was drenched with sweat. Her husband was wiping her face with a wet cloth, while speaking comforting and encouraging words. By the look in her eyes, I could tell that she was frightened and in great pain. I asked if they needed anything else, but they shook their heads no." Joshua was feeling very sleepy and even dozing off occasionally, but he kept himself alert, not wanting to miss this story, as laborious as it was. Beriah also thought to himself that Miss Phoebe's account of that night was explicit, to say the least, but does the woman ever stop to take a breath? Miss Phoebe continued without a stop, "Abe was out tending to the lamb that was being roasted for the next day. I returned to the kitchen and finished baking bread for the following day. I tell you, it was a restless evening. It was shortly before midnight, when I heard the new baby cry. I was happy that the woman's pain was over and the baby was alive."

At this point of the story, Abe said, "A short time later some shepherd knocked on the door. I needn't tell you I was a bit put out. It seemed I wasn't going to get much rest that night. Anyway, they were so excited, they all tried to talk at once."

"What did they say?" inquired a sleepy Joshua.

Abe scratched his beard and slowly shook his head. "They tried to convince me that a host of angels were up in the sky and singing about the 'Lord had come, and a newborn King.' Can you believe that? I looked over my shoulder to see if any soldiers might have overheard them. 'You fools,' I thought. 'You're going to get us killed!" Not that I believed them, mind you. More than likely, they had been hitting the wine skin. They kept mumbling about a star shining over the place. Then they looked up the hill." At this point of the story, Abe paused. Then, shaking his gray head, as if to cast out doubts, he continued, "Strangely, the bright star now hung low over the stable. In fact, the star was brighter than I've ever seen. When I was roasting the lamb, the star wasn't there. When and where it came from passed through my mind. It was like an omen. But what was it's meaning? The shepherds went scurrying in the direction of the stable. I closed my door and locked it. Newborn King indeed! Did they think that a stable would be a fit place for a Kingly birth?"

"Is that the end of the story?" asked Beriah.

"I'm going out to check on the roasting meat. Let Phoebe finish the story," said Abe.

Phoebe pulled out a stool and sat down. "I saw the new baby the next day. He was a fair one. And he didn't squall like most babies. In a few days, the man called Joseph moved his little family into a small house of a deceased widow. The roof was caved in and the door was off its hinges. Soon, however, these were repaired, and the yard and garden was scythed. It turned out that the man, Joseph, was a carpenter. He turned the tool shed into a carpenter shop and was soon earning a living for his little family. The young mother stayed pretty much to herself, except when she came to the well. They blended quite nicely in our little town for about two years." At this point, Miss Phoebe drooped her head and her face took on the expression of deep sorrow. Then in a voice that shook with emotion she continued, "That was about the time when our trouble started."

"What trouble was that?" asked Beriah.

Tears filled the old woman's eyes, "One evening we looked out and there were three men on camels coming up the winding street. Now I've seen wealthy merchants and travelers, but never have I seen anyone as magnificent as these men from the east. Why they looked like kings, the way they carried themselves and all. Abe was completely taken with their reins and other rich trappings on the camels. One was decked out in a brilliant scarlet and gold, one was in purple and gold, and the other was done up in a royal blue and gold. There were golden bells on the fringes and gold threads running through the rich material. The harnesses were interwoven with gold ropes. Oh! They were truly grand!"

"Did they spend the night with you?" asked Beriah. He was so excited by now, he could hardly constrain himself.

"No, as a matter of fact, they kept watching the evening sky. The star that was over the stable, the night the woman gave birth, had moved over the house where they lived. So the three kingly men went there and rapped on the door. I could see all this from our dining room window. By the way, the young mother's name was Mary. I told you earlier, the father's name was Joseph. They named their son Jesus. It means 'Joshua," she said and smiled at Joshua.

"What happened next?" asked Joshua, fully alert now.

"Oh my, according to the old woman at the well, the men from the far east were looking for a new born King. I tell you if that's not something. Why the very idea that a king would be born in Bethlehem is ridiculous. Anyway, they brought him, the baby Jesus I mean, some very rich gifts. Some said gold, myrrh, and uh let's see, oh yes – frankincense. Well, that's what my friend said. You know how we women-uh I mean, some women go on so." The same thoughts were running through Beriah and Joshua's minds, as they looked at each other.

"Did they stay long?" asked Beriah.

"That's strange. It was said, from those who were looking in the house, that these three men bowed to the child Jesus and laid those beautiful gifts at His feet. I declare – that doesn't make a bit of sense! Why a child would rather have a wooden rattle or a noisemaker. The next day, however, the kingly men went away. And a few days later, Mary, Joseph, and their little child left as well. They left in the middle of the night. They didn't tell a soul where they were going. You would think after living in Bethlehem for two years, you would want to say goodbye to your friends, but not them. That's odd, isn't it? Maybe they wanted to go to a bigger city where they could enjoy their riches. They didn't seem to be the greedy type, but one never knows." After this, Miss Phoebe broke down in convulsing sobs.

Beriah and Joshua were stunned. "What's wrong?" they implored.

In a voice just above a whisper, she said, "A few days later, King Herod's soldiers came and killed every male child in the town of Bethlehem; two years old and under. That evil edict included our son, Benjamin. Had he lived, he would have been thirty-three years old. Abe and I were middle-aged before we were blessed with a child." There was nothing Beriah and Joshua could say to the grieving mother.

The following morning, Beriah and Joshua went down the hill to the camel caravansary. Joshua had already fed and watered the donkey and Samson. Beriah carried his harp and Joshua carried Beriah's rug and leather pouch. A short time later Beriah was sitting near the caravansary gate playing his harp. Joshua soon had work with one of the caravans, loading the camels. Then suddenly, the caravan owner asked Joshua, "I've been hearing about trouble in Jerusalem. You said that you came from there. Do you know anything about that? Or are these rumors just a figment of someone's imagination?"

"Well, what have you heard so far?" Joshua asked back.

"Heard?" grumbled the Egyptian. "Why everything from crucifying a rabble rouser to Him coming back from the dead. We even heard that King Herod has lost his mind! One caravan I met had just left Jerusalem. The owner of that one said the Roman soldiers were searching for the dead Jew's followers. He told me that if Caesar got wind of this, heads would roll. Talk is, that Pontius Pilate will probably lose his position and be banished to some God-forsaken island. I think," continued the caravan owner, "If there's any threat to Rome, there will be a bloodbath in the streets of Jerusalem."

Joshua was surprised that the crucifixion and Jesus' resurrection had traveled so far. Joshua continued to listen while the agitated Egyptian related what he had heard about Jerusalem. Finally, Joshua said, "Sir, Jesus, the Nazarene, came into this world to save men like you and me. He was the Son of God who took the debt of sin, on the cross, in our place. Jesus said, 'No man taketh my life from me. I lay it down of my own accord. I have authority to lay it down and the same authority to take it up again. This command I received from my Father.'" The Egyptian kept tying off some lead rope for his camels, but he listened intently to Joshua's account of Jesus. Joshua said, "During Jesus' time on earth, He healed the sick, made the lame to walk, opened up the blinded eyes, cured the lepers, cast out demons, and even raised the dead. He suffered and died that we might have eternal life. It's free for the asking and receiving of His grace and mercy. Jesus asks us to believe that He is the Son of God through faith. He said we must be born again if we are to see the Kingdom of Heaven. To be born again, means a spiritual birth, not physical. We must repent of our sins and ask Jesus to come into our hearts, and then, be baptized."

"We Egyptians have many gods," the caravan owner said. "Is it that simple to have eternal life? Does this mean that when I die, I won't have to travel forever in the underworld of death?" he asked.

"That's correct," said Joshua. "The one true God," Joshua said with feeling, "said the body returns to the dust from which it came. And the soul goes back to God who gave it." At last a big smile broke out on the Egyptian's face. Slowly, he knelt in the dust beside sweating camels, and asked for forgiveness of his sins. Joshua and the man exchanged brotherly hugs before parting. The countenance on the man's face was not the gruff appearance he had when Joshua first encountered him. The caravan then moved slowly along the road to Jerusalem. The owner turned and waved a final farewell to his new found friend. Joshua joined Beriah by the gate and related the story of the new convert for Christ.

After taking refreshments, Joshua rested until another caravan arrived. This one was from Ethiopia. The Afro-Asiatic language of the caravan drivers was unintelligent babble to Joshua and Beriah. Joshua approached a tall, ebony – skinned man who stood with dignity and bearings of a king. Joshua started out trying to communicate with hand language to the leader. The man's grave expression and boring eyes made Joshua feel foolish. At last, the tall man smiled and said in prefect Arabic, "Are you offering your services to help me get settled in?"

Joshua felt even more foolish. Then the two men broke out laughing. "I guess I wasn't doing too well with sign language. But yes sir, I'm offering my services," laughed Joshua.

Joshua worked until almost suppertime. Then He and Beriah returned to the inn. Beriah fed and watered the dog – Samson, who was unhappy about being tied. "I'll take you for a walk after supper," he promised the whimpering dog. Joshua fed and watered the little, brown donkey – Jasper. Both men dusted off their clothes and washed the best they could before answering Miss Phoebe's call for the evening meal. They both were tired but satisfied with the day's work.

Miss Phoebe served mutton, that Abe had been roasting the previous evening, and many savory dishes and fresh bread. After a hardy meal, Beriah and Joshua praised Miss Phoebe for her delicious supper meal. While Beriah and Joshua were relaxing over their second cup of tea, Joshua asked, "Miss Phoebe, did you ever hear what became of the young couple and their baby?"

Miss Phoebe stopped slicing bread and said, "Strange you should ask. For a long time after the tragedy of the children of Bethlehem, I wondered whether or not the soldiers had killed the child before they killed ours. Of course, there's no way of knowing. I guess their leaving before the butchering began, was just a coincidence." Miss Phoebe murmured, "A wise old man said, 'the killing of the children was a fulfillment of a prophesy spoken by Jeremiah, the prophet, who said,

"In Rama, was there a voice heard;
Lamentations, weeping, and great mourning.
Rachel, weeping for her children,
And would not be comforted, because
They were not."

Shaking her head, she said, "Oh well, that's all in the past now. It had nothing to do with today. Abe says I shouldn't keep digging up the ashes of a dead fire. Perhaps not, but I can't seem to help myself."

There was a lull in conversation, and then Joshua asked, "Have you heard about Jesus of Nazareth?" Miss Phoebe nodded she had. "Doesn't the name Jesus ring a bell?" he probed.

"Yes, it's the same as the infant. Since Jesus means 'Joshua' I just assumed there are several children with that name. It is a favorite name you know," said Miss Phoebe with a wrinkled up brow. Joshua shook his head no. Miss Phoebe focused her total attention on Joshua. "Are you saying, the Babe of Bethlehem's stable, is the Jesus of Nazareth?"

Nodding yes, Joshua said, "Yes Miss Phoebe. They are the one and the same." Abe, Miss Phoebe, Joshua, and Beriah sat far into the night discussing the King who was born that night in their stable. Joshua reminded them of the prophesy by Micah, who said; 'But you, Bethlehem Ephrathah,

Though you are little among the thousands of Judea,
Yet, out of you shall come forth to Me, the One
To be ruler of Israel. Whose going forth, has been told?
From everlasting to everlasting.'

The following morning Joshua and Beriah returned to the caravansary to work. Miss Phoebe spread the story of Jesus to the women at the well. Soon, the story of Jesus was being passed from house to house. After a hot, tiring day, Beriah and Joshua returned to the inn. They were met by a throng of men and women wanting to hear more about the Babe who had been born in their mist. Abe warded the crowd off saying, 'Give the men a chance to wash up and eat.' Reluctantly, the people agreed. Abe fed the donkey and the dog while Beriah and Joshua washed up. Miss Phoebe hurried them into the cool of the dining room, where they ate a good, wholesome meal. However, they did not linger around the table.

Soon, Beriah and Joshua were seated on the ground. The courtyard was filled with eager listeners. Joshua told about the teachings of Jesus and His many miracles. Beriah told about him being a witness to Jesus' cruel crucifixion. Joshua picked up the story and told about Jesus' resurrection and how that He was seen talking to over 500 witnesses, before ascending into Heaven. He explained about Jesus sending the Holy Spirit to be our comforter. Once again, Joshua found himself witnessing about the risen Savior. Joshua said, "Christ said that He would come again to receive unto Himself, a glorious people. God did not kill the children of Bethlehem. Satan instigated that. You, my friends, have a chance to see your loved ones again – if you will only believe in Jesus." There, under the Judaen star-studded sky, men and women knelt in the gritty sand and gave their lives to Christ. Once again, the wonder of the Lord flooded Bethlehem.

Chapter Eight

A few days later found Joshua and Beriah on their way back to Jerusalem. Samson was excited to be off his leash. Even Jasper, the donkey, seemed to pick his feet up and set them down carefully. Beriah learned to get his balance and even manage to play his harp. The little donkey's ears flopped up and down, and his tail swished back and forth to the rhythm of the harp. What a funny sight this little traveling quartet made. Even Joshua laughed at the antics of the music-loving donkey. Samson chased rabbits and quail and even a few buzzards.

The happiness over the Bethlehem converts showed in the spring of Joshua's walk and the way he used Beriah's staff. Strangely, they made the trip to Jerusalem in one day. Beriah purchased the evening's meal while Joshua took Jasper back to his uncle's barnyard. Around the fire in Beriah's cavernous home, they ate and discussed their Bethlehem adventure. It was wonderful to be back home, but they missed their friends, Adonis and Heber. Beriah's eyes burned as they began to tear up, thinking about his friends.

The rest of the week was spent as usual. Joshua worked with the camel caravansary and Beriah played his harp at the well. Throughout the day, the merchants wandered over to the well to welcome Beriah back home. And as friends came by, Beriah related Joshua and his Bethlehem experience. Beriah's friends were equally excited about the new converts for the Lord Jesus Christ. Beriah told his friends that in a few days he and Joshua were going to Bethany and on to the Sea of Galilee. Beriah's friends told him they were equally concerned about Beriah traveling so far. Beriah explained to them that he would be riding on Jasper and walk just a little while. "Please don't worry about me. I'll be traveling with Joshua, my brother in Christ." Everyone wished him a safe journey and said they would pray for his safe return.

A week later found Joshua, Beriah, Jasper, and Samson on the road to Bethany. The village of Bethany laid a day's journey to the east of Jerusalem. Bethany was sprawled out on the sunny slope of the Mount of Olives. There were orchards and gardens here and there among the houses and the surrounding rolling terrain. Bethany was on the road between Jerusalem and Jericho. When approaching from the plains of the Jordan River, the road continued to climb. It was a steep road and pilgrims who climbed the road often stopped in Bethany to rest before continuing to Jerusalem.

The two men were on their way to visit Mary, Martha, and Lazarus. Only a month before Jesus had been crucified, he had raised Lazarus from the dead. Many people from the village and from Jerusalem had witnessed this miracle. This was the final miracle, which caused the Priests and Saducees to determine to have Jesus killed.

In Bethany that morning, Mary and Martha had begun the day's work early. Mary carried the water from the village well, while Martha took barley from the large storage pot and ground the kernels between the millstones. When Mary returned with the water, she dipped out a small bowl-full and crumbled in a small piece of fermented dough, that had been saved from the day before. The day old dough was used as leaven for today's bread.

When Martha's barley was ground enough, she blended the flour, leaven and water in a large bowl. She then kneaded the dough in a kneading trough and left it to rise for a few hours. Martha then rolled up the sleeping mats and swept the roof and outside stairs. Martha put clothes to soak in a large kettle before making curds from goat's milk in a goatskin churn. Mary placed oil in the lamps, trimmed the wicks, and gathered fresh vegetables for the evening meal. Then she hung a kettle of beans over a fire in the courtyard. Later, Martha planned to soak dried fish, while she fried sweet cakes. Mary loaded a tray with nuts, figs, grapes, and pomegranates. Covering them with a clean cloth, she then placed them on a low table.

After the preparation for the evening meal, Mary worked at the loom – weaving a garment. Martha scrubbed the clothes. Their brother Lazarus had gone out at daybreak to tend the fields. Martha had fed Lazarus curds, honey, bread, and goat's milk to sustain him for the day. Lazarus, as usual, had filled a pouch with figs and dates to munch on between breakfast and supper.

Even before the bread making, Martha had milked their three goats and watched the sunrise fill the sky with a glorious array of colors. Mary had strained the milk and placed it in an underground storage area where it would stay cool, along with the vegetables and grain. The two sisters went about their work with a song in their hearts. They knew that Jesus had risen from the dead and someday would return for His elect.

It was nearing the evening meal, when Joshua and Beriah rode up to the little stone house of Lazarus and his sisters. Lazarus had just finished washing up. Seeing the weary travelers, he bade them to come in and rest. Joshua introduced himself and Beriah. He told the brother and sisters, that he and Beriah were followers of Jesus and that they were tracing the footsteps of the Messiah.

Around the evening meal, Joshua and Beriah told about witnessing the crucifixion of Jesus. Mary and Martha sat with tears streaming down their cheeks as they heard the gruesome details of the death of their beloved friend. Over the next few hours, Lazarus quizzed his visitors. Joshua answered questions to the best of his recollection. He also told what he had heard and believed about Jesus' resurrection. "We had the privilege of seeing Jesus before He ascended into Heaven," said Lazarus.

"I understand that you too, were raised from the dead," stated Joshua. Lazarus nodded his head.

"Do you remember anything at all about being in the tomb?" asked Beriah.

Lazarus shook his head no. "The last thing I remember was running a high fever and being very sick. The next thing I knew, I was hearing my name called. It was a compelling, authoritative voice that said, 'Lazarus! Come forth!' I remember I sat up but everything was dark. My movement was hampered by something that was binding my body and legs. Yet, I knew I had to obey. I moved toward the direction of the voice, in a slow, hobbled walk. I didn't know I had been dead or was even in my tomb. That is until I heard Jesus say, 'Loose him.' And then I saw the grave cloth. My sisters and I have always believed that Jesus was the Son of God and our Messiah. After a miracle like mine, how could anyone doubt it?" finished Lazarus.

"Did Jesus know you were sick?" asked Beriah.

Mary spoke up, "We sent word to Jesus right away. He was teaching beyond the River Jordan at the time. We waited and waited but He didn't come."

"That's strange, I wonder why, since you were among His best friends," said Joshua.

"I asked Jesus about that after I was raised from the dead," said Lazarus. "Jesus said it was for the furtherance and accomplishment of the glory of God."

Martha suggested the men retire to the roof and talk, since it would be much cooler up there. The three men climbed the outside stairs to the roof, where a small breeze was blowing, helping poor Beriah, as he inched his way up. Mary followed shortly with a tray of nuts and fruit. She then hurried back to help Martha so they could wash the pottery and pans. By working together, they quickly finished up and climbed to the roof. Both women wanted to hear the men talk about Jesus.

The men and women talked far into the night. Later, Joshua told how he and Beriah had met. He talked about Adonis and Heber. "In other words," Joshua said, "Beriah rescued us and gave all of us a place to eat and sleep in safety." As the evening progressed, Joshua explained about Beriah's sandals and staff and the miracles that were performed.

Mary's eyes sparkled as she touched the sandal and staff. "It's like Jesus said, 'I am the Good Shepherd.'"

Martha also spoke, "Before Jesus left, He said, 'Feed My sheep,' by feeding, He was referring to spiritual nourishment. I think Jesus would be pleased you're leaning on His staff Beriah. Where will you go next, on your journey, to trace the footsteps of Jesus?" asked Lazarus.

"We plan on going to Jericho tomorrow," said Joshua. "We only travel in the morning and rest in the heat of the day."

"Won't you tarry longer? You're more than welcome," said Martha.

"Yes, must you go so soon?" asked Mary.

"Maybe on our way back," said Beriah. "Joshua has a schedule mapped out which will take us up the Jordan River, then to the east of the Sea of Galilee. Then around the north end to Capernaum. From there, along the west coast of the sea and over to Nazareth, and eventually back southwards toward Emmaus, Bethany, and home to Jerusalem."

Lazarus laughed, "That's quite an ambitious journey. If you stay but a few days in each place, it will take you almost two and a half months. Then another two and a half if you visit a short time in each place. And that doesn't account for any trouble you might encounter."

"What kind of trouble?" asked Beriah.

"Oh, illness, or something could happen to your donkey, accidents, or bandits. Many things happen when traveling. It's always safer traveling in groups. However, I'll pray for your safety and a fulfilling journey." Lazarus went on, "Mary will fetch us mats and throws to sleep on. We men will sleep tonight under the stars, where it's cool. Martha will pack you enough food for a two-day journey. However, you should make Jericho in one day. I'll wake you at daybreak. Goodnight my brothers in Christ."

Before the sun rose, Joshua and Beriah were on the Jordan road heading in the direction of the village of Jericho. As the men traveled, they discussed their newly found friends. Jasper walked with care, and Samson chased everything that crossed his path, or flushed out along the roadside. At one point, Samson became fascinated in trying to catch grasshoppers. Each time he pounced, he came up empty. The grasshoppers seemed to stay one jump ahead. Jasper's spirit seemed to be down and he hung his head low. Smiling, Beriah took out his harp and began to sing softly. Immediately, the little donkey's head came up. He walked more sprightly. His long ears flopped up and down as his tail swished. The little donkey let out a long bray, and if possible, his body seemed to sway with the rhythm of the music. Joshua and Beriah broke out in hearty and happy laughter.

Between the sixth and the ninth hour, when the sun was at its zenith, the little party rested beneath the shade of a sprawling tree. Samson, tired from his grasshopper chase, lay down and was soon asleep. Joshua staked out Jasper. The donkey was quite content to munch on some grass. Joshua leaned against the tree and Beriah lay down on his rug. The rest was a welcome relief. Each man dozed. Waking occasionally to swat at flies. Samson had placed his paw over his nose to prevent bites from the pests. Even Jasper seemed to be dozing in the shade of a smaller tree. His body remained still except for the swish of his tail when a fly became annoying.

The little group rested peacefully until Jasper began a series of terrified brays. Instantly Joshua and Beriah were on their feet, but not before Samson made a mad dash in the little donkey's direction. Using his staff, Beriah wasn't far behind. What happened next took both by surprise. A big wolf was circling Jasper and snapping at his shanks. Jasper, though, put up a good fight. He was kicking up both hind feet. The big, mangy animal looked half starved. "Well," said Beriah, "you may be hungry, but Jasper won't be your supper." Samson, who was barking and snarling, began to circle the wolf whose mouth was now dripping with saliva.

Joshua, who had also picked up a stick, cautioned Beriah. "Don't go any closer Beriah. The wolf has rabies."

To Joshua's anguish, Beriah was not deterred. "Wolf, lie down, in the name of Jesus," he commanded in a loud forceful voice. For a moment the wild crazed animal looked at Beriah, then stood still trembling. For a few more moments, he remained weaving. Then slowly he sank to the ground and continued to shudder. Joshua and Samson stood still. Jasper's eyes, which had been rolled back in fear, began to focus. The donkey stood trembling, but was otherwise, unharmed. Had not Joshua been watching; he would have had a hard time believing what took place next. Beriah, as though in a trance, began to talk softly to the rabid wolf. "Poor boy, you're pretty sick aren't you? Lie still and let me help you." Beriah rubbed his hands up and down the staff, and then laying the staff on the ground, Beriah slowly approached the sick, frightened animal. Laying his hand on the shaggy, gray head, he commanded in a loud voice, "Be healed, in the name of Jesus!" The wolf reacted as though he had been struck by lightening and fell over as dead. The stunned Joshua watched in amazement, not moving, and holding his breath. Beriah was oblivious to everything around him, except the sick wolf. Dropping to his knees, he ran his hands over the head and body of the wolf. Crooning to the animal, as he ministered to it's needs. Before Joshua's eyes, the shaggy, gray hair changed to a thick, lustrous gray coat. The wolf's body also grew plump. "Come boy, awake," commanded Beriah.

Slowly the wolf's eyes were opened. The look of a wild animal, in for the kill, disappeared and was replaced with an adoring look of love. Slowly, the wolf sat up and began to lick Beriah's hands and face. Laughing softly, Beriah gathered the big dog creature in a bear hug. "Now go on home," he said as he ruffed up the now healthy fur. Strangely, the wolf was reluctant to go. First, he made friends with Samson, and then Jasper, the donkey. When he turned to Joshua, it was almost more than Joshua could bear. Beriah laughed, "He's quite tame and healed now Joshua. Go on, pet the fellow, after all, he's just trying to make amends."

Hesitantly, Joshua stroked the big head and was rewarded by a wet kiss. Turning to Beriah, he said, "I think I've lost a year's growth over this healing." The two young men watched Samson and the wolf get acquainted.

"You know," mused Beriah, "Those two look like they came out of the same litter." Instead of the wolf going away, he lay down beside Samson.

Joshua shook his head. "Will wonders never cease," he laughed. "Beriah, I believe you've acquired another friend. What are you going to call him?"

Beriah looked over at the healthy wolf. Smiling, Beriah said, "I think I'll call him Gray Boy." Joshua looked at Beriah, but kept his thoughts to himself.

An hour later, the little group was once again on their way to Jericho. Samson continued his chase. Gray Boy walked beside Jasper and Beriah. Joshua, carrying the staff, walked a little way to the right. He was in deep thought. His mind went over and over the wonder of Gray Boy's healing. Silently he prayed, "Lord Jesus, thank you for my friend Beriah. Lord, as you know, he bears his affliction without complaint. Father, next to his faith, mine is so weak. But I'm asking you to heal this compassionate young man. I ask it in thy name. Amen."

Talking was down to a minimum for a while. Then Beriah asked, "Joshua, do you know much about Jericho?"

"I know some of the history that has been handed down from father to son over the centuries," answered Joshua.

"Old Jobah told me many stories but I do not recall one about Jericho," said Beriah.

"There have been three Jericho's," said Joshua. "The first and second were destroyed. The one we are going to is not much larger than a village. But the greatest story is about Joshua of old. He was the man chosen to lead God's people, the Israelites after Moses died. You see Beriah, although Moses led his people out of the bondage of Egypt, he did not get to go into the Promised Land. It was Joshua who did that. God told Joshua to take his men and destroy the wicked city of Jericho. If my memory serves me right," said Joshua, "Jericho means 'fragrant place.' At one time it had palm trees everywhere. It stands back on the edge of the plain, where the brook Kelt and the road from Jerusalem come together. The mountain has tall cliff formations and many caves. In the low lands are gardens and orchards. This would be the first Jericho. Now taking Jericho seemed to be an insurmountable task. First of all, it was completely surrounded by thick, tall double walls. Secondly, it was heavily guarded and fortified from within. Joshua had the faith, that if God said take the city, he would have help from God. Strangely, before Joshua even started to take Jericho, a man stood before him with a sword drawn. Joshua challenged the stranger. He said, 'who are you? Are you for us or against us?' To Joshua's surprise, the strange man with the sword said, 'I am the commander of the Army of God.' And then he revealed God's message. 'Joshua, you are to make this formation for battle. Place your mighty men of valor in front. Next in line, place seven priests with trumpets of ram's horns. Then have other priests carrying the Ark of the Lord. Lastly, bring on your rear guard.'"

"Gee, how did they fight; lined up like that?" asked Beriah.

Joshua smiled and said, "That's the beauty of God's plan. God said that Joshua and his men were to march completely around the city once every day for six days. Not a man was to shout or make a noise with his voice. The priests with the ram's horns are to sound a loud blast as they marched along. On the seventh day, they were to march around the city seven times. And the priests are to blow the trumpets, of the ram's horns, and all Joshua's people are to give a loud shout. Joshua carried out the orders of God. When they finished marching around Jericho the seventh time, the trumpets blew, the people gave a loud shout, and all the walls of Jericho came crashing down flat! Joshua and his men destroyed the people and the city. God commanded the city of Jericho never to be re-built."

"Wow!" was all the wide-eyed excited Beriah could say. Thinking the story over he finally said, "When did this happen Joshua?"

Laughing, Joshua said, "About 570 years ago."

They rode along quietly for some time while Beriah mulled over the story. At last he said, "If it was destroyed and God said don't rebuild it, then when was Jericho re-built?"

"It was rebuilt about five hundred years ago. It's told that Jericho was the scene of defeat of Jedekiah, the last King of Judea," said Joshua.

"Who defeated King Jedekiah?" asked Beriah.

"The story says that it was the Chaldeans under King Nebuchadnezzar II. The last King to use Jericho was King Herod the Great. He made his capital there in the winter. He built palaces, an amphitheatre, and other impressive buildings. King Herod the Great had lots of enemies, so he strengthened the fortification of the city. As you recall, King Herod the Great was in power when Jesus was born. And he had all the first-born sons under two years of age killed in Bethlehem. The King himself died a horrible death in Jericho. Someday I'll tell you about it. After his death, the slaves revolted and burned the second city called Jericho. That was only thirty years or so ago. Now a new village has sprung up on yet another site and that is where we're going Beriah. This village is where Jesus healed two blind men and talked to Zacchaeus, the tax collector. This happened on Jesus' last journey through Jericho, before He was crucified," said Joshua.

Chapter Nine

It was nearing the evening meal, of the second day, when Joshua, Beriah, and the animals arrived at the village of Jericho. Joshua located a stall that was still open. He bought bananas, oranges, figs, cheese, and bread. Joshua asked the fruit merchant, "Could you direct us to the well?"

Pointing toward the center of the village, the man said, "It's down that street. Just a short way beyond is a small inn; they will also put up yours animals. Their fee is fair and the food is good. Have you traveled far?"

Joshua smiled, "We're from Jerusalem, but we stopped overnight in Bethany. We spent an enjoyable evening with Jesus' friends – Lazarus and his sisters. I'm sure you've heard how Jesus, a month before He was crucified, raised Lazarus from the dead?" The merchant nodded that he had heard about it. Joshua went on, "Beriah and I witnessed the cruel crucifixion of our Lord Jesus, the Messiah." To Joshua's surprise, the man began to cry. "Are you alright, sir?" asked Joshua.

The weeping man wiped his eyes. "I don't know why they killed a Godly man," he said.

"Did you know Him well?" Beriah asked.

The man nodded his head no. "Only for a moment in time, but that was enough to convince me Jesus was extraordinary. You know, as though He wasn't of this world."

"What do you base your belief on?" asked Joshua.

In a voice above a whisper, the man said, "My name is Bartimaeus. I was once known as 'Blind Bartimaeus,' I am the son of

Timaeus. I was blind all my life, or at least up until the day Jesus gave me my sight."

"How were you healed? Asked Beriah with interest.

"I was sitting with another blind man in our usual place beside the road. I heard a crowd of people shouting, "It's Jesus!" Jesus is passing by! I couldn't see Him and had no way of getting through the crowd. I remember I panicked. This was my only chance of being healed and Jesus didn't even know I was there. So I stood and shouted as loud as I could, 'Jesus, Son of David, have mercy on me!' The crowd tried to make me be quiet, but I shouted more. They had no idea what it was like being blind."

There was a pause in the narrative of Bartimaeus' story. "Don't stop now," begged Beriah. "What happened next?"

"Well, Jesus heard my cries and ordered me to be brought to Him. Someone took me by the arm and parted the crowd. Jesus said in a compassionate voice, 'What do you want me to do for you?' My knees were so weak. They shook like palsy. For a moment I couldn't speak. Then, swallowing my fear, I humbly said, 'Lord, I want to see.'" Jesus said, "Receive your sight. Your faith has healed you."

"What happened next?" Whispered Beriah.

A wet-faced Bartimaeus said, "I took Jesus' outstretched hand and kissed it. 'Thank you Lord,' I said. Jesus laughed at my joy. Then for the first time in my life I saw the beauty God had made. I wanted to run, shout, and sing at the same time. I ran from object to object asking what it was. You see, I had only seen by the touch of my fingers. I knew things by smell and hearing. And nothing in the world of the person who is blind looks like it does with sight. In fact, I'm still learning," laughed Bartimaeus. Joshua and Beriah were thrilled for Bartimaeus' healing. Bartimaeus continued, "After I was healed, I followed Jesus and glorified and gave praises to God."

At last Joshua asked, "What happened to your blind friend? Was he healed also?"

"Oh yes," said Bartimaeus, "my friend also received his sight. For the first time in my life, I saw how a blind man looks. And how unsure he is around unfamiliar surroundings. My friend groped and stumbled through the crowd with arms outstretched to ward off danger. His eyes were glazed over with a milky-white skim. He kept calling, 'Jesus, Jesus where are you?' Jesus stopped talking to some other people, who were under a large tree. He walked toward my friend. Softly, He said, 'I'm here young man.' My friend fell to his knees and clutched Jesus' robe and said, 'Lord, would you heal me too?' Jesus gently lifted my friend to his feet and said, 'I will.' And Jesus touched his eyes. You could tell at that moment that my friend's sight had been restored. It was as though his mind could not take in all the wonders. My friend looked upon the smiling face of Jesus and said, 'Thank you Lord! Thank you,' he kept repeating again and again. 'Follow me,' said Jesus to the crowd, and you shall see the glory of Heaven."

"What happened after that?" probed Beriah.

Bartimaeus continued, "Jesus passed through Jericho and the crowd followed Him. A man by the name of Zacchaeus, who was a chief tax collector, had gotten quite rich. He was a very short man I recall, and wanted a closer look at Jesus. Now understand, as it is with your people, people of Jericho hate tax collectors. No one would let Zacchaeus through the crowd to see Jesus. Forgetting his pride, Zacchaeus ran and climbed up a Sycamore tree – rich clothes and all!" Bartimaeus said laughing.

"Could he see Jesus then?" asked the excited Beriah.

"He sure could," smiled Bartimaeus. "It was strange though, Jesus knew who Zacchaeus was even though they had never met before."

"How do you know that for a fact?" asked Joshua.

"Because Jesus said 'Zacchaeus make haste and come down, for today I must stay at your house.' Zacchaeus looked surprise, to say the least, because most people wouldn't mix with a tax collector. Zacchaeus' face was flooded with joy. He scrambled down the Sycamore tree, but in his haste, he snagged his rich cloak. Then the crowd began to grumble because Jesus had chosen Zacchaeus' house to eat and rest instead of theirs'. So they began to say, 'Look. He's gone to be a guest with a sinner," said Bartimaeus.

"They seemed to have forgotten that we were all sinners," finished Beriah. "Was anything else said that you can recall?" asked Beriah.

Bartimaeus paused a few seconds then said, "I heard Zacchaeus say, 'Look Lord, I give half of my goods to the poor, and if I have taken anything from anyone falsely I will restore it four-fold."

"What was Jesus' reaction to Zacchaeus pledge to make restitution on the taxes?" asked Joshua.

Bartimaeus replied, "Jesus said to him, 'Today, salvation has come to this house.' He went on to say that Zacchaeus was a son of Abraham, so he was a Jew, not Roman. Jesus then said something that gives all men hope. He said, 'The Son of Man has come to seek and save that which was lost,'" Beriah nodded, "And whether we're in a rich man's home, a hut, a cavern, or a sycamore tree, Jesus can find us." A short time later, Joshua rented a room for them at the inn. He fed, watered, and secured the animals for the night. After a wash-up and a good meal, Joshua and Beriah sat out in the courtyard enjoying the cooling breeze. They reminisced about the day's events and the wonderful story that Bartimaeus had told them.

The news that Joshua and Beriah were witnesses to the crucifixion of Jesus soon spread throughout the village of Jericho. The courtyard began to fill with people wanting to hear a first-hand account of Jesus' brutal murder.

Joshua and Beriah told about Jesus' resurrection, the empty tomb, and the trouble in Jerusalem. After answering questions, they told about the mighty, rushing wind of the Holy Spirit and how Jesus' disciples were filled with the Holy Ghost and began to speak in other tongues. They told about Peter, who had denied Jesus during the trial, but now speaking boldly about Jesus being the Son of God. "Every person in the crowd heard Peter's message," said Joshua. "They believed and were baptized in one day."

"Saved," said a man in the courtyard. "How can a man be saved?"

Beriah answered the man, "Jesus told Nicodemus, the Pharisee who visited Jesus in the night, that no one can see the kingdom of God unless he is born again."

"That doesn't make sense," said the man. "Why it's impossible! Every man knows you can't go back to the womb again!" Turning to the people the man continued to speak, "Did you ever hear such nonsense?"

For a few moments there was murmuring between the people. At last, on old man near the front of the group said, "Why don't we listen to how Jesus answered the Pharisee?"

"That's a good idea," spoke up another man.

Beriah waited until the buzzing voices stopped. "According to Nicodemus, Jesus said, 'I tell you the truth, no man can enter the Kingdom of God unless he is born again of the water and the Spirit. Flesh gives birth to flesh, but the Spirit gives birth to spirit.' You see," said Beriah, "we are all born of the flesh. However, when we believe that the Lord Jesus is the Christ, and the faith that He is able to save us, then we repent of our sins and ask Jesus to forgive us. By Jesus' shed blood on the cross, we are washed clean of all unrighteousness and receive His Spirit to dwell in us. That is being born again. It is a spiritual re-birth, not a fleshly new birth."

"Why must we be baptized?" asked a woman.

Joshua spoke up, "Water cannot cleanse us but it is a public declaration that we are born again believers of Jesus Christ. It is also the Lord's commandment. From this point on in our lives, we have declared to the world that we will live our lives to God's teachings."

Another man spoke up, "What did Nicodemus do after Jesus told him how to be saved?"

Joshua answered, "He believed and gave his heart to Jesus. In fact, he was one of the two men who came to the hill of Golgotha to take down the crucified Christ. Joseph of Arimethea, a rich merchant, who was a follower of Jesus, was the other man. Joseph of Arimethea laid Jesus in his own new tomb and Nicodemus brought spices and aloes to anoint Jesus' body for burial."

"How do we really know He was resurrected from the dead?" shouted a man toward the outskirts of the courtyard,

"Because he was seen by over five hundred people. Those included His own disciples as well as Lazarus and his two sisters. Of course, Lazarus had no problem believing Jesus had come out of the tomb since he had been raised from the dead, only a month before. Lazarus' resurrection also had many witnesses. This was the final miracle performed by Jesus which caused the Priests and the Saducees to plot His death," answered Joshua.

"Why did Jesus have to die?" asked another woman.

Joshua looked at the woman with a compassionate understanding. "Jesus died in our place. He defeated death, hell and even the grave so that we could have everlasting life. It's free, just believe in Him." The talk around the group continued on. It was midnight before Joshua and Beriah went to bed.

Early the next morning, Joshua purchased a ball of heavy string and some fishhooks. A short time after sunrise, they said goodbye to the innkeepers and Bartimaeus. With Jasper, the little donkey, Samson, and Gray Boy, they began their journey in the direction of the Jordan River. They hoped to reach Bethany beyond Jordan by nightfall. "Why are we going there?" asked Beriah

"Because I believe that's the area of the Jordan River where John the Baptist was baptizing the new converts. In fact, it may be the area where Jesus was baptized."

The little entourage made good time in their travels. In the afternoon, they would rest and nap, hopefully under a large tree, if one could be found. Evening time found the little group on the banks of the Jordan River. It was with mutual consensus that the small party would camp out for the night. It was a welcome relief to be able to bath and wash their clothes. The animals seemed to enjoy drinking and splashing in the cool water before chasing rabbits. While the clothes were drying, Joshua cut two long poles and soon converted them into fishing poles. Beriah had never fished before and found the sport to be rewarding when he pulled in an eighteen-inch fish. Meanwhile, Joshua caught three smaller ones. Cleaning the fish wasn't nearly as enjoyable. However, sitting around the campfire, roasting the fish on skewers set all their saliva glands into motion. It was hard to wait for the fish to cool as they plucked off the white, flaky meat. The meal was rounded off with bread, cheese and oranges.

That night sleeping out under the stars was a wonder itself. Beriah had spent most of his life sleeping in an underground cavern. And here he was with the canopy of God overhead, instead of limestone. The stars seemed as plentiful as the sand of the seashore. Now why, he wondered, had he made that analogy? Beriah looked up at the stars and wondered if his friend Adonis was also looking at the sky while crossing the Mediterranean. With this thought, the miles that separated them didn't seem so far.

Morning came all too soon for the resting party. The stars began to disappear one by one. The half-moon was already fading and a light mist was moving slowly over the tall grass and the banks of the Jordan River. The air was still cool as Joshua built a small fire and heated water for tea. Joshua had the foresight to pack two cups and a small pan in the donkey's saddlebag.

A drowsy Beriah washed up at the edge of the water. At the point of their crossing, the water was low. Beriah removed his sandals and waded out into the Jordan River. He looked up and down the river. He then sat down on a large boulder in the middle of the river. He wondered if this was one of the boulders carried there by Joshua's men of valor, to mark the place where God rolled back the Jordan River so they could destroy Jericho. He could almost visualize the water rolling back as forty thousand men crossed on dry land. A short distance from the Jordan, lay the village known as 'Bethany beyond Jordan.' The little village was just beginning to stir. Women with clay water pots on their shoulders or heads were on their way to the well. Here and there, a goat was being milked. Barley and wheat was being ground for bread. Sleepy, tousled-headed children were looking around open doors or their mother's skirt-tails. Old women were weaving or churning, and old men were sitting under a tree. The market place was just opening for the day and merchants were putting out their wares.

Joshua, walking with the animals and Beriah riding Jasper, stopped to buy bread, cheese, and fruit for their journey to the Sea of Galilee. The morning sun began to rise higher in the pale blue sky and the coolness of the morning air began to dissipate. Joshua knew it would be just a matter of minutes before the village began to hum with activity.

Joshua filled the saddlebags with bread and fruit, and Beriah's leather shoulder pouch with dried beef and cheese. The saddlebags were secured on the donkey and Joshua carried the pouch. Beriah picked out a sweet smelling melon. Then he and Joshua made for the tree where the old men of the village sat. Joshua took a rope and tied the donkey. Beriah commanded Samson and Gray Boy to lie down. Greetings were exchanged between the newcomers and the old men. Joshua cut the melon, gave Beriah half, and let the old men have time to look them over. While chewing on the sweet melon, Joshua too, was sizing up the men. "Come far?" asked one old man. Joshua didn't speak but nodded that they had. There was a few moments pause before the spokesman of the group continued, "I guess traveling has been rough, with all this heat."

"Yes sir, rough," agreed Joshua.

"Hmm," murmured the old man to one of his cronies. "He's a silent one, he is."

The crony watched Joshua licking the juice off his fingers. Taking a more direct approach, the man asked, "Come as far as Jerusalem?" Again, Joshua simply nodded that they had. Beriah, whose head had been turning back and forth between the men and Joshua, was bewildered. What's happened to Joshua? He's not talking about Jesus. This puzzled Beriah. Then Beriah began to see through Joshua's strategy. The bored, cynical old men spent their days reliving their by gone glory. Joshua was laying the groundwork on getting their minds and eyes on the future. And that future was the Risen Savior, Jesus Christ, the Messiah.

Joshua had been watching Beriah's face. He knew the moment when Beriah understood. Smiling at Beriah, Joshua said to the men who were now eager to listen, "We came from Jerusalem, the Holy City. Except it's not so holy now after the vile murder of an innocent man of God."

The men began to inch forward in anticipation. "What man?" demanded a man near the tree. "Talk louder boy. I don't hear too good."

Raising his voice, Joshua said, "Why Jesus, sir. You've surely heard of Jesus, the one who was foretold by John the Baptist. You do remember John the Baptist don't you? He had his head cut off by King Herod."

Another man in the group answered, "Of course we know about John the Baptist. He baptized hundreds down on the Jordan, where you probably crossed over. John came preaching 'repent and be baptized.' Take me now; I reckon I was the meanest man around until I listened to John. I repented and waded up to my waist and was baptized. I've never regretted it. I was mighty glad to make peace with God."

Joshua smiled, "Beriah and I have also been baptized. Not by John, but by Peter, one of the Lord's disciples. Have you men heard of the horrible crucifixion of Jesus and His resurrection from the dead? Or His ascending into Heaven?"

"A little, not much," said the old man who had been the first to speak. Beriah was amazed at how Joshua had orchestrated the men into wanting to listen. However, Beriah was taken off guard when Joshua said, "My friend Beriah followed Jesus and the Roman soldiers to the Hill of Golgotha and witnessed the cruel crucifixion of the Son of God. That was a sad day that will be remembered throughout all eternity." Waving his arms toward Beriah, Joshua said, "Go on Beriah, tell the men what you saw." Beriah, who had been watching and listening to Joshua maneuver the conversation and was unprepared by Joshua's statement and the shifting of eyes from Joshua to himself.

The old man near the tree said in a loud voice, "Go on son, and tell us what you saw. Now don't forget to speak up."

Beriah looked at the man with long, white, flowing hair and beard. He said to the other men, "Could some of you bring the gentlemen up to the front so he can hear? I assure you, my story about the death and resurrection of our Lord and Savior, Jesus Christ, is worth hearing. After my story, Joshua can tell you about the mighty rushing wind that filled the heavens and how the Holy Ghost and fire fell on Jesus' disciples and a crowd of 3,000 people who were filled with the Holy Spirit."

Chapter Ten

Looking at the sleeping Beriah, and saying goodbye to Joshua, was one of the hardest things Adonis had ever done. He felt he would forever carry the picture of Beriah and Samson, curled up together asleep by the flickering firelight. With eyes filled with tears and a heavy heart, he and Heber joined Abdul's camel caravan. As the dawn was breaking, they had left Jerusalem and were traveling toward the sea.

The red and orange rays of the rising sun filled the sky as birds began to twitter and small animals ventured out of burrows and dens. The plodding camels were heavily loaded. Their destination was the Port of Sycaminum. From there, the supplies and treasures would be shipped to ports in Rodes, Cyprus, Islands in the Agaen Sea, and Greece. If they made it in time, then the Athene would buy most of Abdul's cargo.

The trip was long and arduous. The caravan moved at about twenty miles per day. By evening, the men and their beasts were ready to eat and rest. There was not much lingering around the campfire. The camels were carrying about a thousand pounds each. Though the camels had the stamina to travel forty miles a day, in the hot, sweltering sun, the men did not. Keeping up with thirty-six long legged camels was a tiring job. Abdul had four saddled camels along for the sick or weary. The men, when necessary, could ride and rest for a couple of miles, while they gained new strength.

In the afternoon of the fifth day the Port of Sycaminum came into view. The camel drivers had their hands full controlling the camels. When the camels smelled the water, they broke into a run. The men smiled. They were in sympathy for the big brutes. They too wanted to run toward the beautiful, blue Mediterranean Sea.

It wasn't the sea that Adonis wanted to run to, but rather, his father's ship. The merchant galley ship, with its bowed-out blue and white sides and goddess Athene as it's maidenhead, and folded white sails. It rode high and proud in the lapping water. Adonis was nervous as he and Heber climbed the gangplank. Once on deck, Adonis came face to face with a stern-faced Captain Strabo. "So the runaway son returns!" he spat angrily. "You left me to have my head chewed out by your father! Adonis, I was the one that had to face your mother and father. Yes, it was I who had to tell them their precious son spurred their love and ran away. It was I who watched your mother weep in anguish and saw your father grow old before my eyes. If it were left up to me, you would walk back to Greece! You had it all Adonis. You were spoiled, arrogant, and a fool. Yes, a fool! You left this ship looking like a prince and now you return, smelling like the dung of camels."

All the time Captain Strabo shook with anger, Adonis stared at his feet. When the Captain was finished, Adonis, with tears of repentance in his eyes, looked up and said, "You're right Captain Strabo. It would serve me right if you made me walk the long way home. And if I must do so, I will. You see, I have a message for my father and mother, that I'll walk through hell to tell them."

"So important that you would travel through the dangerous country of Turkey to tell them Adonis?" asked Captain Strabo.

Adonis looked into the aging face of the Captain. Shaking his head yes, Adonis said, "Yes sir. Important enough to walk or crawl through Turkey,"

The shrewd Captain studied Adonis' face. Gone was the young man's arrogance. Gone was the laughing young fool. In it's place, was a serene, knowledgeable countenance. After a moment's hesitation, the Captain extended his hand, "Welcome home Adonis." Their hands clasped for a few heartfelt moments.

"Thank you sir." Motioning to Heber, Adonis made the introductions.

Turning to the first-mate, Captain Strabo directed, "Show them to my cabin Themos."

"Yes sir," answered the first-mate.

"Just a minute Sir," Adonis interrupted. I'd rather you place us with the work crew. After all, we will be working." The surprised Captain looked Adonis up and down. Gone was the lazy, spoiled look of a rich man's son. In his place, stood a young man with a stalwart demeanor and calluses on his hands.

Smiling his approval, Captain Strabo said, "Very well, Themos, find these crewmen some sailor's clothes and give them a bunk. Tomorrow, assign them a job. However, for tonight, they're having supper in my cabin. Adonis and I need to have a talk."

Over the evening meal, Adonis told the Captain all the things that had happened to him; from the time he jumped his father's ship, to arriving in Jerusalem. Adonis told of the bad times, when he slept in alleys and stole to eat. He then told about the crucifixion of Jesus, and how he had come to be living with Beriah. As the evening progressed, Adonis told about becoming a believer and follower of Jesus, the Son of God. "That's all well and good that you believe in the new God. I guess another god won't hurt. However, we already have dozens of gods; so why do you need another one?" asked the cynical Captain. It was well after midnight when Adonis finished telling the attributes of Jesus and Father God – The Great Jehovah.

The Captain wasn't buying the story of a risen Jesus. Nor that He had risen up into the clouds. In disgust, Captain Strabo declared Adonis had been caught up in some sort of hallucination. At last the Captain said, "You two best turn in, we'll be sailing with the morning tide."

On the way across the deck, Heber said, "I don't think you'll ever convince the Captain that all his gods are false."

Adonis smiled, "You know the old saying 'Rome wasn't built in a day.' However, we've given Captain Strabo something to think about. Heber, there's one thing about the life of a seaman you should know;

and that is, he's a mighty superstitious person. They go by signs and omens. If the omens are bad, they won't sail. Are you sleepy, Heber?" asked Adonis.

"No, not in particular. I've never been on a boat, much less a ship, and I'm a bit uneasy," said Heber.

"Oh well, that's only natural," laughed Adonis. "Now take me, I've been sailing since I was a small child. Yet at times I get a bit queasy. And especially if we run into a tropical storm."

"We'll be using the sails?" asked Heber.

"When we have the wind in the right direction. Otherwise, we row," answered Adonis.

"Row? You surely don't think you can row across the Mediterranean Sea?" stated Heber. "Why this boat is too big!"

Adonis broke out laughing. "Let me take you on a tour Heber. First of all, this is a one hundred twenty-eight fool long Merchant Galley Ship. Rome began putting these sails on their warships. So father hired a Roman shipping company to add two more masts to this ship. When we have the breeze and the three sails unfurled; along with the wind we sail fairly well, otherwise we row. This ship has three banks of oar ports and three decks. On the lower bank of the ship there are over fifty-four oarsmen. On the second bank and second deck, there are fifty-four additional oar ports and oarsmen. And on the top back, there are around sixty-two oarsmen. That my friend makes over one hundred and seventy oarsmen. They row in short shifts; they are on four and off four hours. The crew is staggered. That way, there's always a rowing crew. By relieving the men at different intervals every oarsman doesn't get tired at the same time. Of course, in the event of a storm, all hands will man the oars. Besides the oarsmen, we have a crew of fifty men. They cook, clean, man the sails, and take care of the cargo. The first mate, along with the Captain, plots the course and steers."

How does the Captain find his way across all that water?" asked Heber.

"He plots his course by the heavens, time, speed, and recognizing landmarks, when he sees them. I assure you Heber, Captain Strabo is a very competent navigator," said Adonis. For the next hour, the two men wandered from deck to deck and decided to sleep out under the stars. Breakfast was served before dawn to the sailors and the oarsmen going on duty. Next, breakfast was serviced to the oarsmen who were coming off their shift. Sure enough, the Athena left the Port of Sycaminum with the outgoing tide.

Adonis and Heber stood on deck and watched the receding wharf and building become smaller. As the oarsmen rowed like a might team, the rocks and trees on Mount Camel were just spots and eventually the mountains became just a speck. Adonis' heart ached. He knew he was leaving behind a man he loved as a brother and another as a dear friend. Looking back across the water, He made a vow that if it was God's will, he would return someday.

Heber was assigned the job of assistance to the cook, while Adonis' first job was to swab the deck. Many of the older sailors had known Adonis before he jumped ship. They were now enjoying watching him work up a sweat as he mopped the deck. Adonis took their catcalls with a good-natured spirit. Later, over the noontime meal, he told a few of the old-timers about the death and resurrection of Jesus and what it means to mankind. During the evening meal, he sat with a gang of oarsmen who had just been relieved of duty. Again, Adonis relayed the story of Jesus to the men.

By mid-morning of the third day, three burly sailors cornered Adonis, "Hey, rich boy, come and tell us your spook story."

Adonis could tell the three bullies were looking for trouble. Smiling, he said, "I could use a break." And he sat down on a coil of rope.

"Swabbing decks sure isn't the kind of work you're use to, is it Prince?" mocked the sailor.

Laughing, Adonis said, "I'll say not, but it's a sight easier than my job in Jerusalem.

"Huh?" snarled the leader of the trio. "You poking fun at me boy?"

"No, I'm really laughing at me. You see, I ran away from home as you've probably heard," explained Adonis. "Well, let me tell you something. My big, fabulous job was mucking out camel stalls and unloading ten-foot long camels carrying a thousand pounds each. My boss, Abdul owns a caravan of thirty-six camels. Now you fellows remember how hard it was to unload and re-load those contrary beasts, at the land port? Now I could tell you a story or two. Why the first day I worked with Abdullah, he assigned me to the biggest, contraries camel I've ever had the misfortune to meet. You won't believe this, but that stubborn animal deliberately sat down on my foot. That big brute weighed as much as one of those elephants from Borneo. Not to mention he was carrying a thousand pounds." By now the three antagonists were sitting near Adonis and literally eating up his story. Adonis paused in the narrative.

"How'd you get the beast off?" asked the shortest of the trio.

"Get him off, I couldn't. He wouldn't budge. In fact, he began to bellow that catowalling sound that only a camel can make. And the next thing you know, all thirty-six camels were doing the same. Abdul finally rescued me. I bent over to check my foot to see if it was broken and the beast turned around and bit me in the seat of the pants. Then he had the nerve to raise his head and look down on me. He even wrinkled back his lips like a stubborn mule and laughed." By now the three men were chuckling. "Then, if that wasn't bad enough, the ugly animal spit in my face. Friends, swabbing decks is easy compared to working with camels. Sorry fellows, I rather got carried away. Now what was it you wanted to know? Oh yes, I remember," Adonis lowered his voice, looked first to the right and then to the left and whispered, "You wanted to hear about my ghost story. Well, I don't have time right now; I still have the middle deck to swab. But if you're off duty after our evening meal, I'll tell you about a man that cleansed the lepers, made blind eyes see, raised people from the dead, walked on water, and could even walk through walls." Extending his hand, Adonis said, "My name's Adonis, I didn't get yours."

The spokesman said, "Name's Kouras, and here's Zorba, and over there's Kosmas. We're oarsmen but we're off from supper 'til midnight."

"Great," said Adonis. "Shall we meet near the Aft rail where it's cool? Hopefully, my friend Heber will be free by then. He's also from Jerusalem." The other two men shook Adonis' hand and said they would see him later. Adonis returned to his work with a song in his heart. If he could win the ship's bullies over, then others might listen about Jesus.

That evening as the sun was sinking into the sea, the three sailors met with Adonis near the ship's rail. Heber was still working, so Adonis decided to tell his story while the rough men were still interested. Adonis asked, "Have you heard about Jesus, the Miracle Worker?"

Only Kosmas had heard that Jesus was suppose to be some kind of god. "If He was a god," quizzed Kouras, "then what god and goddess were His parents?"

"If He is a god," stated Zorba, "then why isn't He in one of our temples in Greece?"

"These are good questions," said Adonis. "I've been trying all afternoon to think how to best tell you about Jesus of Nazareth. Now fellows, I can't tell you the story all at one time. It's too long. But first I want to go back years to a man named Isaiah." Adonis told them all about Isaiah's prophesy concerning Jesus' birth. He also told the sailors about other prophets, and how their prophecies came to pass about Jesus. Adonis goes all the way to where Mary was betrothed to Joseph. "But before the marriage ceremony, Mary became pregnant. And it wasn't Joseph's."

"Great day in the morning!" exclaimed Kosmas. "Did he dump her?"

Adonis replied gently, "He planned to do so but an angel from God said that the baby was conceived by the Holy Spirit of God. You see Mary had never been with a man. The baby which was implanted in her was God's own Son."

The three sailors looked baffled. "How can this be?" asked Zorba.

"Now that's the question that will mystify men for centuries to come," said Adonis.

"Who is this God?" asked Kosmas.

Adonis smiled, "He's the Great Jehovah. The One that made the heavens and this earth…the seas, all people, and animals. He's the great God that flung the stars across the sky and named them one by one. He made the dew of the morning, and the rain that falls." On and on Adonis credited God with His creation and doings. "He is the only true God."

"Where does He live?" asked Zorba.

"Look up," said Adonis, "See the Milky Way?" The men looked at the sky. "That's the first heaven…beyond that is the second heaven…and beyond that is the third heaven, where God dwells."

"How far away is it?" Kouras asked.

"I don't know. The second heaven is where Satan and his demons live and operate. They're the ones that cause all the evil and trouble on earth," replied Adonis.

Kouras went on duty at midnight. He had skipped his nap by talking to Adonis. However, he did have a late meal. As Kouras rowed, he thought about this new God that Adonis had discovered. Kouras didn't know the gods of Greece, Rome, or Egypt, for that matter, but who could make such a claim as Adonis' God? During a lull in rowing, Kouras asked the questions, "Have any of you fellows ever heard about this God called Jehovah and His Son, Jesus?"

"Who's that?" asked one oarsman from the back.

"The God that created the world and all that's in it," said Kouras.

"Naw, never heard about Him," laughed another oarsman. "Can't say that I would believe that there is such a God if I had."

"Whose been filling your head with such nonsense Kouras?" shouted a sailor to the front.

"I didn't say I believed that there is such a God, I just asked if any of you had heard of this God called Jehovah," said Kouras in his defense.

After some insulting catcalls died down, a sailor sitting near Kouras said, "I've heard of the Great God Jehovah, Kouras. My forefathers have known about Him since the creation of man."

A sailor from midsection shouted, "How long ago was that, Ahaz?"

"A long time ago," answered Ahaz.

"A long time ago," mocked another voice, "the Jew can't even tell time!" Again, there were calls and laughter.

Finally, Kouras said in an angry voice, "Shut up you worms of a thousand gods! Let Ahaz speak!"

In a more gentle tone, Kouras said, "Go ahead Ahaz tell us what you know."

Ahaz was surprised to find himself the center of attention. "My ancestors have told, by word of mouth, the story of man's beginning on this earth. They did this by events that happened during the life span of a person or generation of people."

"How?" laughed a sailor named Ioannis. When did they start counting Jew man?"

"From the first man, God the Great Jehovah made," said Ahaz.

"Who was that?" Ioannis laughed.

Ahaz was unshaken, "That was a man named Adam. His wife Eve was created as a companion when they lived in the Garden of Eden."

By now questions were flying from the banks of oarsmen on each side of the forty-five foot wide galley ship. "How many generations ago was that?" came from the bank on the right side.

"That was fifty-eight generations ago," said Ahaz

"Awe, go on!" laughed a sailor named Georgio. "Nobody can go back that far."

"You're right Georgio. Why fifty-eight generations would go back hundreds of years, maybe even thousands," stated Angelos, "and nobody can go back that far!"

Undeterred Ahaz repeated, "I can and it covers a span of four thousand years."

"Four thousand years, come on Ahaz, admit you're just joking," kidded Agelos.

All was quiet for a short space of time. At last Kouras said, "You're serious aren't you Ahaz?" The short Jewish man nodded yes.

"Well!" shouted Georgio, "Name them!" Ahaz didn't respond. With Ahaz not speaking, jeers and hoots broke out on both sides of the galley ship. For the last half-hour, the ship had been skimming along the sea by the wind in her sails. The Captain, of the oarsman on the upper bank, had let the men rest. He saw no harm in their heckling Ahaz. The Captain walked away and let them have their fun. Laughing with a loud boisterous mimic, Georgio picked up the jeering, "What's the matter Jew-boy, did you forget who your grand pappy was?"

Amid roars of laughter, Ahaz placed his oar in its safety slot. He then arose from his bench and stepped out into the center of the aisle. All of a sudden, the laughter and talking stopped. Ahaz looked around at his fellow oarsman, who waited in anticipation. He didn't disappoint them. In a loud, well-modulated voice, he began, "God created Adam and Eve, who begat two sons." On and on Ahaz related the story, from creation until their present day. He spoke of Noah, and the great flood, Seth and Enoch, he reiterated what Adonis had said about the first, second, and third heaven. Ahaz looked over at the Captain of the oarsman, "Do you want me to stop, Phaidon?"

"The winds are still holding Ahaz, so go on," said Phaidon.

"I'll move a little faster," said Ahaz. He continued the genealogy of Jesus Christ, even up to Abraham's son Isaac. The sailors were quiet during the rest of their shift. They were beginning to see that Ahaz had indeed been instructed about the genealogy and lineage of Jesus. And that he had been brought up knowing about the Great Jehovah.

Chapter Eleven

It wasn't long before the story of Ahaz began to circulate around the ship. The top bank of oarsmen began to share the story with the middle bank, and they in turn, passed it on to the lower bank. Kouras, Zorbo, and Kosmas continued to seek out Adonis after the evening meal. Adonis told about the wonderful birth of Jesus in Bethlehem. And how a great host of angels filled the heavens singing about the newborn King. Adonis left out not one tittle of the narrative. From having no room at the inn, King Herod's insane massacre, Joseph and Mary's flight into Egypt and their safe return. On and on he went, giving great detail, even of Jesus raising the dead.

Over a period of ten days, the trio drank up the information about Jesus – His birth, His growing up, His ministry, the trial, His crucifixion and resurrection from the dead, His ascension into Heaven, the baptism of the Holy Spirit, and the Great Commission.

The three sailors could hardly wait to go on duty. Each man was an oarsman on a different bank, and each man repeated Adonis' stories. The ship was erupting with excitement. The stories were told over and over and retold off duty. Ahaz continued to give the lineage of Jesus, along with many ancient heroes. The days were filled with stories of Moses, Samson, Joseph, King David, Goliath, Samuel, and on and on. Ahaz was careful to point out that not all were in the direct line of Jesus. However, the sailors, young and old, enjoyed the adventure stories.

The time seemed to fly. Cyprus was reached. The ship unloaded and re-loaded. And the galley ship sailed on to Rhodes. From there, the Captain sailed south to Crete to unload his cargo and pick up a load for

Athens. Adonis and Heber had noticed that whichever harbor they entered, the sailors were spreading the story of this wonderful new God Jehovah, and His amazing Son, Jesus, who came back from the dead. Strangely, the hardened men of the sea were telling the story as if they believed Jesus would someday raise them from the dead, and they too would live forever in this wonderful world called the Third Heaven. Adonis wanted to shout that Jehovah God was not new but had existed before time eternal, but thought rather to hold his tongue. Adonis remembered how excited he and Beriah had been when they learned about Jesus and His unconditional love for man. Instead of speaking, he watched and listened and marveled at how fast the story of Jesus was beginning to spread across the Mediterranean Sea.

The journey was now in its eighth week, due to all the stopping at different ports. Fortunately, the weather remained warm and balmy. The breeze blew in their favor, and the nights were filled with radiant stars.

It was shortly before the galley ship arrived in Athens that Captain Strabo approached Adonis. Clearing his throat, the Captain said, "Adonis, you have turned my ship upside down. I don't know what there is about your new God and this Jesus, but I have never had a happier, more congenial crew, since you came aboard. There has been no complaining or shirking of work. In fact, it's been the opposite. The men can't wait to go on duty. We've had no quarreling or fights, nor even jumping off ship. Laughter and songs fill the air and there is a sense of camaraderie between men who have been enemies for years. Seemingly, even the sun and wind smiles upon us. Young Adonis, after you spend time with your parents, will you tell me about this great Jehovah and His Son Jesus?"

Adonis on impulse embraced the rugged old sea Captain. "I'll be more than glad to sir." Captain Strabo said no more. He cleared his throat and took out a neckerchief, wiped the moisture from his eyes and blew his nose. The Captain went over to the rail and stood, staring at the beautiful blue water of the Mediterranean. Adonis too leaned on the rail and looked down on the wharf. Already, a crowd of gaily-dressed people gathered. Dockworkers were hurrying to and fro. Smaller boats were hastily moved out of the way to make room for the galley ship to dock. The oarsmen gently dipped the oars and moved the blue and white ship forward. The Athena glided into the port like a graceful swan.

Adonis hungrily searched the crowd for a familiar face, but saw no one. His heart was filled with disappointment. Over the laughing, wagging tongues of the crowd, Captain Strabo said, “I see your father made it.”

Adonis’ heart leaped, “Where?” he whispered as his inward being flooded with joy. The tough old sea Captain studied young Adonis’ face. Drawing on his pipe, he let the smoke blow around his head, then slowly removing the pipe and using it as a pointer, Captain Strabo motioned to a lone figure standing on the west side of the dock.

Captain Strabo watched Adonis’ countenance as he caught a glimpse of his father. Gone was the smile as Adonis’ face registered shock. There before the eyes of this rich young man, was the end result of the rash action he had taken a year ago. Gone, was the robust figure of his father who once stood tall and self-assured. The raven-black hair and the tidy clothes of his father was only a memory in Adonis’ mind. In their place, was a thin, stooped shouldered man carelessly dressed. At the moment, his hands were in his pockets. His silver-gray hair blew in long wisps about his face. Adonis’ father stood looking out over the placid, blue waters of the Mediterranean. Soft, puffy, white clouds were on the horizon. Seagulls swooped, dipped and dived, while making their racareous cries. Adonis’ father didn’t even bother to look at his beautiful galley ship now tied to the wharf with the gangplank lowered.

As the older man turned toward the hills of Athens, Adonis sprang to life. Racing down the gangplank, he rudely pushed people out of the way, as he called out, “Father! Father! Please wait for me!” Tears were falling so fast, Adonis could hardly see. The gray-haired man, whose feet had been shuffling as though they were made of lead, stopped. Turning slowly around, his eyes searched for the voice that was in such a panic, but yet sounded so familiar to him. At last he saw a long, black-haired young man with a full beard and dressed in shepherd's clothing.

Shaking his head, the man said aloud, "No one I know," and turned to go on.

At this point, Adonis cried out, "Father, please wait, its Adonis!"

The older man looked at Adonis, "Young man, is this some sort of a cruel joke? I don't know you."

"Oh papa," sobbed Adonis. "Beneath this bushy beard is your 'Little Donnie Boy.'" The old sea Captain, standing on the bridge, saw the two men fall on each other's shoulders and weep. Slowly, he removed his neckerchief once again and wiped his own tear-filled eyes. Then clamping his worn, dark teeth on the pipe stem, he turned away from the happy reunion.

Alexander Palamos put his arm around his son. Together they climbed the hill toward the white palatial villa with the colonnade walks and porticos. The villa sat like a sparkling jewel among the flowering shrubs and roses. Graceful statuaries were placed beside goldfish ponds and fountains. Chairs and recliners were under vine-covered arbors. There were various baths and pools in secluded places. Each one looked as inviting as the cool lagoon. To Adonis' surprise, his father did not take him immediately to his mother. Instead, he took him to a bathhouse. Sitting beside the sunken pool, Alex gave a series of orders. Within a short time, Adonis was scrubbed, shampooed, shaved and his hair trimmed. Next, a servant rushed forward with a new white mid-thigh tunic, heavily embroidered and tied with a gold-trimmed sash. He was powdered and covered with sweet-smelling aloes. Finally, new sandals were placed on his feet. Adonis turned around for his father's inspection. His father smiled with pleasure. Then the smile disappeared as he lunged for the chain around Adonis' neck. Pulling the chain none to gently over Adonis' head, he demanded, "Where did you get this necklace!"

Adonis was totally unprepared for the emotion on his father's face, and in his voice. In confusion Adonis stammered, "In, in Jerusalem."

"I heard you," said his father. "But where exactly and from whom?" Alexander Palamos' voice was urgent.

Adonis was alarmed, "It was given to me by my friend Beriah as a going away gift."

"How did your friend acquire this?" demanded the agitated Greek father.

"I don't rightfully know," acknowledged Adonis. "He wore it under his robe. Even though I lived with Beriah, I had never seen it until the night before I left Jerusalem."

Alex studied his tall, handsome son. "How old is Beriah?" he asked.

Adonis studied his father's face. Why is he so interested in Beriah's necklace? "Uh, Beriah is four years older than me."

"What does he do for a living?" Alex probed.

Adonis was getting uneasy. Did his father think the rare coin was stolen? "Beriah plays his harp and begs for alms while he sits beside a well on a busy street."

"Is this young man a lazy tramp?" inquired his father.

"Oh no Father, Beriah is one of the most upstanding men I have ever met. He stands for everything that is good, kind, and noble; that can be found in mankind," said Adonis.

"Then what's wrong that he's not working for a living?" demanded Alex.

Adonis' eyes filled with tears, "Because he's a cripple," he said softly. "His back is deformed and he walks like a crab."

"Other than being a cripple, what does Beriah look like?" probed his father.

Adonis' face lit up, "Father, Beriah looks like a Greek statue of one of the gods. He is absolutely beautiful in facial features."

"How tall would your friend be – that is, if his back was straight?" continued his father.

Adonis though a moment, "He would be about my size. In fact, his hair, eyes and skin coloring are about like mine. We could pass for brothers except he is far superior in looks."

Adonis looked at his father. At that moment, Alex's face was wet with tears, yet it was radiant. Looking at the silver chain and coin, Alexander Palamos said, "I have a friend who's a coppersmith. I took a small painting of my mother to him. I asked that I have three coins made with her picture on both sides. I had these coins hung on silver chains."

"Father, what are you saying?" interrupted a nervous Adonis.

"Listen, I am saying, I wore one, you, being only two months old, I had put one away for you. The third one, I put around my eldest son," said Alex.

"Your eldest son?" I thought I was the only child.

Shaking his head, Adonis' father continued, "Your brother, Nicholas is four years older than you. We called him Nico. He was a handsome, bright child. On a whim, I decided to take four-year-old Nico on the galley ship to Tyre. Of course this was against your mother's wishes. Nearing the coast of Israel, we were caught up in the tropical storm. Young Nico was washed over board."

'Overboard, overboard, overboard,' echoed in Adonis' mind. Then finally Adonis whispered, "Overboard, but why was he on deck, in a tropical gale, in the first place?" quizzed Adonis.

"I left Nico in my cabin while I helped with the sails. Every hand on deck was urged into action to keep afloat. Too late, I spied Nico out of the corner of my eye, just as a huge wave swept his small body overboard. Adonis, I died a million deaths right there. He was nowhere to be seen. We limped into port. After some repair work, we cruised up and down the coast, but no Nico. When I returned to Greece, the news almost killed your mother."

Now at long last, Adonis knew why his mother lived seemingly in perpetual sorrow. "Father, are you sure this coin, uh Beriah's coin, matches your own?" Without a word, Alexander Palamos removed the chain he had not taken off for twenty years. They were identical in every detail. Turning to a man servant, Alexander gave orders like his old self. "Andre, go down to the Athene. Tell Captain Strabo to make ready to sail on the morning tide. Tell him to take only enough supplies for a trip to Israel and back. Be sure to tell him not to take on any other cargo. I want the Athene to skim across the Mediterranean like a Roman galley ship of war." Turning to Adonis, Alexander put his arm around his young son's shoulder. "Come my boy, let's go tell your mother we're leaving tomorrow to bring home her lost son."

Adonis' mother was sitting in a latticed covered arbor. Her needlepoint lay idly in her lap while she gazed wishfully out to sea. Silver threads shone in her black hair and her sweet face had aged since Adonis had last seen her. Hurrying, Adonis rushed to his mother. He dropped at her feet and laid his dark head in her rose-colored lap. For a moment, she didn't move. It was as though she was afraid of having an illusional dream and that it would disappear, as it had many times before. At last, Adonis looked up. "Mama, please say something. Say you forgive me for bringing you pain." Adonis' mother tentatively reached out her hand and stroked his head. Then she gathered him into her arms.

Weeping, she whispered, "My son, my son, my baby, you've come home."

Adonis' homecoming was more festive because he brought hope that their lost son was found. Adonis told eager parents about making Beriah's acquaintance on the Hill of Calvary, the terrible day Jesus was crucified. He told how the tenderhearted Beriah prayed for the suffering Jesus. He also explained, that when Jesus died, he picked up Jesus' sandals and gave them to Beriah.

"Why would you give your broth, uh, I mean Beriah, well your unbeknown brother to you," stammered Alex, "a dead Jew's shoes?"

"Because sir, Beriah's were worn out," said Adonis.

"Couldn't you have bought Nico a pair of shoes Adonis?" asked his mother.

Hanging his head in shame, Adonis said, "No mother, I had no money, no job, no food, and no home. I stole for food, slept in back alleys among the garbage, and even thought about robbing a priest of his decorative jewels." There was a horrified cry from his mother and a look of disbelief came over his father's ashen face. "Meeting Beriah was the best thing that happened to me. He took me home with him, he encouraged me to clean myself up, and he gave me clean clothes, good food, and a place to sleep. But more importantly, Beriah encouraged me to take a long hard look at my inner man. That night I did a deep soul searching and I didn't like what I found. The next day I got a job with a man named Abdul, unloading his camel caravans."

"How did things go from there until you decided to come back home?" asked his father.

"Believe it or not, we were happy together. Beriah rescued a young man from two thieves. Well actually, they wouldn't even make good thieves." Adonis chuckled at this statement. "Beriah also brought these men home to live with us. Next, he rescued a big dog from a group of angry camel drivers. Father, you won't believe this, but the dog turned out to be my dog, Thor. The dog had jumped ship and followed the caravan to a caravansary in Jerusalem. Mother, Beriah is so loving and compassionate, he would take in every stray or help any person in trouble. Oh mother! You will totally love Beriah. He's a son to be proud of. He is also a believer, like myself, that Jesus Christ is the Son of God, the Great Jehovah. And that Jesus died for our sins."

"If He died for your sins Adonis, then how can He help you, seeing that He is dead?" asked a disturbed Alexander Palamos.

"That's just it father, Jesus arose from the dead on the third day and was seen walking around for forty days by over 500 witnesses. In fact, I came home to tell you and mother about this wonderful God," said Adonis.

Adonis' father looked sternly at him. "Where is this Jesus now son?" asked his mother.

"Jesus went back to Heaven to prepare a place for us. He wants us to live in Heaven forever. A group of His followers watched Him ascend up into the heavens. He also promised that He would return some day, so where He is, we can be also. Oh mother, Jesus' world will be so wonderful. There will be no more sickness; no dying, no sorrow and no parting with loved ones. There will be joy unspeakable! No more war father. Men will beat their swords into plowshares. Just think we will be able to live in perfect peace." By now Adonis' face and eyes were flushed with excitement. "You see, I found Jesus' walking staff and gave it to Beriah to help him walk. Ever since he has worn Jesus' sandals and used his staff, Beriah was given a gift of healing. Well, actually Beriah has no power, but it is in his firm belief in the healing power of Jesus, that does the healing."

"Wait!" Adonis was not ready for his father's outburst of unbelief. "If Nico has such a connection to his Jesus, then why is Nico still a cripple? Why won't Jesus heal my son?" Adonis and his parents talked far into the night – question after question was asked by his parents. However, by early dawn, Alexander Palamos and his younger son set sail for Israel-to find, and bring home, the lost Nicholas Palamos, who had been washed overboard twenty years ago.

Chapter Twelve

By mid-morning on the next day, Joshua and Beriah once again, found themselves sitting under the tree with the old men. A crowd had begun to gather. They had heard through the old men about Joshua and Beriah witnessing the crucifixion of Jesus. Joshua and Beriah were asked to repeat their story. Be the ninth hour, a man in the crowd asked the crucial question. With tears in his eyes he asked, "Joshua, what can I do to be saved?"

Joshua looked at the young man, who was trembling under conviction of the Holy Spirit, and answered, "Believe that Jesus is the Christ and that He is the only begotten Son of God, the Father. You must also believe that Christ died on the cross and shed His blood in our place. Believe that Jesus rose again from the dead and ascended into Heaven. Repent of all your sins and ask Jesus to cover those sins with His shed blood. He will then come into your heart and wash you as white as snow. Jesus is faithful and just. He will forgive you of your sins and give you everlasting life. He commands us to confess Him before men and be baptized. Jesus himself was baptized by John the Baptist. Not that Jesus was sinful but rather to set the example for us to follow."

The young man listened carefully to Joshua's words, then humbly said, "I believe and ask forgiveness of my sins. I hereby now declare before God, my friends and neighbors, that I believe Jesus Christ is my Lord and Savior. Now Joshua, will you baptize me?" Before Joshua could answer, the 'and me,' 'and me,' began to ring out all over the crowd.

Joshua was amazed but happy. "When would you all like this done?"

The young man had a quick reply, "Why not now? The banks of Jordan are not that far away." With emotion running high in the crowd, they began to follow Beriah as he rode on the donkey. Joshua found a low spot on the Jordan and he and Beriah waded in the water, up to their waists. Beriah kept his balance with the staff of Jesus. The crowd lined the banks trampling down the tall grass and wild flowers. The elderly sat under the trees so they could witness their many friends and neighbors being baptized. Small birds were flitting among the bushes and trees, singing their joyous songs. Butterflies floated on the morning breeze and soft, white clouds floated in a bright blue sky. The crowd talked in low voices and insects hopped and hummed in the background.

Before making camp for the night, Joshua and Beriah had baptized over 300 converts. After their evening meal, Joshua and Beriah talked over the day's events and prayed for their new brothers and sisters in Christ. And once again, they slept under God's blanket – the starry sky.

For the next three days, the little group stayed on the path that followed Jordan. The path itself was well worn by travelers, and the ground was packed and firm. It was wide enough for two horses to ride abreast. The scenery was tall grass, wild flowers, rocky slopes, scrub bushes, and tall trees. They found out it was cooler traveling close to the water. It was also nice to be able to bath and wash their clothes. Each evening they fished and cooked over a campfire. The nights were chilly but with the fire and their rugs, they managed to stay warm. Beriah continued to enjoy sleeping under Gods canopy of stars.

On the morning of the fourth day, the men ran into their first encounter with trouble. A short way up on the side of the hill, a lamb was entangled by a thicket of briar; while nearby and moving closer, were three wolves. The terrified lamb was bleating loudly for its mother. But the mother was nowhere in sight. In fact, no other sheep or shepherd was in sight. The poor wandering lamb was helplessly caught. Beriah and Joshua watched in horror. The lamb was too far away for them to reach it in time. However, Gray Boy and Samson did not feel the same. With a bound, they were off and running. Gray Boy was out distancing Samson and was first to arrive on the scene. He did not hesitate; rather he lunged immediately for the leader of the pack. Samson coming in second, snapped at first one wolf's hindquarters and then the other. The fight was on. Gray Boy was first on top and then on bottom. There were growls and howls, torn fur and flesh mingled with blood went flying in the air, before finally, all three predators gave up and went slinking off into the underbrush. Beriah was all for going up the hill at once. Joshua took hold of Jasper's bridle. "Wait Beriah, the mangy wolves may just be licking their wounds and haven't given up the fight." Joshua knew if he let go of the bridle, Beriah would go to the lamb's rescue, regardless of the danger.

Both men were surprised at what happened next. Gray Boy took hold of the wool on the lamb's side and began to pull the frightened animal forward. The lamb moved a few inches. Next, Gray Boy began to pull at the brambles that were holding the lamb. This process was repeated again and again. Samson, looking confused, cocked his head and sat down to watch. At last Gray Boy latched on to a mouthful of wool and gave a mighty heave. Gray Boy and the lamb fell to the ground, as the final strand of wild rose bramble broke loose from the frightened lamb. Samson, at last, got in on the action by licking and washing the face of the animal. Between the two, the lamb was nudged down the hill in the direction of Beriah and Joshua. Beriah was elated. Joshua let out his breath. Until that moment, he wasn't aware that he was holding it. Shaking his head, he said to Beriah, "Had I not seen this happen, I wouldn't believe it. Beriah, you rescued Samson from being killed at the camel caravansary, and Gray Boy from a horrible death of rabies, and now they repaid their debt by rescuing the lamb." Beriah checked out the dog and the wolf. Luckily, their injuries were minor. The lamb wanted no part of being looked over. While Joshua and Beriah were trying to decide what to do with the lamb, Gray Boy herded the scared animal to a low spot in the river. There, the dog, the wolf, and the lamb drank together, all the while, Joshua pondered to himself, 'What kind of wolf and dog are these creatures?'

"What will you name the lamb?" asked Joshua.

Beriah smiled and said, "I believe I will name her Rosa. After all, Gray Boy got her out of the roses."

Joshua chuckled, "That's a good choice. Rosa it will be."

A short time later the enlarged party was again on the move. Joshua walked beside the donkey, and the lamb walked alongside her rescuers. They traveled in this fashion until the sun became almost unbearable. At last they stopped to rest under a large sycamore tree. After a drink and some fruit, they laid themselves down for a nap. The donkey, tied to a tree, closed his eyes and only moved when swishing flies. Samson laid his head in Beriah's lap. The wolf curled up with the lamb and Joshua leaned against the tree and dozed.

This was the strange scene the two Arab men came upon, as they were traveling in the direction of Jerusalem. The taller of the two men was having trouble with his camel. Since morning, the beast had balked, sat down at times, and bellowed in loud, agonizing cries. His owner was thoroughly exasperated. Upon seeing the sleeping men and the docile little donkey, the Arab cried out, "My friends, would you like to sell your donkey?" Instantly, the men and animals were on their feet. Joshua grabbed the startled lamb so it wouldn't run away. "Sorry – I wake you. My name is Trubal. We on way to Jerusalem." Beriah noticed the Arab's attempt in trying to speak in broken Jewish dialogue. "This contrary Beast of mine, no want to carry me. This is my friend, Umar," said Trubal slowly.

Joshua stepped forward, "I am Joshua and this is my friend, Beriah."

Beriah nodded and smiled, "What seems to be the trouble with your camel?"

"He's quite a handsome animal," said Joshua. Just as Joshua finished speaking, the camel let out a long, agonizing screech. He moaned louder than Abdul's big camel.

Beriah, who had been leaning on his staff, staggered forward. Looking at the man on the camel, he said, "Will you step down sir and let me look your animal over?"

The surprised Arab had the camel to kneel, and stepped off. As Beriah moved toward the kneeling camel, Trubal yelled, "Don't get close, mean camel – run over you!"

Beriah ignored the Arab's plea and began to croon and talk softly to the camel. The big, intelligent head began to rise up. As Beriah came closer, the camel turned his head sideways but still managed to watch Beriah out of the corner of his eye. Beriah continued to talk directly to the camel. "You don't feel good today, do you boy? Now just rest and let me check you out. Your jaw is swollen. Did something bite you last night? I don't see a wound with all that hair." Joshua motioned the camel's owner to come under the shade tree. There they watched in astonishment, as the sick camel responded to Beriah's hands. "What's his name?" asked Beriah.

"His name is Qasim," said Trubal.

Beriah continued to talk. Rubbing his hand up each side of the camel's cheeks, Beriah crooned, "Qasim's a nice name for a fine fellow like you." Periodically, Beriah rubbed the staff and continued to stroke the sides of the camel's head and cheeks. By now, Qasim was looking hypnotically into Beriah's eyes. "It's alright boy, you're pretty sick and you're allowed to cry if you want to. I understand all about crying." And to the astonishment of Trubal, Umar, and Joshua, big teardrops formed on the camel's long eyelashes and slowly overflowed. Gently, Beriah put his arm around the camel's neck and laid his head against the camel's forehead. The camel continued to shed silent tears. Then slowly, the camel arose to his feet. Joshua motioned the Arabs to remain still. Beriah then reached the staff upward to the side of Qamir's head and said, "In the name of Jesus, be healed of this affliction." This Beriah said in a demanding voice. To Trubal's horror, his big brute of a camel fell over on his side as though it were dead.

Shaking his fist at Beriah, Trubal yelled and flung Arabic curses at the little cripple. "May the wrath of Allah strike you!" Through all the verbal abuse, Beriah just simply smiled. Then he sat down in the sand, placed the camel's head in his lap. Thus he sat, stroking Qasim's face and crooning. At last, Beriah quickly stepped out of the way, as a vile; blacking substance began to drain out of the camel's mouth. The drainage continued for another ten minutes. By now Trubal, Umar, and Joshua were bent over studying the strange, smelly material.

"What is it Beriah? Is it an infected tooth?" asked Joshua.

"No. Much more serious I fear," answered Beriah. "Qasim has been bitten by a poisonous reptile."

"Reptile – oh no!" gasped Trubal. "Then he dies?"

Beriah looked up at the sweaty, turbaned head and said, "No. Not this time sir. Our Lord Jesus is removing the poison. Joshua, take the men back under the tree and give them some refreshment. In their haste to reach Jerusalem, they didn't take time to eat this morning."

"Two very confused Arabs looked at first, Beriah, and then Joshua. At last, Umar asked, "Is he a magician?"

"Not at all," smiled Joshua. "We're believers and followers of Jesus Christ. Beriah has just had a word of knowledge from Jesus."

"Does the cripple have the power to heal people?" asked Trubal.

"Not at all," answered Joshua. "Beriah called on Jesus, our Lord to heal a sick and dying animal. Beriah has the faith that Jesus will honor his plea. From the look of things, your Qasim's body is getting a thorough purging. He'll soon be well. Just believe and have patience."

A short time later, Qasim lumbered to his feet, shook, and let out a happy bellow. Then he put his nose to Beriah's cheek like a kiss. Beriah laughed and reached up and hugged the big animal's neck. Over his shoulder he called out, "Joshua, quarter about five apples."

As the Arabs stood smiling and thanking Allah, Joshua said, "You men are thanking the wrong god. It was Jesus of Nazareth, the Son of God, who was resurrected from the dead, that healed your camel."

Trubal turned big, wet eyes toward Joshua, "Who this Jesus – who performs miracle?" While Beriah fed Qasim apples and continued to console him, Joshua told Trubal and Umar about the wonderful Jesus who was the Savior of all mankind.

The four men spent the afternoon and night eating, talking and sleeping under the tree. When morning broke early, the men smiled at Beriah and his menagerie. Beriah fell asleep while leaning against Qasim's broad side, with Samson, the dog, lying near by. At Beriah's feet, lay the wolf and the lamb. Joshua shook his head, "If we pick up any more strays, we can start an animal show."

As the two Arabs prepared to leave, Tubal did a strange thing. "Joshua, no wake up Beriah. We leave – we give Qasim to friend. Yes, Yes. Tell friend Qasim belongs to him. Stubborn camel fell in love with young healer."

"Are you sure Trubal?" questioned Joshua. "That's a very expensive animal."

"You no spoil my pleasure. I give camel in spirit of your Jesus. Umar and I thank you – you share story of wonderful God," said Trubal.

To Beriah's surprise, when he awoke, the two Arabs were gone, yet Qasim remained. "Why didn't they take the camel?" asked a perplexed Beriah. "Didn't Trubal believe that Qasim was healed?"

"Oh yes Beriah, Turbal and Umar believed in the miracle. But the best news of all, they believe in the Lord Jesus Christ as their Savior. Beriah, Trubal gave you the camel out of brotherly love," said Joshua. Beriah was exuberant. He could hardly believe that he was the benefactor of such a handsome animal. In fact, an animal, which at the moment, was bestowing slobbery kisses down the back of Beriah's neck.

Riding in the saddle on Qasim was an experience. Beriah had to hold the long-legged camel back, so Jasper, the donkey, who was now carrying Joshua, could keep up. By evening time the party of seven turned off the Jordan River and headed in the direction of Gadera. The turn off was only about five or six miles from the Sea of Galilee. For about two miles they followed the Yarmuck River. It was here, on a little grassy slope, that they pitched camp. The animals drank and forged for themselves. Strangely, Jasper had made friends with Qasim. Beriah and Joshua ate cheese and dried beef for the evening meal and topped it off with fruit. By the time the moon was riding high in the clear sub-tropical night, Joshua, Beriah, and the animals were fast asleep.

At the early morning light, Joshua had purchased vegetables, fruit, cheese, and bread from a farmer and his wife. He inquired about the little village that lay in the distance. "Is not this the village where Jesus healed a demoniac man?"

"Yes, that's true," answered the farmer. "But it's an unfriendly village." Being told that, Joshua decided to turn north in the direction of the Sea of Galilee. By both men riding, the miles were more quickly covered. By mid-afternoon, they caught their first glimpse of the Sea of Galilee. The water was cool and calm. The blue-green water made a fellow want to own a boat. The eastern side of the Sea of Galilee was a series of shallow to steep slopes. At last, finding a pleasant, grassy slope, the little party took a meal under a gnarled, old fig tree. The wind picked up and blew a cooling breeze over the water. Here and there, a silver-blue fish leaped into the air; delighting the onlookers before it would fall back with a splash. Momentarily, the small sprays of water sent out tiny teardrops of rainbow colors. Slowly, the rainbow drops fell back into the water and became one again with the Sea.

For the next two days, Joshua and Beriah took their time traveling. They washed their clothes, bathed, and fished in leisure. On the third day, after arriving on the banks of the Sea of Galilee, they came across six fishermen who were mending the rips and tears in the nets. Warm greetings were exchanged. "You come far?" asked the leader of the men.

Joshua nodded yes. "We come from Jerusalem after the death and resurrection of Jesus Christ. There's a lot of trouble in our Holy City," said Joshua.

With this statement, there was a barrage of questions. "Have you seen Jesus? What do you think of His teachings? Is Jesus really the Messiah promised to the Jewish people? Have you seen our neighbor Peter? How is Mary, Jesus' mother holding up? Are Jesus disciples in hiding? Did Judas, who betrayed Jesus, really hang himself?" The questions went on and on and flowed for the next two hours. The mending of the net was put aside as these eager Galileans hungered for news.

Joshua and Beriah answered each and every question to the best of their ability. "Where are you going from here?" asked the big fisherman.

"We're following the footsteps of Jesus which were mapped out by Peter," replied Joshua. "Tomorrow we'll stop at Gergesa, where Jesus cast demons out of a man."

The fishermen looked among themselves and then slowly shook their heads. "Make your stop brief," said Big John, the spokesman. "It's a most unfriendly settlement." Beriah and Joshua felt a slight chill at this cryptic warning. Swiftly changing the subject, Big John said, "This is the place where Jesus, seeing the boat carrying his disciples, decided to join them." However, Jesus didn't have a boat and His disciples didn't seem to be aware that He was on the shore, due to the storm."

"That was a problem," smiled Beriah. "How did Jesus get there?"

Big John laughed, "That would have been a problem for me or you, but Jesus simply walked on the water to the disciple's boat.

"A man cannot walk on the water!" stated Beriah.

"Correct," said Big John, "Man can't walk on water, but the Son of God can! And He did! It was right out there where those two sea gulls are circling."

Beriah's eyes were huge with wonder. "Well, what did the disciples think?" asked an equally surprised and stammering Joshua.

"They thought He was a ghost," said Big John. "At last, Peter asked to walk on the water and Jesus said, 'Come.' Peter climbed out of the boat, into the stormy sea, and walked on water, until he looked down. Then his faith was overcome by fear and he began to sink. Peter was terrified as he began to sink into the cold, turbulent sea. 'Lord help me!' Peter cried in panic. Jesus took his hand and asked him, 'Wherefore did you doubt me' When Jesus helped Peter on board, the storm ceased. The waves and the wind were still."

Shortly thereafter, the men prepared to cast off. "John, I have another question before you go," said Joshua. "Why wasn't Jesus with his disciples in the boat?"

John smiled, "I'm glad you asked. That was the day that a crowd of 5,000 men, not to mention women and children, had followed Jesus on the mountain. They wanted to hear Jesus teach. As the day was getting late, the crowd was hot, tired and hungry. Jesus asked His disciples how much food was in the crowd. All they found were five loaves of bread and two fish. Jesus had the people to sit down. He prayed over the bread and fish, and started breaking the food into pieces. He kept breaking and breaking and breaking, until everyone had eaten his or her fill. His disciples took up twelve baskets of what was left over."

"No wonder He was tired," said Joshua.

Big John agreed. "I don't believe that it was so much the miracle, as the fact the people were pressuring Jesus to declare Himself as King. Jesus sent his disciples to the other side of the sea, while He went farther upon the hill to pray. You see Joshua, praying was Jesus' way to revive himself, as it's our way to renew our strength. Jesus kept saying that setting up a kingdom now was not His purpose at this time."

"What was His purpose if He didn't want to set up His kingdom?" asked Beriah.

There was a long pause before Big John answered, "Jesus came to die on the cross to pay for our sins, so that we might have eternal life. But someday, Jesus will return, in all His Heavenly glory and set up His kingdom. Never doubt nor fear, Jesus will return." With this said, the big fisherman got into his boat and they were soon rowing across the Sea of Galilee.

Chapter Thirteen

The following morning Beriah and Joshua proceeded along the seashore to the region of the Gergesa. Fisherman John had warned them the Gergesian people were most unfriendly. Climbing up the steep slope of the hill, they tapered off to a more level road. This narrow dirt road leads past a ravine where the dead were buried. There were many tombs cut out of solid rock. And there were many graves dug directly into the ground with leaning tombstones. Some stones were broken and others had turned porous and dark gray. This was caused by years of seawater being sprayed on them, from the Sea of Galilee, during the storms.

Joshua, Beriah, and the animals acted a little skittish as they passed by the forlorn place of the dead. Long before the little party reached Gergesa, they began to get an unpleasant whiff of the odor of swine, which was carried by the breeze. "There must be a large herd of the ghastly beasts nearby. Two or three pigs would not give off that much of an offensive odor," declared Joshua. Beriah agreed. Within a quarter of a mile, they saw a hillside literally covered with the animals. The swine were lazily forging for themselves. The herdsman was resting beneath a tree near the road. He didn't seem too concerned about the movement of the animals. The swine seemed content to root beneath the brush and roots of small trees.

Joshua and Beriah greeted the herdsman cordially. The man spoke but did not smile. In fact, his demeanor was one of sullen suspicion. "You have quite a herd of swine," said Joshua as a way to open up a conversation. "Do you roast the meat?" asked Joshua.

The man under the tree was outraged. “If you’re Jewish, then you should know that it’s forbidden to eat swine’s flesh!”

“Well, yes – but what do you do with them?” asked the confused Beriah.

“Not that it’s any of your concern, but I sell them,” answered the herdsman.

“Is that a fact?” interrupted Joshua, in hopes of getting Beriah off the hook. “I thought Gergesa area was a Jewish community. So who buys your pi, uh swine?” asked a flustered Joshua.

“Kind of nosey, aren’t you?” stated the herdsman.

Joshua, taken aback, just smiled and said, “Sure does sound like it, but my friend Beriah and I are from Jerusalem. We don’t know much about rural living, however, right now we are tracing the footsteps of Jesus.”

With Joshua’s explanation, the herdsman jumped to his feet. “You fools!” he shouted. “Let me tell you a thing or two about that trouble maker.” While the Gergesian was shouting, Beriah began to gag and cough. “Come,” said the herdsman, “we’ll go down wind so you city fellows don’t pass out over a little whiff of rural odor.” Joshua and Beriah followed the long flowing robe of the angry herdsman. He moved quickly for a man of small stature. Traveling about another quarter of a mile, the man sat down beneath a straggly, wind twisted pine and motioned for the men to sit down. Here the air took on a more pleasant smell. It was scented with scrub pines and wild mint weed. Here and there, bunches of sage and wildflowers, made pleasant the scenery on the hillside. The view of the Sea of Galilee was breathtaking and the air was without the odor of swine.

Joshua and Beriah’s little party alighted and was soon resting and waiting for their guide to explain why he didn’t like Jesus. Sitting down, Joshua said, “My name is Joshua, and this is my friend Beriah.”

The herdsman nodded his head but did not offer his name. He asked what he thought was a retalitorial question back to Joshua, “Where did you get all of your menagerie?”

Joshua began to answer, “Well.”

"Never mind. Just spare me the details," interrupted the quick-spirited herdsman. "Now let me tell you about this Jesus, whose footsteps you're following," chuckled the herdsman in mockery. "He's no friend to the poor."

"Really?" feigned Joshua. "We were led to believe Jesus was particularly kind to the poor."

This said Joshua tried to pull the man into a deeper conversation. "Haw!" snorted the man. We're poor around here and this Jesus killed my neighbor's whole herd of swine. It was one of the best herds he ever had. There was a thousand nice, fat head of swine, and Jesus killed them all! And at one time! My neighbor already had them promised to a Roman soldier."

"Really? Why and how did Jesus do that? Was it because if it was wrong to eat swine, then is it wrong to sell them to others to eat?" asked Beriah.

The herdsman glared at Beriah for his burning question. He then turned to Joshua, "Did you travel along the seashore?" he quizzed.

"Yes," said Joshua, "and it's a pretty dismal place."

"You can say that again," chimed in Beriah.

"Well," said the herdsman, "it has a reason to be eerie. For years two demoniac men lived in the tombs. They wore no clothing and had supernatural strength. Why it would take fifteen men to get them in chains. But it didn't do any good. The older of the two men seemingly, had more strength. He would break his chain as though they were baling string. Then he'd help the other demoniac man break free."

"Oh! it was ghastly! How did you know they were demoniacs?" asked Joshua.

"They were possessed by some evil spirit. Why, they were nothing but walking skeletons. Their skin was gray; their shaggy, matted black hair had turned to a dull gray. The saliva drooled down the sides of their mouths. They shrieked and moaned, day and night. They took stones and cut themselves. In fact, they self-mutilated their bodies. When a few of us would venture close to try to talk to them, it seemed that there were evil intruders looking out of their reddish-colored eyes.

Whoever, or whatever was looking out of those bodies was not human. Whatever possessed those men, were demonic. And as sure as I'm here, that evil thing came from the pits of Hades!" The herdsman voice was raised when he said, 'Hades'; at this, Samson raised his head and made a guttural growl.

"Be still boy," comforted Beriah.

The herdsman continued, "The morning that Jesus came by was the day my neighbor's swine were feeding on nuts near the ravine. My friend was nervous about being close to the tombs. So he didn't get too close. Anyway, when Jesus got near the tombs, a loud, low gravely voice came from the strongest man."

"What did he say to Jesus?" asked Beriah.

The herdsman looked annoyingly at Beriah, and then stated, "I was getting to that. The demoniac said to Jesus, 'what do you want with me Jesus, the Son of the Most High God? I beg you, don't torture me! And Jesus asked him, 'What is your name?' 'Legion, for we are many. We beg you don't order us into the abyss.' My friend said the demoniac man looked over at the herd of swine and said, 'Let us go into the herd of swine.' Jesus looked at the demon controlled man who had sunken eyes and said, 'Go!'"

By now Beriah could hardly sit still. "What happened sir. Did they go?"

The man, a little more gracious to Beriah this time said, "They all came out and went into the swine. Now, there are a thousand demon-crazed pigs." This was the first time, Joshua noted, that the herdsman related to the swine as 'pigs'. "They went wild with fear and began to squeal until the hair began to raise on my neighbor's head. The pigs had lost control of themselves, and in panic, ran down the steep hillside and plunged into the Sea of Galilee, and drowned – all 1,000 of them! His herd was completely wiped out. His income was at the bottom of the sea."

"Well, it seems that the demons killed the herd of swine, not Jesus. He only gave the demons divine permission to go into the pigs," said Joshua.

"It amounts to the same, they were just as dead," stated the disgruntled herdsman.

"What happened to the men when they were free of demonic power?" asked Beriah.

"They were back to being normal. The disciples put clothes on the men and they were lying around Jesus' feet giving Him praise. Why, they even wanted to follow Him."

"Did they?" asked Joshua.

"No, Jesus told them to go home and tell their families and neighbors what God had done for them. But let me tell you a thing or two. By the time my neighbor told everyone how that Jesus killed his herd of swine, no one in Gergesa wanted Jesus around here. As a matter of fact, the Gergesians asked Jesus to leave." The little Jewish man acted quite pleased that Jesus wasn't welcome in his area.

"What became of the two delivered men?" asked Joshua.

"If you follow the seashore north, you'll find them tending sheep on the side of the hill," replied the herdsman.

Joshua and Beriah thanked the herdsman for his story and started back down the path to the seashore. As they were descending the path, they could hear the herdsman call out to his herd, "Get away from those rocks, my little filthy, unclean swines!" Beriah, Joshua, and their little party turned north. Following the seashore, they by-passed Gergesa and it's unfriendly inhabitants. They traveled slowly and talked over the strange story of the demoniac men.

The mid-morning air was still pleasant as it blew across the beautiful waters of the Sea of Galilee. The water was calm; the gulls swirled, dipped, and dived. The pelicans, with their boat-like bills, scooped up crayfish on the sandy seashore. About three miles north of the village of Gergesa, they spotted the fleecy flock of sheep up a shelly incline. Turning the animals to the east, they carefully followed a well-worn path to the grassy plateau near the sheep.

The larger of the two shepherds left the flock in the care of the smaller man, and approached Joshua and Beriah. The man bade them to sit a spell under a towering fig tree. After the hostility of the swine herdsman, it was a pleasure to see a friendly face. Qasim kneeled so Beriah could slide off his back. Joshua, who had been walking, staked out Jasper. Gray Boy took the lamb off and away from the flock to graze. And Samson laid down under the tree. Joshua introduced himself, and Beriah, "They call me, 'Fish," said the shepherd. "Have you come far?"

"We've come from Jerusalem where Jesus, the Son of God, was crucified, buried, and was resurrected from the dead. After His resurrection, Jesus was seen by His disciples and over five hundred witnesses. After forty days, Jesus ascended into Heaven to make intercession to the Father on our behalf. But we were left with a wonderful promise," said Joshua.

"What's that?" asked Fish, who was by now crying.

"Jesus said, 'I go to prepare a place for you. That where I am, you shall be also.' Jesus promised to come again someday and gather His own." Joshua looked at the man's swarthy face, flowing with tears running into his beard, and deep sorrow in his eyes. "Friend, are you a follower of Jesus Christ?" asked Joshua.

Fish sat with shoulders hunched. Nodding he said, "I'm a follower of Jesus now, but I wasn't always. In fact, I had traveled so far down the road of depravity, I couldn't find my way back. Had Jesus not come by the tombs that day, I would either be dead, or worse – still living there in a deranged state. You see I was a demoniac. I was filled with hundreds of demons – possibly thousands, from the pits of Hades. I had no say over my life. The demons moved within my body and did with me as they pleased." By now Fish was sobbing great body racking sobs.

"How did the demons get in?" asked the frightened Beriah. "What I need to know is if the demons took over your body and mind, can they take over mine or Joshua's?"

Fish looked first at Beriah and then Joshua. "Anyone can succumb to the demon forces by his moral depravity. When a man gives himself up to sin and gratification of the lowest desires, they open themselves for the invasion of evil spirits. The deeper a man sinks into degradation, the more they are open to demonic powers. Through sinful appetites and lust, he opens his body and soul to the devil and his demons. Once they take possession of a man, he can't get rid of them without the help of God. They called me a lunatic I was so far gone. I wore no clothes and I lived in the tombs."

Beriah and Joshua sat quietly while Fish regained control of his emotions. At last Joshua said, "Would you mind sharing how you let yourself become open to the supernatural power of demons?"

Fish sat a few moments in deep thought, then began, "Like everything else, it began small. I was about thirteen, when I began to take pleasure in tying a string on the legs of big bugs. I would let them try to escape until their legs pulled off. Next, I would pinch off the end of fireflies and wear the light like a ring. From there, I began to enjoy killing little birds with my sling. I next graduated to torturing and killing cats and then stray dogs. By the time I was fifteen, I stopped going to the synagogue. By sixteen, I began to lust after my neighbor's wife. Then I became angry because he had so much more than my widowed mother. So I began stealing things I wanted. I would lie to my mother about how I acquired my new treasures. By the age of eighteen, I began to drink heavily. I no longer believed in the Great God Jehovah. Next, my sexual appetites became more depraved. I began to pay young boys for sexual favors. The more I sinned and did evil, the more my body lusted after something different." Looking around at his flock of sheep, Fish dropped his head and shamefully remarked, "I am ashamed of what I had become and what I gratified myself with." Beriah and Joshua could see the shame and remorse over Fish's face. He continued, "My mother, who could no longer control me, died of a broken heart. Shortly thereafter, I heard of an old woman, who lived in a remote area that was able to talk with the dead. I thought this would be an interesting thing to be able to do. So I traveled to see her. She called herself a witch and declared to worship Satan." Looking at the two faces before him, Fish said, "This was the final push to completely open my mind and my soul to the entry and total takeover of demonic spirits. The demons delighted in tormenting me twenty-four hours a day. You see fellows, sin starts out small but sin is progressive, sure, and deadly. Be sure to guard your mind and soul, and let Jesus be your watchman. Since Jesus rescued me, I have no fears. God always watches over us. God says, 'He never sleeps nor slumbers' and that's good enough for me. I call myself Fish, as a symbol to the world that I am a believer and follower of Jesus Christ, the Son of God."

It was amid hugs, and handshakes that Joshua and Beriah took their leave. Traveling at a leisurely pace, the little party followed the Sea of Galilee. In the distance, they could see three fishing boats bobbing in the gentle waves. Again and again, the fishermen cast their nets into the cold water and brought up great catches of fish.

A short way from the village of Bethsaida, they came across a fishing boat near shore. Its sail was lowered and the men were eating a mid-afternoon meal. Seeing the little group, one of them called out, "That's a strange assortment of animals. I suppose there's a story behind how you acquired them."

Joshua laughed, "There is, come ashore and we will tell you how we got them. We also witnessed a murder we'd like to tell you about." Joshua really knew how to get one's attention ready for his witnessing, thought Beriah. Joshua told the fishermen all about Christ's crucifixion, His burial, and resurrection. Joshua also related to them about the Day of Pentecost and the phenomena of tongues, which was brought on by the indwelling of the Holy Ghost, as prophesied by Jesus.

"How do you know all this?" asked one fisherman as he was climbing out of his boat.

"Because I was one of those who was filled with the Holy Spirit," said Joshua. "Peter, the big fisherman, baptized me."

A short time later, the fishermen were roasting fish over an open fire for Joshua and Beriah. As they were eating the savory meal, they told about Judas, and his betrayal of Jesus. They told what Adonis had seen and heard in the Garden of Gethsemane. By evening, they had relayed the story of the earthquake, the torn veil in the temple, and the opened graves. Beriah told about the trouble between the merchants and the Roman soldiers. Lastly, he told how Joshua, Adonis, Heber,

Samson, Jasper, Gray Boy, Rosa –the lamb, and the camel Qasim had come to him.

The fishermen were enthralled by the story told by the soft-spoken cripple. Before leaving, the fishermen left a string of fish in the water for Joshua and Beriah's supper meal and for breakfast the following day. "We're from Capernaum. That's to the northwest of the Sea of Galilee. Be sure to plan on staying a while with us. We have many more questions to ask, and things to catch up on about our neighbors." Joshua promised. The men waved goodbye and let their sail fill with the evening breeze. A short time later their boat was just a speck on the rippling, blue water.

The following morning, after breakfast, Joshua and Beriah continued their journey northward. They were still following the seashore. A flock of grebe birds, along with the gulls, dived for fish, while tortoise and crayfish crawled along the wet, sandy shore. The breeze of the water blew tall grass in rippling yellow waves. Stopping by a little hut along their trail, Joshua bought cheese, figs, grapes and olives. Beriah looked longingly at the newly baked loaves of bread. The old women, seeing Beriah's wistful look, cut off half a loaf and handed it to the young cripple. Beriah carefully wrapped it in cloth for their afternoon meal. The woman refused pay for the bread. Joshua lingered long enough to tell the woman about Jesus.

By evening, the two men had talked to a man in Bethsaida, whose blind eyes were healed by the spittle of Jesus. Beriah was curious, because in Jericho, a blind Bartimaeus received his sight, by Jesus only speaking to him. However, the man who received his sight in Bethsaida could practically see after Jesus touched his fingers to his own tongue and laid them gently against the blind man's eyes. The man recalled, "Jesus asked me if I could see. I told Him I saw men walking around like trees. Jesus again, put spittle on my eyes and I could see clearly. I had been able to see many years ago. But now, the first face I saw was the loving and compassionate face of Jesus. I tell you, I haven't seen anything so beautiful." Near Bethsaida was the mountain where Jesus fed the 5,000 with the five loaves and two fish.

Joshua and Beriah listened to the villagers give an account of the event. "Not only did Jesus feed 5,000 men, but women and children as well. There must have been close to 8,000 people who were fed that day," said an old man near the front of the crowd. Joshua and Beriah told the villagers about the crucifixion and resurrection of Jesus. They spent the evening telling about the strange happenings in Jerusalem. That night, they slept on the roof of a house that belonged to a man named Aaron. They were fed a good breakfast and were loaded down with provisions. Joshua and Beriah had made friends with the people of Bethsaida, so it was with heavy hearts that they said goodbye, and began their journey to Capernaum.

Following the northern plains around the coast of Galilee, they could see, in the distance, the snow covered top of Mount Hermon. The lofty mountain stood towering toward the sky, displaying the majesty of God.

Before leaving Jerusalem, Peter, the disciple of Jesus, asked Joshua and Beriah to stop by his home in Capernaum. He wanted his family and neighbors to know that he was well. Simon Peter also wanted Joshua to tell his family, that he was on a great commission, given to him by Jesus, to take the gospel to the ends of the earth.

Chapter Fourteen

Leaving Bethsaida, Joshua, Beriah, and the animals followed the plains around the northern end of the Sea of Galilee. According to the villagers, it was here, on the slopping hill, that Jesus taught them. The plains were yellow with waving grain. In places, small grape vineyards were rich in bluish and purple color, and the sweet aroma of ripening fruit permeated the air. The sky was as blue as the Mediterranean Sea. It was pleasant traveling, after the rugged terrain of the eastern slopes of the Sea of Galilee. Looking across the valley to the hills, with steep rocky sides, they could see clouds of pigeons. They flew in and out of the rugged cliffs. The local people called it 'Pigeon Valley.'

From where they were traveling, Joshua and Beriah could see a mountain that was broad in the middle and rose higher on each end. The mountains were known as Horn of Hattin. It was a rugged path, which led to the plateau. Once there, the climb was worth the effort. It had a wide, beautiful view of the meadows, checkered with the different colored crops. Far to the north, was the majestic snow-capped Mount Hermon. Below was the Sea of Galilee. It was here that Jesus told the multitude, which followed Him, the 'Blessing.'

A man named Eber invited Joshua and Beriah to spend the night with him and his wife. Sitting on the roof at a low table, the men enjoyed a rich mutton stew. Fresh vegetables and fruit were served along with freshly baked bread. Joshua and Beriah praised the wife Dinah for the delicious meal. When the dishes had been removed, Eber told about the day a great crowd had followed Jesus to a wide, level place on the hill. Jesus gathered his disciples around him and gave a talk that was both touching and unforgettable. Jesus said,

*'Blessed are the poor in spirit, for theirs is the kingdom of Heaven;
Blessed are they who mourn, for they shall be comforted;
Blessed are the meek, for they shall inherit the earth;
Blessed are those who hunger and thirst after righteousness, for they shall be filled.
Blessed are the merciful, for they shall obtain mercy;
Blessed are the pure in heart, for they shall see God
Blessed are the peacemakers, for they shall be called the Sons of God.
Blessed are those who are persecuted for righteousness sake; for theirs is the Kingdom of Heaven,
Blessed are you when they revile and persecute you and say all kinds of evil against you falsely, for my sake.'*

And Jesus ended by saying, '*Rejoice and be exceedingly glad for great is your reward in Heaven, for so they persecuted the prophets who were before you.'*

Jesus went on to say that we are the salt of the earth. He warned us about how salt loses its flavor. He said we were the light of the world. And not to put our light under a bushel. Rather, let our light so shine before men, that they may see our good works and glorify our Father in Heaven.

"I tell you, when Jesus would finish teaching, a man would have enough to think on for weeks," said Eber. The three men went over the blessings, one by one. They were deeply touched by the simple, yet deep lessons of Jesus. That night, sleeping under the stars on the roof, both, Joshua and Beriah prayed to the Savior whose love for the lowly was so great.

The following morning, the little band of pilgrims rode to Capernaum. After inquiring as to the location of Simon Peter's house, they were directed to a modest home by the side of a narrow road. Peter's wife was in the process of baking bread, and his mother-in-law was churning. Both activities were taking place in the courtyard. There was a well nearby where Joshua found a watering trough. It was here, that he drew water for all the animals, Jasper, the donkey was staked out to graze. Qasim was content to lie down to sleep under a tree. Samson and Gray Boy took the lamb, Rosa, to a small meadow that was dotted with blue flowers and tall grass.

Joshua introduced himself and Beriah, and told the women that Peter sent his greetings. During a meal and afterwards, they told all about the crucifixion of Jesus and His resurrection. They tried to explain about the troubled times in Jerusalem, and how Peter, John, and the other disciples fit into the scene. The women received the news of Peter's fulfilling Jesus' great commission with mixed emotions. "I have known from the moment Jesus called Andrew and Simon, that Simon would never turn back. Some in the village have asked how I can tolerate a husband who stays gone all the time. I really don't consider this to be their affair. But had the Master called me, I too, would have left everything and followed Him. You see Joshua, Simon Peter doesn't love me less. He was one of Jesus' chosen and he obeyed and I understand. I love Jesus too. He spent many hours in our home. Jesus no longer felt at home in Nazareth. He even said Himself, 'That a prophet is without honor in his own country.' When Jesus was in Capernaum, He felt at home and relaxed," said Peter's wife.

At last, the older woman spoke up, "We've all had some exciting times during Jesus' visits."

"Such as," asked Joshua. "One day, Jesus sat down to eat when a neighbor, over the way, came to this house, begging to see Jesus. I tried to put him off until Jesus finished eating, but the poor man was in a terrible panic. He said his daughter was gravely ill, and at death's door. Our neighbor's name was Jairus. He was known to be an upstanding man so I wasted no time telling Jesus. Later, when they returned from Jairus' house, Simon told how the young girl was already dead when they arrived. Simon said Jesus had ordered the mourners out of the house and raised the young girl from the dead." The old lady smiled a toothless smile that set a multitude of tiny wrinkles into motion. "Isn't that a marvelous story?" she asked.

Beriah, with eyes shining, had been hanging onto every word. "Yes maam, it's a wonderful story and event. Do you know of other healings?" he asked.

"I agree," said Joshua, "to give a child life and restore her to her family, is a wondrous, touching story."

"In answer to your question," said Peter's wife, "we had many, wonderful events. Why on Sabbath, our courtyard was filled with people from all over the district. Most were sick, or had brought friends and loved ones who were ill, that day they even filled our home. Some were blind, others lame or infirmed. There was even a child that was demon possessed. Jesus made deaf ears hear and dumb tongues to speak. That particular day, four men came carrying their friend on a stretcher, but couldn't even get to the door. So what did they do? They climbed to the top of our roof, began tearing at the tiles and let their friend down through the hole – right in front of Jesus!"

By now Beriah could hardly contain himself, "Did He heal the man?" he asked.

"He sure did," smiled Peter's wife. "And everyone else that had come that day."

Peter's mother-in-law picked up the story. "Peter told us about Jesus healing a young boy who was demon possessed. The boy foamed at the mouth, threw himself down on the ground, rolled around and then become ridged. Jesus rebuked the evil spirit and commanded it to come out. When the demon left the body, the boy became as dead. But when he came to, he was no longer deaf and dumb, but was normal. The father was ecstatic. Peter said when Jesus would see the lame and sick healed, He would smile with enjoyment."

Mrs. Simon picked up the story of Jesus, "I believe He showed more compassion for the blind and the lepers. Peter said sometimes the lepers had body parts already rotted off."

"Rotted off?" asked Beriah.

Nodding Mrs. Simon continued, "Yes Beriah, some were missing ears or noses. Others had fingers and toes to drop off. More severe ones had lost hands or feet. It's a slow, horrible, and painful death that just rots your body." Beriah's eyes had filled with tears and they finally overflowed. "We could tell you stories about Jesus' wonderful miracles for days. And the Elders and Pharisees, at the synagogue, would find fault with Jesus for healing on a Sabbath."

At this point, Joshua broke into the conversation. "I find the hypocritical Elders and Pharisees to gag at a gnat and swallow a camel when it comes to the laws of the Sabbath. I hope that Jesus put them down."

"He sure did," laughed Peter's mother-in-law. "Jesus said that it was lawful to water your oxen and asses on the Sabbath. And He felt that mankind was more important than these." And with this, she broke into peals of laughter and slapped her bony knees. "They couldn't come up with an answer to that." She continued to laugh at the way Jesus outwitted the leaders of the Synagogue. Her laughter was so infectious that Joshua and Beriah joined in. During the next few days, Peter's family told them about Jesus' healing the Nobleman's son, also about the healing of the man with dropsy. There was a woman infirmed for eighteen years, healed by the power of God. On and on, the women told of healings and miracles of Christ. Each day, the women would recall more events. After five days in Peter's home, Joshua and Beriah reluctantly took their leave.

By passing Nazareth, they traveled to the outskirts of Nain; there, they located the home of Big John, the fisherman. It was from Big John that they learned about Jesus helping a widow woman in the village of Nain. "It was the talk of the countryside," said the fisherman. "This poor widow's only son died. She did what any Jewish mother would do. With the help of some neighbors, she had her son bathed, dressed, and laid out in a new coffin. The custom is to bury the dead before sundown. But the broken-hearted mother refused. Instead, they sat up with him three nights. The rabbi came and spoke the proper words and prayed. After three days, the funeral procession was on the way to the cemetery. Picture this; there was a cart with the coffin, the chief mourners, and most of the villagers following, when they met Jesus.

Now Jesus saw the broken-hearted mother and was filled with compassion."

"What did Jesus do?" asked Beriah.

"He did something alright. To everyone's surprise, Jesus stopped the procession and ordered the son to arise," said Big John.

"Arise," interjected Joshua. "But how can a dead man arise?"

Laughing, Big John said, "But that's the miracle. The young man was no longer dead. He sat up in the coffin. Looked around in amazement at the funeral procession and hurriedly scrambled out onto the road. Amid hugs, laughter, and cheers the funeral turned into a whole village celebration of the area. It lasted for three days."

Joshua was smiling, "I don't blame that young fellow for scrambling out of the coffin."

"What did Jesus do?" asked Beriah.

"What did He do? Why He just smiled and went on down the road," said Big John.

Beriah was thrilled by Big John's story. At last, Beriah said with reverence, "What a wonderful Lord we serve."

"That we do Beriah," said Big John, "That we do."

The following day Big John had his son to watch the animals while Joshua and Beriah spent the day on the Sea of Galilee. It was a beautiful sun-drenched day. Off on the horizon, the sky was translucent blue, sea gulls filled the air with their cries and movement. The lakeshore had several boats drawn up in the sand. Other fishermen were busy, some were getting their catch or mending their nets, and others were mending their sails. Birds waddled along the beach harvesting tid-bits that the fishermen would throw away. On shore, the pelicans scooped up large beakful of fish parts. All in all it was an exciting hive of activity.

Near the shore, grebes floated and dived for fish and crayfish. To Beriah, they looked like small floating ducks. A few yards further, one mother had a nest of three fluffy chicks hidden in the bushes. Beriah didn't touch the nest, but was thrilled as he watched the grayish and brown baby chicks. Beriah was sure he would treasure the wonders of this day forever. Watching Big John and his men haul in nets of fish was a thrilling experience. The breeze was just enough to ripple the water. The men were in a jovial mood. Shortly before noon, Big John ordered the fishing boat to shore. Time and time again, the nets were cast into the water, and came back full of wriggling, flopping fish. By mid-day the boat was filled to capacity. It was here on the sandy beach, a fire was built to roast the fish. Beriah and Joshua enjoyed the food as they watched fluffy clouds float over the blue waters. It was with reluctance that Joshua and Beriah bid their friends goodbye.

Leaving the village of Nain, Joshua and Beriah turned back toward the northwest. They traveled over the rocky terrain and crossed washed out ravines made by seasonal freshets. They followed a winding, hilly trail. The landscape was dotted with blue, yellow, and white flowers, which intermingled with the tall waving grass. Scrub oaks, cedar, acacia, and an occasional sycamore grew in small groves, giving travelers welcome shade.

The animals forged ahead but returned often to check on Rosa. Rosa still rode Jasper when she tired. And a bond had grown between the donkey and the lamb. By the time Joshua and Beriah arrived in Nazareth, both were filled with fatigue. They spent the night in a small cave and felt very much at home. Thinking on this, Beriah began to miss his little, private cavern back in Jerusalem. The following day they arrived in the village of Nazareth.

Following Big John's directions, they found the carpenter shop of Joseph. The shop was only worked part-time since Joseph had died. At the death of her husband, Mary had turned the shop over to her younger sons; James, Joses, Simon, and Jude. They, in turn, left it to follow their elder brother's teachings and commandments. But it was not until Jesus rose from the dead, that they truly believed in Him. Jesus' sisters told Joshua and Beriah about their older brother's compassion, and His loving character. They explained about the village children following Jesus around. They were in His lap, between His knees, and around His feet. The children felt free to wrap their arms around His neck from behind Him. "Children, animals, the elderly – they all adored Him.

Everyone loved Jesus, except the powers of evil; including that of the Synagogue. They accused our brother of speaking blasphemy," said the eldest sister. "I said it was nothing but hogwash. They always wanted to find something wrong with Jesus. They were so hypocritical."

"Why did they accuse Jesus?" asked Joshua.

The eldest sister replied, "Jesus went to the synagogue on the Sabbath and there was delivered to Him the scroll of the prophet Isaiah to read. He found the place where it was written,

> '*The Spirit of the Lord is upon Me.*
> *Because He has anointed me to preach*
> *the gospel to the poor. He has sent*
> *Me to heal the broken-hearted, to preach*
> *deliverance to the captives, and recovering*
> *sight to the blind, to set at liberty, them that*
> *are bruised, to preach the acceptable year*
> *of our Lord.*'

And He closed the roll and gave it back to the Scribe He began to say to them, 'This day is the scriptures fulfilled in your ears. Verily, I say to you, No prophet is accepted in his own country.' And the entire synagogue was filled with wrath and they raised up to cast Him out of the city. They were always trying to set traps for Him. Even here, in our own village, He was an outcast."

"Well, at least they didn't try to trick Jesus with coins like they did in Jerusalem," said the younger of the women.

"What trick was that?" asked Joshua.

"One of the Priest's cohorts ask Jesus if they should pay taxes to Caesar. Jesus asked them whose head was on the coin and the man said Caesar's. So Jesus said, 'Render then to Caesar that which belongs to him. And render to God, that which belongs to God.' Wasn't that wonderful wisdom?" smiled the sister.

"It sure was," laughed Joshua. As the sisters talked about their half-brother Jesus, their eyes sparkled and their voices were filled with love. The sisters were aware that Joseph was their natural father. As the sisters talked, it was evident that this was a close-knit family. A family filled with love and understanding.

The eldest sister began speaking again, "Only once did my brothers take offence with Jesus. They went to see Him and there was a large gathering around the house. My brother Jude sent a message to Jesus, by a servant, saying His mother and brothers were outside. Jesus said, 'Who is my mother; and whom are my brothers?' Pointing to His disciples, He said, 'Here are my brothers. For whoever does the will of my Father in Heaven, is my brother, sister, and mother.' Our brothers took offence to that and felt slighted, but not our mother. She was not hurt. For in her heart she cherished a secret of Jesus' destiny as told by the angel messenger years ago."

As the morning progressed, the sisters began to try to narrow down the wonderful stories of Jesus. The eldest of the two said she believed one of the most heart wrenching healings was the one of which their brother, James, told. It concerned ten lepers.

"Ten lepers? Did Jesus heal them one by one?" asked Beriah.

The sister smiled and said, "No Beriah, He healed them all at once."

Joshua was puzzled like Beriah. "That's quite a feat, to heal ten lepers at the same time, considering what leprosy does to the body," said Joshua

"Did He lay hands on them?" asked Beriah.

"No, Jesus just told them to go and show themselves to the priest," the sister said.

"I don't understand," said Beriah.

"Well then, we'll tell you as James told it to us." The sisters spent a great deal of time giving Beriah and Joshua the details of that great miracle. Even to the point that only one of the cleansed lepers thought enough to return and give Jesus thanks

"Only one?" asked Beriah.

"Yes, just one," said the sister. "You see Beriah, even though they were all healed, the spread of leprosy stopped, the Samaritan, who returned to tell Jesus thank you, got not only the healing, but the miracle as well. Jesus was so touched by the man's gratefulness, that Jesus told him to go his way, for he was made whole. Beriah, the man's limbs began to grow back! His nose returned and his arms were back on him. Everything that leprosy destroyed was miraculously returned to him!"

"Praise God!" shouted Joshua.

"Yes, Praise God indeed!" echoed Beriah. That's a marvelous story," declared Beriah. "It's a good lesson on the benefits we have from thankfulness, praise, and worship."

"One of my favorite stories," said the younger sister, "is about the faith of the Canaanite woman. Jesus had withdrawn Himself to the region of Tyre and Sidon, when the Canaanite woman begging for a cure for her daughter who was suffering terribly from demon possession approached them. Jesus heard, but did not immediately answer her. She kept calling, 'Lord, Son of David, have mercy on me. My daughter is suffering terribly from demon possession.' James said Jesus wouldn't even answer her a word. But she kept on begging. The disciples wanted to send her away because she was annoying them. At last, Jesus said to her, 'Woman, it's not right to take the children's bread and feed it to the dogs.'"

"Dogs?" said a shocked Beriah. "Do you mean Jesus called the Canaanite woman a dog? Didn't He have compassion on her?"

"Beriah," said the youngest sister, "the term Jesus used when He said 'children' was referring to the children of Israel. The Jews refer to the Gentiles as 'dogs.' The woman knew the context of the reference, but it did not deter her. She said 'Yes Lord, but even the dogs eat the crumbs that fall from their master's table.' Jesus was pleased with her answer. He smiled and said, 'Great is your faith' and He healed them both."

Next, Beriah and Joshua were told about the miracle at Cana. There, at a wedding, Jesus made wine at mother's request. That wine was the sweetest that anyone had ever tasted. It was the purest of the vine. John told one of the most recent stories the sisters heard after Jesus ascended into Heaven. He and his brother James, and their friend Simon Peter, had accompanied Jesus up Mount Tabor. Here before their very eyes, Jesus had transfigured into a radiant figure. His face shone like the sun, and His clothes became white as the light. And, even Moses and Elijah appeared and talked with Jesus. While they were talking, a cloud enveloped them and a voice said from the cloud, 'This is my Son, whom I love; with Him I am well pleased. Listen to Him!' John said they were so scared that when they heard the voice of God, they fell face down on the ground. Then Jesus came and touched them and said, 'Get up, and don't be afraid.' Can you imagine being on the same mountain with a transfigured Jesus, Moses, and Elijah, hearing the voice of God at the same time? Of course, no one could.

The following day, Joshua, Beriah, Qasim, Samson, Gray Boy, and Rosa were ready to leave Nazareth. Before leaving the little town, Joshua and Beriah took time to look around one last time. Already, women were at the well with their water pots. A man, who was a dyer, was hanging his cloth out to dry. The rings of the smithy hammer against the anvil could be heard in the clear morning air. A potter threw clay on his wheel and begun to form a jug. Women were washing wool and the carpenter's shop was still closed. Nearby, a man was working his lathe. Goats were being milked and children were at play.

Off in the distance, stood the majestic snow capped Mount Hermon. And farther away, the sky was a soft purple, and the tip of the Mediterranean Sea could be seen. At the base a little town, could be seen, the meadows in their checkered board outlay of different colored crops. And not far away, was the Sea of Galilee, with its hills and meadows and sandy beaches. Palm trees waved in the breeze, and old men gathered under a myrtle tree. The smell of fresh baked bread and roasting meat mingled with the sweetness of grapes, flowers, and figs. It was a poignant moment for Joshua and Beriah as they tried to absorb the sights, sounds and the aroma that must have assailed Jesus' nostrils as He walked these narrow streets. Then, slowly, they descended the steep, winding trail.

Chapter Fifteen

Ever since the Athene left the port of Athens, the weather stayed cool and balmy. The sun shone each day, however, and the wind filled the sails. Heber returned to the kitchen with Phelix, while Adonis swabbed decks against his father's wishes. When he was off duty, men wanting to hear more about this Jesus who had overcome the grave would surround Adonis. After all, wasn't death what every man feared? Didn't everyone want to know that there was a better life waiting for them on the other side of the veil? While Adonis told stories and taught the way of salvation to those on the upper deck, Ahaz was teaching to those below deck. Ahaz, the little Jewish man, was again asked to continue with the genealogy of his people. A rough looking sailor, to the right, yelled, "Hey Jew boy, you left off when Abraham had Isaac. Now go on and tell us more of your history." The sailor's request was echoed around the deck.

Ahaz looked at Phaidon, the Captain of the oarsmen, for permission. Phaidon nodded, "Go ahead Ahaz, I'm as anxious to hear more stories as the other men."

Ahaz secured his oar and stepped out into the front and center of the deck. This gave everyone a chance to see him as he talked. Though Ahaz was small in stature, he had a nice resounding voice. He spoke so every man could hear. Ahaz resumed the genealogy of Abraham. "Abraham had been chosen by God to be the father of a great nation. However, he and his wife Sarah had no children." Ahaz told all the story of Abraham and Sarah's life together. "God had promised Abraham and Sarah a son in their old age. Sarah, in her frustration, gave her Egyptian handmaid to Abraham. It was custom in that day that the handmaiden's baby would belong to her mistress." There were some hoot and catcalls in the crowd at this statement.

"My old woman would never stand for that!" yelled one sailor.

"Nor mine!" said another.

"It doesn't seem fair to the handmaid, to let her do all the suffering and then take away her baby," said a tenderhearted Dionysoin.

Ahaz waited until all was quiet, and then he continued. He told the sailors about Hagar giving birth to Ishmael, the contention between Hagar and Sarah, Isaac's birth, and the lineage of Isaac. On and on, and what seemed like hours, the sailors listened to Ahaz's recount of the Jewish nation. From the twelve tribes of Israel to Boaz and Ruth to even going back to the creation of the earth. Ahaz told them about Noah and the flood that destroyed all living things except for Noah and his family. At the end of the great flood story, Ahaz returned to his oar. Amid groans and the sailors begging for more stories, Ahaz simply said, "Later."

On the upper deck, Alexander Palamos watched the hardened sailors gather around his son's feet on their off duty time. Gradually, he began to stand on the fringe of the gathering so he could hear what this strange, mature son of his was saying. Alexander was surprised to discover that Adonis was quite an orator. However, he couldn't bring himself to believe that Jesus was crucified and came back from the dead.

It was a wonderful story but hard to believe. Yet, Alexander listened carefully to the miracles performed by Jesus. How could a mere man cause the lame to walk, the deaf to hear, and the blind to see; unless He was some kind of god? No mortal man had the power to cleanse lepers, drive away evil spirits, and what? Even raise the dead? Alexander's mind went around and around, trying to figure out this man called Jesus. And what kind of power does this Jesus yield over my son? Yet, Alexander saw that Adonis was made the better for it. But like a magnet pulling metal, Alexander continues to stand closer to hear the lessons.

One morning, Phelix the cook, asked Heber if he knew anything about this Jesus that the men were talking about. Heber said that he did, and he started from the time he entered Jerusalem after the crucifixion and resurrection of Jesus from the dead. "Phelix, I know it's hard to believe, but when Jesus died, there was great earthquake and the graves were split asunder and sealed tombs were opened. Some of the dead were seen walking about in the city."

"I saw the open graves and tombs with missing bodies. When Jesus was on the cross around the noon time hour, a blackness fell on Jerusalem as black as the night. The people were terrified. Even today, there's great trouble in that city. The Roman soldiers are arresting anyone who professes to be a believer in Christ Jesus. But Jesus told his followers to take his word to the entire world. This is what Adonis and I are going to do," Heber said.

"Hmm, We'll talk about this later," said Phelix as he returned to his cooking. As Phelix stirred the cooking stew, his mind was stirring up images of Heber's stories.

That afternoon, Ahaz was again telling the stories of his people. He was telling the sailors in great detail about Sodom and Gomorrah and God's destruction of those wicked cities. "There is nothing left to show the wicked cities ever existed," said Ahaz. "God surely doesn't want men to desire men or beasts. Nor does He want women to desire women, or relations outside of marriage. Drunkenness and sexual perversions go against God's plan for man. So, when people will not turn away from their sinful lifestyles, God will judge their evil deeds. The wrath of God has been poured out, in times past, against the wicked and their offspring; including their animals."

Late that evening, when the sailors were gathered around his feet, Adonis retold the story of the mighty rushing wind of the Holy Spirit. Part of the men had heard the story and requested it to be told to their friends. At their request, Adonis explained that Jesus said He would send another comforter, who would be our helper, to guide and comfort us in times of need. "He is known as the Holy Spirit," said Adonis.

An old sailor asked, "How can we get this wonderful helper to live in us?"

"Yes," said the others, "and speak up so we can hear you."

Adonis began, "First, you must repent of your sins and confess the Lord Jesus Christ as your personal Savior. We must live our lives the way Christ teaches us to live them. When we confess our sins, Jesus is just and right to forgive us of our wrongs and sins. We are pardoned and washed clean by the shed blood of Christ. Then we can receive the indwelling of the Holy Ghost. Because sin no longer reigns in our being."

That evening, with the Mediterranean Sea lapping against the ship, and the stars shining brightly overhead, a group of sailors bent their knees in prayer, on the ship's deck. Each man silently made his confession for his sins. And asked the Lord Jesus to be his Lord and Savior. Alexander Palamos observed from the fringes of the group.

There was rejoicing among the sailors. To be a son of the mighty God was an exciting, exhilarating feeling. Adonis said to the happy men, "Jesus commanded that we acknowledge Him in public and be baptized. So when we get to the port, I'll baptize you." As the evening progressed, Adonis told of Jesus' teachings that he had heard from Joshua and Simon Peter, a disciple of the Lord's. Alexander and Captain Strabo discussed the strange stories that Adonis had been teaching.

Captain Strabo said, "Alex, I have listened to Adonis ever since we left Israel. And now I find myself listening to him again. I have come to the conclusion that Jesus is the Son of Almighty God." Alexander began shaking his head. Captain Strabo raised his hand, "Wait friend, hear me out. I too, grew up in Greece, where we worship many gods. Wooden gods, stone gods, brass and golden images-but they are just that. These 'gods' a mere creations that a potter or a glass blower conjures up. What do they or have they done for us? Do they heal the sick? Do they, say, give a blind person back their sight? Alex, can they even raise the dead? My friend, when we look at these images, they are just innate objects that can do nothing. I don't know about you

Alex, but I need this God that Adonis has been speaking of, a God that can do all things. And when I stop sailing this ship of life, I want to have a harbor of rest on the peaceful shore of Heaven. What about you old friend? Shall we secure our passage to Heaven by Jesus Christ, our Savior?" With tears flowing down their faces, the two men knelt and gave their lives to Jesus, who in the sojourning will chart their course in life.

Strangely, Alexander Palamos felt as if the weight of the world had been lifted from his shoulders. Gone was the terrible burden of depression. He wanted to shout, sing, and dance. Later, when Adonis saw his father, he knew something monumental had happened. Alexander's shoulders were held back and he walked with a spring in his steps. He was laughing and talking to the sailors, whom he usually avoided. But what was most striking was his overall countenance. His face was radiant. He looked ten years younger. Adonis knew his father had accepted Jesus as Lord of his life. He walked into his father's open arms and unashamedly wept. No words were needed between father and son.

As the Athene slowly made her way across the beautiful Mediterranean Sea, it became a ship filled with joy. Each day a few more men accepted Jesus as their Lord and Savior. There were praises on their lips instead of curses. There was willingness to lend a helping hand; as well as, a feeling of brotherhood. While below deck, Ahaz continued his stories of great men and women of God. "What are these rules or commandments, as you call them, that God laid down to Moses for His children?" asked Melos. Ahaz slowly began to enumerate them:

1. Thou shalt have no other gods before me.
2. Thou shalt not worship any graven image
3. Thou shalt not take the Lord thy God's name in vain
4. Remember the Sabbath day, to keep it holy
5. Honor thy father and mother
6. Thou shalt not kill
7. Thou shalt not commit adultery
8. Thou shalt not steal

9. Thou shalt not bear false witness
10. Thou shalt not covet.

"These, my friends, are God's laws for direction and guidance. These commandments were written with the finger of God," said Ahaz. There was no more boredom on the Athene.

Above, on the ship's deck, stood Adonis; teaching the men how to give thanks and praise unto God. The next morning when the sailors saw the shores of Joppa, a round of shouts filled the air. Amid the shouts, they reminded Adonis to not forget to baptize them. Slowly, they lowered the sails, and the Athene sailed safely into port. The gangplank was lowered and Adonis and his father, Alexander, set foot on Israel's soil.

That evening, Adonis baptized ninety new converts, including his father, Captain Strabo, and Phelix the cook. On the ship that night, they had a great feast and a time of rejoicing. The following morning, Adonis rented camels and their owners. Adonis and Alexander Palamos turned in the direction of Jerusalem to find the lost son and brother.

Chapter Sixteen

After leaving Nazareth, Joshua and Beriah went to Tiberias, by the Sea of Galilee. This was a beautiful, thriving city. The Galilian area was ruled by one of King Herod the Great's sons. Tiberias became the capital for King Antipas. Here he built a castle with an oriental influence in its design. Tiberias had hot springs, the Sea of Galilee, and was flooded with fruits and vegetables all year long. It was also a retreat from the troubles in Jerusalem. Joshua and Beriah only stayed long enough to purchase supplies and went on their way through the rugged land of Samaria.

There were many tales about the bandits who roamed this area and robbed lone travelers. There were many caves in these rocky mountains for the bandits to hide and live. After much discussion and prayer, Joshua and Beriah decided to travel on. In order to travel in Jesus' footsteps, they would need to stop at Sychar, at the foot of Mount Ebal. It was here that Jesus had talked to a woman who came to Jacob's well. Jesus asked the woman for water. She was surprised, because Jewish men had nothing to do with the Samaritan people. Jesus told the woman he could give her water and she would never thirst again.

A few miles before they reached Sychar, they ran into trouble. It happened along a lonely stretch of road in a rough looking section of country. The hills were barren and pocked with caves. Out of the underbrush, on each side of the road, rough looking men surrounded them. "Peace be with you, my brothers," said Joshua as though they were long lost friends. The leader of the clan was a big man. But one look told Beriah that he was a mighty sick man. The leader's face was flushed and was beaded with sweat. His eyes were glassy and he shivered as though it was zero temperature weather.

Without waiting to find out what the bandits wanted, Beriah had Qasim to kneel. With his staff in hand, he hobbled up to the sick man. "Friend," he said, "you're a sick man. I'm a follower of Jesus of Nazareth. He has blessed me with the gift of healing. Would you like to be healed?" By now Joshua was standing beside Jasper. He was amazed at Beriah. It seemed when there was a sick person or animal, Beriah had no fear. The rest of the men were watching Beriah in amazement. This was not the usual reaction of terror they were accustomed to getting. "I'm Beriah and this is my friend Joshua. What is your name?" asked Beriah.

"Name's Ebez," grunted the sick man.

"I'll tell you what Ebez," said Beriah, "sit over here in the shade. Is there anyone else in your group ill?"

Ebez answered, "My wife, my mother, eight other adults, and three children."

"Beside the fever, what other ailments do you have?" asked Beriah.

"Vomiting and – well, diarrhea," answered Ebez.

"It sounds like you've gotten hold of some bad water. First, I'll set about healing the sick. Then you boil the water before using it. And find another source of water." Quickly, Beriah rubbed his hands down the staff and laid them on the sick man's fevered brow. In a commanding voice, he said, "Be healed in the name of Jesus!" Ebez's body jerked and he fell flat on his back as though a bolt of lightening hit him. Quickly, Ebez's men drew knives from their sheathes.

Joshua held up his hand and yelled, "Wait friends! Beriah is only driving the sickness out of Ebez's body." Slowly, they put their knives back in their sheaths. Ebez lay flat on his back. Beriah continued to touch the staff, then the unconscious man. He rubbed his head, his eyes, and his ears.

Motioning to two men, Beriah said, "Get on each side of Ebez. When I say arise, you slowly lift him up. He may be dazed for a few moments but that will pass." Reaching out his staff, Beriah touched Ebez above his heart. "Arise Ebez and be healed," commanded Beriah. Ebez opened his eyes and the two men lifted him to his feet.

Puzzled, Ebez said, "Did I sleep too long?" He yawned and stretched and said, "I feel great! In fact, I haven't felt this good in years." There was a roar of laughter as his men told how Beriah had healed him.

"No not by me," said Beriah, "but by Jesus Christ. I am only a tool He uses to bring about healing. Now you can lead me to the other sick people so Jesus can heal them too."

"They're up the hill, in two caves," said Ebez.

"Then I'll ride my donkey instead of the camel. Jasper is a sure-footed little animal," said Beriah. Joshua helped Beriah onto Jasper's back and then rounded up the other animals to go up the hill. It was a strange looking group that climbed the winding path toward the caves. First went Ebez, and then Beriah and Jasper, following them came Joshua, Qasim, the lamb Rosa, the wolf, and Samson, the dog. Following behind these was an assortment of dirty, rough-looking men.

Once in the pine torch-lit cave, Beriah was appalled by the stench and the filth. He ordered the sick to be carried outside into the fresh air. "That cave is working alive with multiplying germs. Is there another cave where you can live until this one is cleaned and aired out? Ebez if your family is not in clean surroundings, you will only keep infecting each other. Burn all the mats, boil all the clothing in clean water, and don't forget to do the same with your bedclothes. Get rid of all the water and food that is not in a sealed container. In the future don't wash clothes near your drinking well. You will need to dig a new well and fill this one up with dirt and rocks."

Ebez looked around at the men. "You heard the healer! Carry the sick outside. Then bring everything outside and burn it. We have shovels in the other cave. Start shoveling until you lower the floor of the cave a foot." Soon two women and three very sick children were carried out into the fresh air.

"Where are the other eight adults?" asked Beriah.

"In the cave to our left," said Ebez.

"Then send your men to get them into fresh air. Next, clean their cave in the same way as this one," said Beriah. Ebez issued orders, and the hill became a hive of activity.

Quickly, Beriah set to work on healing the sick. Within minutes the women were well and on their feet, directing the clean up. The children were well, laughing, and chasing each other up and down the hill. There was much rejoicing and thanks from Ebez and his family. Next, Beriah, through the majestic name of Jesus, healed the eight bandits. Later, Joshua and Beriah sat down on the side of the hill and told the band of men about the crucifixion, burial, and resurrection of Jesus. They told them that Jesus was the Son of God and had ascended into Heaven. They told of the promises of Christ, returning for His own. Beriah told the men that Jesus is God's gift to mankind and that, by accepting Jesus, they would have eternal life. "So I say to each of you, choose you this day whom you will serve. Will it be God, who will lead you into Heaven, or will it be Satan, who will lead you into the pits of hell?"

Beriah added, "Everyone here is able-bodied. There's not a one among you who could not get honest work. Think over what Joshua said. It's a known fact that every man will die. Is sinning today more important then where you will spend eternity? I, for one, want to live forever in that wonderful land Jesus promised. It's a land where there will be no more tears, nor sorrow. In a time when the lion will lie down with the lamb. Your swords will be turned into plowshares. Beautiful flowers will be more fragrant and bountiful as never before."

Many heads were bowed and many eyes flooded with tears. A short time later, Joshua asked if anyone wanted to give their lives to Jesus. Ebez's family was the first to say yes. Then one by one, over half the men knelt and asked forgiveness for their sins.

The men cooked a meal for everyone who was out on the side of the hill. While the meat was roasting, Ebez's eight-year-old son walked up to Beriah. "Do you heal animals?" asked the young boy. Before Beriah could answer, Ebez scolded him for bothering Beriah.

"He's no bother," said Beriah. "Do you have a sick animal? asked Beriah.

El-don, Ebez's son replied, "It's my goat and my donkey."

"Take me to them El-don," said Beriah.

Together the two of them followed a trail around the hill to a cliff stable. There lying on their sides, were two very sick animals. Beriah touched them with his staff and commanded them to be healed in the name of Jesus. Slowly, the little, brown nanny goat got to her feet, swished her tail, and went to El-don, who put his arms around her neck. Next, the little donkey got to his knees and then to his feet. He shook himself and let out a happy bray. Beriah and El-don broke out laughing at the frisky little donkey. Together, Beriah, El-don, the donkey and the goat returned to the circle of men.

There was much rejoicing and giving praise in the camp that night. The following morning Joshua and Beriah were on the road to Sychar. They had rejected Ebez's offer of an escort. Joshua's answer was simple, "The Lord will provide." There were handshakes and hugs as the brothers in Christ departed.

After spending a few hours in Sychar and drinking from Jacob's well, they located the Samaritan woman whom Jesus had the conversation with. She had indeed been married five times and had lived with a man who was not her husband. This woman had asked Jesus for His living water and had received it. She was shocked and devastated with the news of Jesus' crucifixion. However, she was happy Jesus arose from the dead. "Jesus promised that He would return someday and take us all back to Heaven with Him. Hold onto your faith. Get involved with someone's home ministry. Tell others about Jesus." On and on they went, testifying to the woman.

In the afternoon, Joshua and Beriah went to the city of Shechem. Here they visited the tomb of Joseph, who had risen from a slave, to being the Governor of Egypt. When the children of Israel left Egypt, it was Joseph's request that they take his body with them and bury it near his father's home.

Joshua brought provisions. The next day, they traveled to the town of Modim. There, they paid their respects to the Maccabees. While visiting the tomb, Beriah said, "Jobah told me a little about the history of the Maccabees and how they tried to take control of Israel out of foreign hands. What can you tell me about them Joshua?"

"It would take months to tell you their heroic deeds, but I will tell you a few things. The Syrian King, Antiochus IV, attempted to stamp out Judaism in Jerusalem. He took over the temple and stole the golden candlesticks, the gold cups and bowl, censors, the table of shew bread, and the golden altar. He took all the valuables and hidden treasures. All of these things belonging to the Temple of God Jehovah, King Antiochus removed and put them in his capital city of Antioch," said Joshua.

"How horrible," said Beriah.

"Well wait-it gets worse," said Joshua "A heathen altar was set up, and they sacrificed swine."

At this, Beriah gasped aloud. "Why that profanes the temple!"

"Yes Beriah, God's Temple. The temple was then rededicated to the Olympian Zenus. These heathens were more interested in a sports deity than the one true God. Judas Maccabaeus, with his brothers, raised an army and recaptured Jerusalem. The temple was cleansed, purified, and rededicated to our Lord God. This revolt happened in 170 B.C., before Christ was born. In the autumn of 169, some Jerusalemites began to see things in the sky," said Joshua.

"What kind of things?" asked Beriah.

"Now this is hard to believe, but for forty days, people in Jerusalem saw golden-clad horsemen charging through the air, in companies fully armed. Things were terrible in Jerusalem for a long time. Once, the Syrians rode thirty-two, battle trained elephants, into battle. The elephants were clad in leather armor. The elephants carried troops in wooded cages. The Syrians fed the elephants wine to make them crazed beasts, and to charge ferociously. Judas Maccabaeus' older brother killed the largest elephant, thinking it carried the king; however, it didn't," Joshua said. "Sadly though, Eleazar Maccabaeus was killed when the dying elephant fell on him. Later Judas' got rid of the temple prostitutes, cleansed and rededicated the temple. Later, in an uprising, Judas was killed. His brother, Jonathon became the leader of the army. Much later, he was killed. Both were brought here to be buried with their family. Jerusalem has a long and troubled history. It will only see a lasting peace when Jesus comes back to set up His kingdom on the throne of David."

Beriah agreed with Joshua. "There seems to be no peace for Jerusalem."

Modim was only nineteen miles from Jerusalem. Here they spent the night in a small cave. The next morning, they were up bright and early and headed in the direction of Emmaus, where Jesus first appeared to His disciples after the resurrection. Two days later, the tired pilgrims stopped at the well in Emmaus to water their animals. While there, two women came for water.

"Have you come far?" they asked Joshua and Beriah.

"Oh yes," said Beriah, "we have been five months following the footsteps of Jesus."

"Where did you go?" asked the youngest woman.

Joshua gave the women the full itinerary of their travels and what they had encountered. On and on he went, giving the women the accounts of the things he and Beriah had witnessed. Joshua concluded, "...and from there we visited the tomb of the Maccabees in Modim. And now, we are here, because Jesus appeared here after his resurrection."

The two women were beside themselves with excitement. "You must come home with us. I'm Mary Magdalene and this is Rhoda. Rhoda had a child-like quality about her even though she was a full-grown woman. She simply smiled and kept her head down during the introduction. "I've been living here since the crucifixion. I come from the town of Magdala, located on the Sea of Galilee, just a little north of Tiberius. I was quite an evil woman until I met Jesus. He cast seven demons out of me. I have faithfully followed Jesus ever since. I was at the crucifixion with Mary, the mother of Jesus, and His disciple John."

"I saw you there," said Beriah. "I sat off to the side in the shade of a scrub tree. And Joshua stood on the fringe of the crowd."

"That was the saddest day in the history of the world," said Joshua.

The two women sadly agreed. "At the moment, Simon Peter, and John are resting at my house," said Mary. "I know they will want to know all about this marvelous trip."

In a short time, Joshua and Beriah were securing the animals in the field, in back of Mary's house. Then they followed the women into the modest house. And there, bigger than life was Simon Peter, eating fruit and cheese. Over to the side of the room was John, sipping on a glass of juice. Immediately, Peter was on his feet, engulfing both, Joshua and Beriah, in bear hugs. John also was glad to see his new friends and embraced them.

"Here, sit down," said Peter. "How was the trip? Did you see my family? Was tracing the footsteps of Jesus worth the effort? Tell us where all you went and what you saw."

"Peter, Peter," scolded Mary. "Slow down! First let's wash their feet and give them something to eat.'

Joshua began to laugh, "The answer is yes, yes, and yes. The trip was wonderful and I hope to do it again someday. Your family is fine. They miss you and send their love. We spent five wonderful days with your family. Your neighbors came by to meet us and they also send their best wishes."

"That's enough talk until these men have washed up and been fed." And with this, Mary Magdalene shoved the men toward the washbasins at the back of the house. Beriah and Joshua quickly washed and put on clean clothing. It felt good to have the dust and grime, of the road, out of their hair. They were also able to shave their beards. It was a different looking pair of men who sat down to a table laden with food.

Throughout the evening, and far into the night, the little group of believers talked. The women were excited about Beriah healing and rescuing Gray Boy and Qasim. They loved the story of the brave wolf and dog rescuing the little lamb. Peter smiled at the story, but was more interested in the bandits being healed and converted. "You say Beriah, through Jesus, healed a whole family and eight bandits? Then at a child's request, he climbed to a cliff stable and healed the child's goat and donkey?"

"That's right," said Joshua. "When Beriah saw the bandit leader was ill, he didn't hesitate to help him."

Simon Peter was in deep thought for a few moments. Finally, he spoke, "It seems Beriah is what Jesus would call a 'Good Samaritan.' He always puts everyone else's welfare before his own. He takes in strays and those in trouble regardless to his own safety. No such love and compassion have I found greater than his; except in our Lord Jesus Christ. Beriah, you are truly worthy to walk in Jesus' sandals, and to carry His staff." Beriah sat with his head bowed. He felt humbled by Peter's compliments. "Beriah," said Peter, "I have been curious about you since we first met. In fact, I have made a point of inquiring about you from the merchants on your street." Beriah looked up in surprise. Peter held up his hands so there would be no interruptions. "In fact, your character record is without blemish. It seems the older merchants have known you since you were four years old. That was when, let's see now, what was his name-oh yes, Old Jobah they called him, cared for you. Beriah, you are always helping others. This is a remarkable twenty-one year record."

By now, tears were streaming down the face of Beriah. Joshua began to wipe his own eyes, for he dearly loved his friend. Peter continued, "Beriah, the Lord stands ready to answer your own prayer of deliverance. You could have had it anytime, but you put the needs of others, before your own special need. Now God is going to give you a special touch. Stand with your back toward me," commanded Peter. Beriah's heart was beating fast as the seconds ticked by. As Beriah followed Peter's direction, Joshua put his hand to his mouth, to stifle his own whimpering cry. Tears filled Joshua's eyes once again, but this time they overflowed onto his cheeks. Mary and Rhoda raised their hands upward and began silently mouthing a prayer. Then, very gently, Peter began to run his hand up and down Beriah's knarled back and shoulders. Beriah's poor spine felt like a twisted, turning trail of a desert snake. Then Peter spoke in a commanding voice, "By the power given to me, thy servant, I command this warped and twisted body to be healed, in the name of Jesus!" The moment that Peter spoke the words, 'be healed!' a heat like a fire raced through Beriah's body, from the top of his crown to the bottom of his feet. Suddenly, as if an awesome light had struck him, Beriah fell to the floor.

Joshua began to cry, "Beriah, Beriah!" Beriah lay prostrate on the floor. Then-you could hear the sound of bones snapping and cracking in place!

Joshua wanted to pick his friend up, but Peter again, put forth his hand. "No Joshua, don't touch him. The power of God is upon him." And indeed Beriah's face was radiant. "Let God do His work and heal His faithful servant." Beriah was on the floor for a good twenty minutes. Slowly his body began to straighten out. Soon, what had been a four and a half foot twisted form was lying in a perfectly straight six-foot tall, well-shaped human body. There was a glorious glow about Beriah's head and a sweet smile was on his lips.

In awe, Mary looked at the young man on the floor. "He is absolutely beautiful," she whispered. "Why, he looks like one of the angels that was at Jesus' tomb."

"And Beriah is just as beautiful on the inside," said a teary-eyed Joshua.

"You're right," said Simon Peter. "It's as though the wickedness of the world never touched this young man."

"What a wonderful representative of Jesus he will be," said Joshua.

Rhoda, with her child-like mind, said, "Do you think that Beriah will be so proud of his body that he will change his way of living?"

Not thinking that Beriah had been doing work for God; already in the body that he had. "Not Beriah, he would do the good works of Jesus, if he was never healed," said Joshua.

"I agree with Joshua," said Peter. "Beriah is the type of man you meet only once in a lifetime."

Shortly thereafter, Beriah opened his eyes and sat up. He was ecstatic! "I just talked with Jesus!" he exclaimed. "He told me to take

His gospel to Greece and to heal the sick there, cast out devils, make the lame to walk, and the blind to see. Peter can you imagine Jesus choosing me, a mere cripple to do his work?"

"And you will obey His calling," said Peter.

Without hesitation, Beriah answered, "Oh yes, I told Jesus that where He lead me, I will go, even to the ends of the earth.

"Perhaps you need to get up off the floor if you're going to be one of Jesus' workers," said Peter. Slowly, Beriah stood up. His back and shoulders were perfectly straight. He looked confused. Everyone laughed and clapped their hands, as Peter said, "Beriah, you have been healed by the power of God. Jesus has made you whole, so you can carry out His Great Commission." With this, Simon Peter enveloped Beriah in his massive arms. "God go with you, my brother, and may you always remain true to our Lord Jesus Christ." Joshua put his arms around Beriah, and for the first time, since knowing his dear friend, Joshua had to practically step on his tip toes to embrace Beriah, at this Joshua began to weep uncontrollably. That night, in Mary Magdalene's humble home, they rejoiced and gave praises unto God.

Chapter Seventeen

The following morning, Joshua and Beriah, amid hugs and laughter, bade their brother and sisters in Christ goodbye. They had promised Mary, Martha, and Lazarus they would stop on their way back from following the footsteps of the Lord. So they turned in the direction of Bethany. They arrived at the house of Lazarus as it was nearing the evening meal. Here they received a wonderful welcome. The sisters and brother were happy that through Peter, Beriah had been healed. Beriah told them he had to adjust to a new way of walking. But he was quite thrilled about his miracle from Jesus.

Around the evening meal, they talked about their trip from the time they left Bethany, nearly five months ago. They had a captive audience from the time they began telling about their saga. They were telling of the journey and the people that they encountered. It was far into the morning before they made the round from start to finish. "Oh how I wish I could make such a trip," said Mary. Her eyes were shining with wonder.

To Lazarus' surprise, his sister, Martha said, "And I too, would like to follow Jesus' footsteps."

Lazarus smiled at Martha and said, "Martha, perhaps at autumn, we all can make that trip."

That night Joshua, Beriah, and Lazarus slept on the roof and under the stars. To Beriah, the heavens looked bigger and more wonderful. Beriah was having a hard time falling asleep. Finally he whispered, "Joshua, are you awake?"

"I'm awake Beriah," replied Joshua.

"Joshua when I go to Greece, will you go with me?" asked Beriah.

There was a pause, and then Joshua said, "I thought you'd never ask."

"So does that mean you're going?" Beriah asked.

Joshua said, "Beriah, when it comes to you, I am like Ruth and Naomi, 'Where thou goest, I will go. Where thou livest, I will live also.'"

"That's wonderful Joshua." Beriah simply rolled over and went to sleep. Joshua stayed awake for a long time. He couldn't let Beriah, in all his innocence, out alone in a hard, cruel world.

The following day, about noon, the strange collection of animals arrived in Jerusalem. Qasim was left at the camel caravansary for the night. Joshua said that he would take Jasper, Gray Boy, and the lamb to his uncles' stable. The friends agreed to meet at the cavern. Beriah said that he would stop by the bazaar and get supper. So the two parted for the time being.

Beriah made his way to the bazaar. People, he had traded with, did not even recognize him. One old woman said, "How did you get the cripple boy's dog?"

"The dog belongs to me," said Beriah.

"No way," she answered emphatically.

"Miss Rebecca, I am Beriah. Two days ago, Simon Peter laid hands on me and healed me," said Beriah.

"Praise be to God Almighty! I'm sorry Beriah, but I just didn't recognize you," said Rebecca.

"That's alright," laughed Beriah. "I hardly recognize myself."

Beriah bought the evening meal and a large bone for Samson. He then purchased matches and candles and headed back for the cavern. When he dropped into the crevice, he lit a candle and slowly descended the time worn steps. As he rounded the corner, where his living quarters were, it looked as though someone was there. A fire was lit and two men stood in the shadows. Samson took off in a bound and leaped into the arms of the first man. Amid slobbery kisses and barks, Adonis tried to regain his balance and stepped into the light. When Adonis saw the tall, healed Beriah, he cried, "Beriah, you're healed!" and flung his arms around Beriah's neck and wept. Beriah and Adonis stood locked in each other's arms.

At last, a wet faced Alexander Palamos stepped forward and into the light. "Nicho, my son," he cried.

Somewhere deeply buried in Beriah's mind, came those words. Stepping around Adonis, Beriah cried, "Father, I'm here!" and he fainted. Alexander and Adonis were on their knees trying to revive Beriah, when Joshua entered the chamber.

"Adonis!" he said in alarm. "What happened to Beriah?" came tumbling out of the mouth of Joshua.

Alexander Palamos stepped forward with extended hand, "I'm Adonis' and Beriah's father. In my excitement of seeing my son after twenty-one years, I cried out 'Nicho my Nicho', and Alexander broke down and wept.

Adonis picked up the story, "I had rushed forward and cried out 'Beriah, you're healed', and while we were locked into an embrace, father called out the name 'Nicho'."

"What was Beriah's reaction?" asked Joshua.

"Beriah stepped out of the embrace, and with a child-like voice, he said, 'Father, father, I'm here' and fainted." Adonis said.

Joshua nodded his head. "That name has been locked away in his brain for many years. But the lost child in Beriah knew his father's voice. Let's let Beriah come out of this slowly and then we'll get everything sorted out."

"When was Beriah healed?" asked Adonis.

"Simon Peter, through Jesus, healed him three days ago. Strangely, while he was unconscious, and being healed, he had a vision. Jesus spoke to Beriah and gave him some direction. I'll wait and let Beriah tell you about the vision," said Joshua.

A short time later, Beriah opened his eyes and looked into the face of his kneeling father. Slowly Beriah reached up and touched his father's face. "Is it really you father?"

"Yes, Nicho my son. It is me." Alexander gathered his long, lost son in his arms and rocked him like a child. There wasn't a dry eye in any of the men.

Finally, Adonis stepped forward, "Beriah, this is your father Alexander Palamos. You were christened Nicholas Palamos. When you were four years old, you were swept overboard, during a storm, from father's ship. I am not only your brother in Christ, but I am also your natural, younger brother." Joshua couldn't remember when he had seen such a reunion of love. Adonis had also purchased food. So while the Palamos family was getting acquainted, Joshua set the table and placed food and juice in the center of the packing boxes.

While everyone gathered around the table, Joshua prayed a long and heartfelt prayer of praise and thanks to God Almighty, who had orchestrated this happy reunion. "I'm curious, Mr. Palamos. How did you know Beriah was your lost son?"

"When Adonis came home, I saw a necklace around his neck. I demanded to know whose it was and how he came to acquire it," said Alexander.

"What was so important about the necklace?" asked Joshua.

Alexander replied, "Because there are only three in existence. I had a silversmith to make these coins with my mother's image on each side. A hole was punched in each. I had the coins hung on silver chains. One necklace I wear. I put one around Nicho's neck and the other one I saved for baby Adonis."

Joshua turned to Adonis, "How did you get the necklace?" he asked.

"Remember the night before I left for Greece?" said Adonis. Joshua nodded yes. "I took off my father's insignia necklace and hung it around Beriah's neck. I told Beriah if he ever changed his mind about coming to Greece, all he had to do was to show this to any Captain of my father's ships, and he would receive free passage."

Wrinkling his brow, Joshua said in a perplexed voice, "But I don't get the connection."

Suddenly the connection clicked in Beriah's mind. "I know it was the necklace I placed around Adonis' neck. I told him that it was just a loan and he was to return it someday."

Alexander nodded his head. "Yes, Beriah Nicho, I placed it on your neck myself. Have you worn it all these years?"

"No," said Beriah. "Old Jobah, who took me in, when a camel driver found me, was quite a drinker of wine. He had lost his job and self-respect as a teacher and scholar. I had been found all alone on a lonely seashore. I was covered with insect bites, cuts, and bruises. My back was broken and I was running a high fever. The camel driver strapped me on a board and then took me to Joppa. No one knew me or wanted me. The kind-hearted man brought me to Jerusalem and Jobah took me and raised me as his own son."

"Did Jobah tell you this story?" asked Joshua, who was hearing this for the first time.

"No, it was his wife, Shua, the soap maker. Jobah had entrusted her to keep the necklace until I was grown. He was afraid that he would sell the necklace in order to buy wine. Jobah had stopped drinking but he wasn't taking any chances. He thought that someday the necklace might be seen and recognized. Old Shua only told me the story and returned the necklace to me after all of you came to live with me. In fact, it was the night that you brought Peter and John home. I put the necklace on but kept it under my clothes. I was going to share my story with you, but then came Pentecost, the visit of Simon Peter, and the baptism. So the story was just pushed into the background. However, the night before Adonis and Heber left, I removed it and placed it around Adonis' neck. It was the only thing that I treasured, so I gave it to him." Beriah's unselfish love was there for everyone to see.

Later, as they sat, talking around the fire, Adonis asked Beriah if he was willing to share his vision of Jesus. Beriah's eyes filled with tears. "While my back was being healed, I left my body. An angel escorted me to the most beautiful land. Everything had such vivid colors. The flowers, the trees, and birds were breathtaking in beauty. Every leaf on the trees were singing praises to the Lord. There was such peace. Then Jesus came walking toward me, with out stretched hands. There were nail prints in His hands. He gathered me in His arms. I felt so loved and so secure. Jesus told me that He wanted me to take His word into Greece. He wanted me to teach and to heal the sick there. He told me that He would give me power to cause the lame to walk, the deaf to hear, the blind to see, and cast out demons. Jesus asked me if I was willing to go. I told Jesus that wherever He would lead me, then that's where I would go. Then I was returned and re-entered my body. Joshua has already agreed to go to Greece with me. Since he followed Jesus and knew Him, he will do better at teaching than me. However, I am learning."

The men were amazed at Beriah's vision, and his faith. Throughout the evening, Joshua related the story of following Jesus' footsteps. Adonis was so excited about Gray Boy, the wolf, and Rosa, the lamb. He was intrigued with the camel, which could cry and give kisses, considering his own experiences with contrary camels. Alex was equally impressed with the healing of the bandits. After this, Adonis told about his trip back home and about the conversion and baptizing of ninety souls, including his father, Captain Strabo, and the cook. Adonis finally asked about Simon Peter and John. "I would like for father to meet them before we return to Greece."

Peter should be teaching in the temple tomorrow. Rather, I should say today, considering the time," said Joshua.

Adonis asked, "Do you think we could attend one of the secret meetings in the cave. I would like for father to hear Thomas teach and testify."

"I'll ask some of the members. If possible, we'll attend," said Joshua.

At last Beriah spoke, "Tomorrow, I would like to introduce father to some of the merchants who have looked after my welfare since I was a little child." It was agreed that Alexander Palamos would accompany Beriah to meet his friends. "Then I'll bring father to the Temple to meet Peter." At last the men lay down to rest. Most were too excited to sleep.

Adonis arose at the break of day and hurried to buy food for breakfast. It was a glorious morning. The sky was like the colors of the rainbow. There was a cool breeze and birds were singing. It was wonderful to be alive and a follower of Jesus. Adonis sang as he returned to the cavern. Joshua woke up next and built a fire. He was in the process of heating water for shaving when Adonis arrived. "What goodies did you buy for breakfast?" asked Joshua.

Adonis had taken Beriah's leather bag and filled it with food. "I have two melons, a fresh loaf of bread, some goat cheese, cream cheese, a dozen bagels, a jar of honey, and some orange juice. I also bought some grapes and a bunch of bananas." With this said, Adonis placed his food on the table.

"Well," chuckled Joshua, "that should hold us for awhile." By the time the water was boiling for the tea, Beriah and his father crawled out of bed. Beriah and Adonis folded the bedding and tidied up around the table. By the time everyone had washed and shaved, they were ready for breakfast.

The plans of the day were already discussed. Beriah and his father were going to meet his friends, while Adonis and Joshua would check on the animals and find out when the next meeting, in the secret cave, would take place. Then all would go to the Temple to see Simon Peter and John. A short time later, the table was straightened up. The bowls and cups were washed up. A fire was made for their return. Then the men set about to carry out their plans.

First, Beriah and his father stopped by Old Shua's soap stall. Not recognizing Beriah, she asked if she could help them. Beriah smiled at the dear old woman. Then her face lit up, "My God in Heaven-you're healed Beriah! How tall and handsome you are! Praise be to God Almighty!" With this she rushed around the stall and embraced the tall, young man. Before Beriah could introduce his father, Shua began calling all the shopkeepers. "Hiram, Elon, Hur, Tola, Amos, Nadab-come quick! Rosh, where are you!" she shouted. Beriah laughed at Shua's excitement. The merchants came running out from their shops. They were concerned at the way Shua called for them. "Look, look," she cried. "God in His mercy has heard our prayers. Beriah's been healed!" All eyes slowly left Shua and they fixed them on Beriah. Beriah's friends literally mobbed him. There were hugs, kisses, handshakes, and tears.

Rosh, the weaver, with tears dropping onto his beard, held Beriah in his arms. "Jesus has rewarded you for all your kindness and faith."

Beriah introduced his father to the merchants. "I've come to thank Miss Shua for returning my son to me."

Shua was surprised, "How did I do that, Mr. Palamos?"

"By saving the necklace, that was around Beriah's neck when he was washed overboard from my ship," said Alexander.

It was well over two hours before Beriah and his father said goodbye to his faithful friends. "When will you be leaving Beriah?" asked Tola.

Beriah turned to his father, "We'll leave at the end of the week." There were more hugs, kisses, and tears.

Alexander told Beriah to give the necklace to Tola. "If, in the event, things become to dangerous here in Jerusalem, come to Greece. Just present this necklace to any of the Captains of my ships. I will help you all get established in your own homes, and help you set up your own business. I want to thank you all from the bottom of my heart, for taking care of my son." Beriah then bade a sad farewell.

Next Beriah and his father went to the Temple Mount. As they entered the courtyard, they could hear Peter in a commanding voice, telling the people to repent of their sins and accept Jesus Christ as their Lord and Savior. "Jesus will return someday and set up His kingdom here in Jerusalem and on the throne of David."

The Priest and Saducees were irate. Peter had become a bigger thorn in their side, since the resurrection. Jesus' followers were growing in number and the Priests and Saducees were unable to stop it. Even the Roman soldiers were beginning to listen. Later Beriah introduced his father to Simon Peter. Alexander Palamos repeatedly thanked Peter for healing his son. "I did not heal Beriah. It was Jesus that did the healing. I was only the vessel in which He worked through. And I would say the healing went to a mighty deserving recipient." Adonis and Joshua joined Beriah and Alexander on the Temple Mount. Alexander invited Peter and John to visit them in Greece anytime they wished.

After the evening meal, Joshua told about a planned meeting in the cavern when it became dark. All four men decided to attend. In the meantime, Beriah brought up the subject on what to do with the animals. "Joshua, do you think your uncle would take care of them?" asked Beriah.

"I'm sure he will," said Joshua. Beriah's eyes filled with tears at the prospect of never seeing his 'other friends'. "I feel like I'm betraying their love and devotion. They won't understand why I won't be coming back." Alexander watched his son and was amazed that he was so concerned about the well being of these animals.

Looking at Joshua he said, "When we leave tomorrow, you and Adonis go to your uncle's and bring the animals with you. We're sailing with an empty cargo and we can put them in the cargo holds."

"Do you mean the camel, Gray Boy and the lamb?" asked Beriah.

"That's correct. I have a small farm on the edge of Athens. The animals can stay there. That way you can visit them anytime you like," said Alexander.

"If Beriah would have found anymore animals to heal, we would look like Noah's Ark," laughed Joshua.

Shortly after dark, the four men crossed the Cheesemaker's Valley to the secret opening into the cave. The meeting hadn't yet started. Beriah introduced his father to the members, and told about his vision of Jesus. "Tomorrow we'll be leaving for the Port of Joppa. From there, Joshua, Heber, Adonis, and myself will be taking the word of Jesus to the cities and villages of Greece. If you know of someone who needs to hide in my cavern, please show them where it is. I am leaving everything behind. They can use it all."

Shortly thereafter, Thomas, who was the leader of the group, began to teach. "Tonight's lesson is, 'What is salvation?' 'Why do we need it?' 'How do we receive it?' 'If by salvation, do we mean eternal life?' and 'What happens to those who do not want salvation?' God wants to save all humanity. Redemption means to buy back someone by paying a price. Our Lord and Savior paid the price for us by shedding His precious blood on an old rugged cross. He paid the price for all humanity. The only thing we have to do is repent of our sins and accept Jesus as our Lord and Savior. Our salvation is a free gift. We need only to accept it. For those who reject this free gift will be forever punished. But those who accept it will have life eternal in Heaven. Friends make sure which road you travel. For truly, you cannot travel the pathway of sin and enter the Kingdom of God." The meeting lasted another hour. Thomas laid the groundwork for becoming a follower of Christ. It was after midnight before the men retired for the night. Perhaps on the road to Joppa they would have time to discuss Thomas' lesson.

Everyone was up before dawn. Breakfast was only juice and fruit. Alex wanted to be on the road by daybreak. Joshua and Adonis went to collect the animals while Beriah packed his leather pouch with a change of clothing. Sadness filled his heart, as he looked around the room. This was my home for twenty-one years, he thought. In his mind he could hear Old Jobah teaching him lessons from the Torah and about the lands beyond Jerusalem. Beriah wondered if Jobah had been preparing him for this day. With a last look, Beriah picked up his shoulder bag, his rug, and harp. He climbed the worn steps into the early morning. He raised his eyes toward the Temple Mount and thanked the God of Israel for loving him and reuniting him with his family.

As the sun broke, in the eastern sky, the strange band of people and animals were on their way to the Port of Joppa. Before Joshua and Beriah climbed the gangplank of the Athene, a Jewish camel driver could be heard in the distance chanting the Wayfarer's song:

The sun shall not smite thee by day, nor the moon by night;

The Lord shall preserve thee from all evil; He shall preserve thy soul; The Lord holdeth His hand over thy going out, and thy coming in, now and forevermore.

At last, the weary travelers were on board the Athene. Beriah was engulfed in a hug from Captain Strabo. He told Beriah that he was at the helm the night Beriah was washed overboard. Joshua and Adonis, with the help of two sailors, secured the animals in the cargo hold. Alexander Palamos gave orders to send ashore for food for the animals, for their long journey ahead, and also, for plenty of provisions for all the men and themselves. "Don't linger because we set sail at dawn."

Joshua, Beriah, and Adonis laid out under the stars that night. "I will be so glad to see Heber too," said Beriah. But there was little sleep that night. There was sadness about leaving Jerusalem. Each man knew he might never return to see the Holy City, until Jesus returned. The following morning Joshua, Beriah, and Adonis stood at the rail, looking in the direction of Jerusalem. Beriah quoted from the prophet Isaiah:

And it shall come to pass in the end days that the mountain of the Lord's house shall be established at the top of the mountains.

And shall be exalted above the hills;

And all nations shall flow into it.

And many people shall go and say, 'Come ye, and let us go to the mountain of the Lord, to the house of the God of Jacob;

And he will teach us His ways,

And we will walk in His paths;

For out of Zion, shall go forth the law,

And the word of the Lord from Jerusalem.

As the Athene slowly left the Port of Joppa, Beriah turned his face toward Greece.

Yvonne Bunn is available for interviews, speaking engagements and personal appearances. For more information contact the publisher at:

ADVANTAGE BOOKS™
PO Box 160847
Altamonte Springs, FL 32716

Here is a list of Yvonne's titles with ***Advantage Books***

Foreshadow of Desolation O'Jerusalem
A Man of Galilee
The Staff and The Sandals
Facing the Tribulation

Coming Soon
From the Stable to the Cross
On the Damascus Road
Beech Hollow
The Healing of the Hills
Opening the Seven Seals of the Scroll of Revelation
Hills of Home
In the Shadow of the Cross

To order additional copies of this book or to see a complete list of all **ADVANTAGE BOOKS™** visit our online bookstore at:

www.advbookstore.com

or call our toll free order number at: 1-888-383-3110

Longwood, Florida, USA

"we bring dreams to life"™
www.advbookstore.com

Printed in the United States
131396LV00004B/3/A

9 781597 550574